THE TRIDENT SERIES

IRISH

Volume 1 – Book 4

———————

Jaime Lewis

The Trident Series - Irish
Copyright © 2020 by Jaime Lewis

ISBN: 978-1-952734-19-9

TABLE OF CONTENTS

CHAPTER ONE

Bailey Anderson smiled and drew in a deep refreshing breath as she passed the sign that welcomed her to Virginia Beach. It was late, close to 11:00 pm, and just her luck, it had started to rain. She'd been on the road for a little over eleven hours since she'd left Birmingham, Alabama. But she had made it, though her eyes were a bit strained, and she was starving. The beef jerky she picked up a few hours ago at the gas station hardly suppressed her appetite. She felt her belly rumble. She had hoped to find a small store open where she could pick-up a few items until she could get to the grocery store.

"Karen," her in-car GPS, instructed her to turn right, indicating she was on the home stretch and just minutes from her new beach-front, two-bedroom condo. The way her eyes burned, maybe she'd forego the store and drive straight to the condo, take a relaxing hot bath before hitting the sack for some much-needed sleep. Sleep hadn't been much of an amenity in the last few days while tying up loose ends and preparing to move. Until her furniture arrived, she'd be sleeping on an air mattress. She was so tired she didn't care. Hell, she'd welcome the hardwood floor if she had to. She was just thankful she could get a night of full sleep without any worries.

She rubbed her eyes and put her blinker on. As she started to make the turn, her front left tire hit something. She heard a pop and her car jerked to the left. She gripped the steering wheel tight to avoid losing control and steered the vehicle into a parking lot, so she was safely off the road.

"Well, shit." She let out a frustrated sigh, wondering what in the hell she was going to do now. She was ashamed to admit it, but she didn't know how to change a tire. It was late and raining, and she knew nothing about this area.

She looked through the windshield between the wipers and got a good look at the place that stood in front of her. The sign above the door read

1

Bayside Bar and Grille, but it looked like a dump from her vantage point. Considering how full the parking lot was, the place must offer something good, especially at this hour. It still made her nervous about going into a bar and asking for help, especially one looking like it had seen better days. She could only imagine the type of people inside.

From where she came from, the local hangout was the Birmingham Country Club, where everyone dressed to impress, and if you weren't in with the society, then you weren't shit. Her parents were wealthy by inheritance and enjoyed playing the part of the rich and famous. They were cruel individuals. They looked down on others who didn't meet their standards. She, on the other hand, hated the lifestyle. Growing up, she was raised by nannies, butlers, and where every damn thing was decided for her. Even whom she dated.

She shivered, thinking about that jerk, Randy Lamonte, who her parents tried forcing on her. He was one of the two reasons she left home. Her parents were the other reason.

After she graduated from college, she was expected to marry Randy. It was what the whole town expected. However, she wasn't down for an arranged marriage, and that had put her in the crosshairs with her parents. It wasn't the first time, and she was certain it wouldn't be the last time she disappointed them.

Just because they thought she and Randy should be together didn't mean she did. Randy was thirty-nine years old, and although he was handsome, he was a complete horses ass who had the same expectations as her parents. He didn't know that she knew all about his nightcaps with other women while he was supposedly courting her. God knows how many women have kept his bed warm. When she mentioned her concern to her mother, her mother responded that if she'd quit teasing him, he wouldn't have to stray to keep himself satisfied. Bailey was appalled, to say the least, although not surprised at the crude comment. Her parents expected her to become the next neighborhood trophy wife.

She thought back to the conversation she'd had with her wicked witch of a mother just this morning before she high tailed it out of town.

2

"You shouldn't be working, Bailey, especially not that job babysitting those little snot-nosed kids," Annette Anderson said as she sat at the breakfast table like she'd done every morning since Bailey could remember, sipping her green tea and eating a half grapefruit. Some things never change.

"I love teaching, mother. When I'm around children, I feel like that was my purpose for living in this world. I'm a natural."

"Pfft...It is so beneath you. You were brought into this world for one purpose," her mother stated nastily and turned her nose upward before dramatically rolling her eyes.

"And what was that, to obey every command given by you and Dad? Because news flash that has never happened and never will."

"No, to marry Randy and spread your legs like a good girl for him and give us an heir to the family bloodlines. Just think of the assets we'll acquire when you marry, let alone with a child made from the two of you." Bailey could only stare at her mother as she sat there with a huge smile on her face as if she truly believed that was going to happen.

"I hate to burst your bubble Mother, but I never planned on marrying Randy, let alone spread my legs for him. You might as well accept that."

Her mother turned on her quickly, and she didn't see the flying hand quick enough. She only felt the sting as the hand made contact with her cheek. "Listen, you, little ungrateful bitch, your father and I spent a lot of money on you through the years, grooming you to become the future, Mrs. Randy Lamonte. You will not screw this up. We've already started spreading the news that you two are engaged. He is a very sought-after bachelor, and you should feel honored he still even wants you after you let some college frat-boy deflower you."

Bailey held her hand to her face because it hurt like a bitch, but she wasn't about to cry and let her mother see she was vulnerable. "If you are referring to the boarding schools you shipped me off to, and all of the beauty pageants you entered me in and, oh, let's definitely not forget Junior League, then you are highly mistaken because all of those things you did were for your own benefit. I don't need you, Daddy, Randy, or any of your damn money. I have my own that I've saved from working in a career that I love. There are plenty of men out there that will love me for me and not my net worth." She wasn't going to venture down the deflowering part.

"Not in this town, you won't because everyone knows you belong to Randy, and no other man is stupid or brazen enough to cross Randy Lamonte."

"Well, then it's a good thing I sold my house yesterday, isn't it?"

Her mother's head whipped around so fast she reminded Bailey of the little girl in the movie the Exorcist. Her mother gave her the evil eye. "What do you mean you sold your house? You never mentioned to your father and me you were looking to sell. Where are you planning on living?"

She wanted to laugh at her mother's contorted facial expression. Talk about shock and awe. "Why would I tell you when it would have ruined the surprised look on your face?"

"You know, your father doesn't like surprises."

"Well, tough shit. I was offered a job, and I'm moving. As in out of state."

Her mother gasped. "What? You can't do that. Where?"

"Like I would tell you where I'm going."

"No, you will ruin everything. I forbid it, and so would your father," her mother shrieked.

"You can't stop me."

She knew they would try, and that is why she had planned everything perfectly and was here now telling her mother this morning. As soon as she left, she would start her drive to Virginia Beach. She was thankful she caught her mom alone without her father around because he could be a little more persuasive, and she wouldn't put it past him to tie her up, lock her in a closet and lose the key. That was after he'd beaten the shit out of her.

"I'm calling your father. He will knock some sense into you," Annette stated as she pulled out her phone, and that was Bailey's cue that it was

4

time to leave. And she did. She walked out the door with a wave as her mother screamed at her.

Everything boiled down to money with them. Based on her experiences, money only caused trouble. Bailey had a hefty trust fund that her grandfather had left her. As far as she knew, nobody knew about it, except for her cousin, Jonathan. Everyone believed that because of her family's status, she was expected to act differently because of their wealth and reputation. In the five years since she was given access to the trust fund, she'd never touched a penny of it. She decided at a young age that she wasn't going to end up like her parents. She wanted a career, something to feel proud about. After she graduated from college, she had bought a little house and got a teaching job. She lived off her teachers' salary and was careful when it came to budgeting. Her only mistake was when she moved back to Birmingham. That was a lapse in judgment on her part. But she was rectifying that by moving on and starting a new chapter in her life.

After applying and receiving multiple offers from school systems in several states, she was lured to Virginia Beach for several reasons. One, being she could enjoy the beach during the summer and two, because of the vast military history in the area, especially with the Naval base in Norfolk being just a hop, skip, and a jump away. Her grandfather had introduced her to military history when she was a child, and she hadn't let go of it. She would sit and listen to her grandfather, who was a veteran, talk about his days in the Army any chance she got. She couldn't wait to get out and explore the area and its history in her free time.

But her new adventure wasn't starting the way she had hoped, as she sat in her car in the pouring rain debating what to do. People got flat tires all the time. It couldn't be that hard to change the tire. The challenge was going to be getting to the dang spare tire. She was going to need to empty the back of her car in the rain. Even if she got to the tire, could she even lift it? Of course, the rain decided right at that moment to come down harder.

"Why now?" She mumbled as she leaned over and pulled her iPad from her purse. There had to be a YouTube video on how to change a tire.

She pulled up the first one, and just as she thought, it seemed relatively simple. She put away the iPad and crawled in the back seat and started pulling bags and small boxes that were in the tailgate area into the back seat. This way it saved her time of being out in the rain. All she had with her were her valuables, some basic essentials, and enough clothes to get her through a few days in case the movers were delayed for any unforeseen reasons.

She looked around the car, hoping she had thrown one of her jackets in there, but she didn't see one. She looked down at the clothes she was wearing to make sure there wouldn't be an issue with them if they got wet because she was going to get soaked. She had dressed for comfort, knowing she was going to be in the car for several hours. Her blonde hair was pulled back with a headband, but since she didn't want her hair in the way, she quickly pulled in up into a ponytail. Once she was all set, she got out, ran around to the back, and opened the hatchback. Quickly, she found the jack and got it in place under the vehicle like she'd seen in the video. Okay, she thought to herself, this really isn't that hard. Until thirty minutes later and looking like a drowned rat, she realized it wasn't exactly easy peasy. The damn lug nuts were stuck, or the freaking Jolly Green Giant tightened them so darn tight that nobody could get them off but him.

She took a deep breath and exhaled as she stood there, soaked to the bone in barely-there clothing. The rain had let up a few minutes ago, but it was starting to get heavy again, and even though the temperature was warm, the dampness from the rain made it seem cooler; she was shivering, and the lug wrench was slippery in her hands.

She looked over her shoulder, back toward the front door of the bar again as the raindrops pelted her face and arms. She was debating on whether she should just suck it up and go in and ask for help. She damned herself for not listening to her cousin Jonathan and enrolling in AAA before she left. He had lectured her on why she needed it, especially since she was going to be on the road alone.

She decided to try one more time, and if she couldn't loosen it, then she'd suck it up and go inside and ask for assistance. She squatted down and pushed down on the wrench with all her might and even heard herself grunt. "Come on, pleaseeee." She felt the lug start to give, and she got excited. "Finally," she said breathlessly. Then she looked at the tire and realized that was only one; she had four more to go. "Son-of-a-bitch!" She was ready to throw the damn wrench at the tire when a deep but humorous voice uttered something behind her, scaring the absolute crap out of her.

"Do you need some help there, sweetness?"

She wasn't expecting anyone to sneak up on her. She was already on pins and needles to begin with. So, the moment she heard the voice, she screamed, lost her balance, and fell backward, landing in a big puddle. If any part of her wasn't wet, it definitely was now. She closed her eyes and muttered to nobody in particular. "What else could go wrong?"

It wasn't until she heard the deep chuckle that she remembered she wasn't alone. How in the hell did he manage to sneak up on her? She opened her eyes slowly as if expecting to see some backwoods hillbilly man with missing teeth and looking like he needed to bathe. But unless she hit her head when she fell and didn't realize it or her eyes were playing tricks on her, her intuition was wrong. VERY WRONG! Standing over her with a sexy grin on his face had to be the hottest guy she had ever laid eyes on. And that was saying a lot because where she came from, the men were always polished from head to toe. But this guy...he was the complete opposite. And she was momentarily speechless. He was tall, but considering she was lying on the ground, anyone would seem tall. His dirty blonde hair stuck up in all directions but in a sexy sort of way because it was wet. He had a firm jaw with a little scruff, and he had piercing blue eyes that held a slight twinkle to them. His dark wash jeans fit snugly through his thighs, hugging his ass, and the red long-sleeve Henley shirt he wore showed just how defined his chest and arms were. But what caught her attention when he shifted and the light hit his face was a scar that ran from his bottom lip to just under his chin. It was sexy looking.

She shook her head. *"Really, Bailey? All that sexiness standing in front of you, and you pick out a damn scar as his most appealing feature?"*

ॐ

The music was cranked up, and the bar patrons were starting to get a little wild at Bayside. A typical night at the local hangout.

Ky "Irish" Daniels scanned the room as he entered, just like he would with the scope of his rifle when out in the field. It was a force of habit, thanks to his job. This place was a hidden treasure in town, as it sat back off a side road right on the beach, mostly only the locals knew about it. A perfect place for the SEALs and other military personnel in the area to hang out and not be bothered by outsiders. The owner, Paul, was a former Marine. He opened the joint when he left the Corps. From the outside, the place looked run down, and no tourist in their right mind would step foot in the place. But on the inside, it was a treasure, decorated in a mix of a Chesapeake Bay meets military theme. What the place was really known for was the food. It was where most of the personnel stationed at the Naval Amphibious Base Little Creek came when they wanted to get out and unwind peacefully without the tourists or women who flocked to town just to catch a glimpse and say they met a SEAL. The locals respected them and gave them their space. That wasn't saying that local SEAL groupies wouldn't frequent the place, especially on the weekends.

It didn't take Irish long to spot Marcus "Ace" Chambers, his team leader and a good friend. The two of them were meeting to discuss the logistics of their "guys" trip this coming weekend. After the fiasco with Frost's fiancé, Autumn, being stalked and nearly killed by her crazy sister-in-law and a guy named Cecil, the guys were planning a getaway weekend. Stitch was hosting the team at his cabin in the Shenandoah Mountains. Since they weren't scheduled for any training or missions, their commander had granted the team a few days leave. Stitch had an awesome set-up at the three-bedroom cabin that sat on five acres of land. He created hiking trails with obstacles, using most of the wilderness provided and even built a mini range for target practice. It was a total "man cabin," and everyone was pumped for a little R&R SEAL style. It was also doubling as a bachelor party for their teammate Frost since he and Autumn were getting married the following weekend.

Irish walked over to the bar and took a seat on the stool next to Ace. Buddy, the bartender, appeared and sat a cold Bud down in front of Irish.

He looked around and saw a few women who were on the prowl looking to land a man. And they weren't just after any man. These women were locals and knew the SEALs hung out here. They were referred to as "frog hogs," but they didn't seem to mind the offensive name as they came back night after night, week after week, looking for a good time and always left with a frogman on their arm. And those "someone's" included himself on some of those occasions. He liked sex. Sex kept him grounded, especially when coming home from a mission, and he needed that stress release. But over the last few months, seeing a few of his buddies and teammates settle down with some pretty amazing women, he started to think about his future and what he wanted beyond the Navy. He questioned himself several times if he wanted a family with the career he led. The secrecy surrounding his job, the long deployments. It was so much easier to scratch the itch when needed. He was always straight forward with the women he slept with. It was always a mutual agreement before engaging in any sexual activity that it was just sex. No cuddling afterward, no sleepovers, and definitely no commitments. But seeing how his friends, Ace, Potter, and Frost have made it work, he wondered if a serious relationship was in his cards. Alex, Ace's fiancé, was always trying to set him up on blind dates. Maybe after he got back from the weekend with the guys, he would give her a call and take her up on her offer. If he wanted to date, he had to start somewhere. He trusted Alex. She wouldn't set him up with just anyone.

Ace slapped him on the back. "Damn, man, you just walk in the place, and they set their sets right for you. Do you have some sort of a pussy magnet on you?" Ace teased him and glanced over his shoulder. "Tell me, which lady is getting lucky tonight?"

Irish glanced over his shoulder, and sure enough, two women were staring him down, grinning and running their hands along their bodies. He knew that look. *"Sorry, ladies, not tonight,"* he thought to himself and took a sip of his beer.

Irish looked at Ace and shook his head as he turned back in his seat, leaving the ladies staring at his back. "None."

Ace choked on his beer. "Excuse me? Are you feeling alright, stud?" He reached up to feel Irish's forehead, and Irish slapped it away, making Ace chuckle. Ace could laugh all he wanted to, but Irish was determined to show everyone he too could find someone. At least he thought he could.

They spent about an hour talking and making plans, then decided to call it a night since it was getting late. Irish was envious of Ace. He had his beautiful fiancé waiting for him at home. How those two met and fell in love was something for the books. Alex was awesome in more ways than one. She was like part of the team, and all the men respected and adored the hell out of her. She could keep up with all of them in every aspect of being a SEAL. But it really wasn't a surprise, considering her father was a SEAL and then being raised by an entire team of SEALs when her father was killed in action. Hell, his commander, a very well-respected man, was her adoptive father.

He and Ace walked outside and stood under the overhang, watching the rain come down.

"Damn, I thought this storm was going to miss us," Ace said.

"Yeah, it's coming down pretty good," Irish replied.

"Well, I'm parked on the other side. I'll see ya tomorrow morning for PT." Ace waved and ran toward his truck.

Irish started jogging towards his car. As he neared his vehicle, his ears homed in on a sound. Was that a grunt? He looked around, and two parking spaces over, his eyes landed on a small Mercedes SUV with the hatchback open and the lights on inside. He was getting wet, but curiosity got to him. Walking closer, he realized the vehicle was jacked up on one side. What he wasn't expecting was to find a woman trying to change a flat tire. Well, she was more like struggling.

He had to hold back his laughter when she finally got the one lug nut off but then realized she still had four more to go and then swore.

So, he used abilities to his advantage and stood back and watched silently for a few seconds. The woman had a great ass from his view. She wore a pair of tight black pants, the kind that Alex loved to wear. She was bent over, struggling with the lug wrench. Was that a southern accent he detected? He waited another minute or so, taking in the sight of her body. Not wanting to stand around perving any longer, he decided to put the poor woman out of her misery and lend her a hand.

"Do you need some help, sweetness?"

He was caught off guard when she screamed and then fell backward into a big puddle, completely soaking her. When she asked herself, "if anything else could go wrong," he couldn't help but chuckle.

He stood over her as she opened her eyes, and when she looked up at him, it was he who almost landed on his ass. He cleared his throat and realized he certainly wasn't being a gentleman, and he held out his hand. "Here, let me help you up." She looked at his hand as if it might bite her, and he smiled. "I promise I won't bite. My mother would spank my ass if she knew I left a beautiful woman lying in a puddle." The woman smirked and took his offering. He lifted her easily, and once she was stable on her feet, he stepped back to get a good look at her. She was a short little thing. He was six-feet-one, and the top of her head only came to his upper chest, probably bringing her around five-two, five-three. She had blonde hair that was pulled back into a ponytail. Her most notable feature were her blue eyes. He had been told numerous times by women how "pretty" his blue eyes were, but the blue eyes staring back at him were fucking insane. The color reminded him of the glaciers he'd seen in Alaska. That color surrounded by her thick black eyelashes, which were spikey from the rain was a showstopper.

He didn't want to look away, but then she whispered a thank you and he was right, there was a southern accent.

"You shouldn't be out here all alone, honey," he told her, and she took on an alarmed expression and looked around nervously. Shit, the last thing he wanted to do was frighten her. As he examined her more closely, he noticed some light bruising along her cheek, and his gut clenched. Had someone hit her? Not wanting her to think he was some creep, he said,

11

"Look, I'm not going to hurt you or anything." He nodded toward the tire. "What happened? I can help if you'd like."

She nibbled on her bottom lip as she ran her hands up and down her pants. He smirked. She was cute. "I hit something in the road," she said, still looking around, seeming a little on edge. He didn't like her feeling scared.

"How long have you been out here?" He asked, bending down to get a look at the tire. Whatever she ran over, it had slashed the tire. A plug wouldn't fix it.

She shrugged her shoulders. "Probably about forty-five minutes or so."

His eyebrows shot upward. "Why didn't you come inside? There were and still are plenty of people in there who could've come out and helped you." But if she had done that, he may have missed her, and that would've been a damn shame because out of nowhere, he was suddenly interested in this beautiful creature.

She looked back toward the building then looked back up at him. "Uh...if you were a woman new to town, would you've gone into a place that looked like that? Especially at this time of night?"

He glanced back at the building. She had a point. To a stranger's eyes, it did appear a little shady, but to locals, it was by far the best restaurant around.

He looked back at the little pixie standing beside him. She was even shorter than his friends Alex and Tenley. She had a cute figure, considering he could see every curve since her wet clothes were plastered to her body. As his eyes roamed over her body, they landed on her abundant breasts, and he could faintly see her hard nipples poking through the material of her bra and shirt and damn if the sight didn't make his cock stir. It was a good thing it was dark out. He tried to be a true gentleman and not stare, but it was hard.

She knew where his eyes were looking too because when she looked down, she crossed her arms over her chest and squinted her eyes at him. But the movement only pushed her breasts up, giving him a better view of her glorious cleavage at the top of her tank top.

12

He grinned and shrugged his shoulders. "Sorry, I'm a guy, and you're beautiful." Her eyes widened, and her eyebrows shot upward. He had caught her off guard. He actually caught himself off guard. He never apologized for looking at a woman. But then again, most women he was around threw themselves at him. This goddess was different. He knew it the moment he looked into her eyes. They held a look of innocence—the perfect submissive type. And there went his dick again.

He needed to get the tire changed and then go home and hop into a cold shower. Or, maybe he would just run down the beach path next to the bar and go for a swim in the ocean. That should tame the beast in his pants.

As he went to kneel, he noticed she was shivering. *Christ, didn't she have a jacket or something in her car?* He had seen a bunch of bags and boxes in the back seat. She mentioned she was new in town, and he wondered if she'd literally just moved.

"Honey, this is going to take a few minutes. Do you have a jacket or something you can put on?"

"No, like I said, I'm new in town. As in just pulled into town. I was on my way to my condo when I hit whatever was in the road. I only have t-shirts and shorts with me, and the movers aren't coming with the rest of my stuff until tomorrow."

"Why don't you go sit in the car?"

He could tell she was thinking about it, but she surprised him. "No, I'll wait out here. I would hate for the jack to slip or something because of me while you're working on the tire. I'll manage," she said as her teeth started to chatter.

He looked up at her as she watched him closely. He was shocked she was looking out for his wellbeing over her comfort. A lot of women he knew would've jumped right into the car without hesitating. He meant it when he told her she was beautiful. Even with her hair wet and matted down, but he couldn't let her just stand here in the rain.

"Hang on a second." He got up and ran over to his Corvette. The metallic grey sports car was his pride and joy. He bought it last year using a portion of his bonus when he re-upped with the SEALs. He opened the

13

passenger door and rummaged through a go-bag he always kept in there and found one of his sweatshirts.

"Here, put this on," he told her, holding the sweatshirt out for her to take.

She looked surprised, and her eyes widened. "Oh, I couldn't. I'll be okay." She crossed her arms, obviously cold.

He gave her a stern look. "I know you're cold, and you said yourself you don't have anything to put on. I don't want to be the reason you wake up with a cold tomorrow. Please, for me." He flashed his flirty smile.

She sighed, but he could see her hiding a smile as she took it from him and pulled the sweatshirt over her head.

Once she had it on, he looked her over. It was huge and hung on her small frame. He immediately felt his chest tighten. A sudden possessive feeling overcame him seeing her in his property. He never let a woman wear any clothing of his. It was way too personal. He shook his head and tried to focus on the task in front of him.

He reached into the back of the car and pulled the spare tire out with ease and placed it next to the car and began to loosen the lug nuts. They both stayed silent for the first couple of minutes.

He looked up at her again and couldn't help but admire her beauty. "Where did you say you were from?" He asked but knew she hadn't said, however, he wanted to make sure this woman had some smarts to her. According to the license plate on her car, he assumed she was from Alabama.

"I didn't say," she replied, giving him a sideways look, and he finished tightening the last lug. He stood up, and she handed him a towel to wipe his hands on. "I'm not in the habit of spilling my life story to men who sneak up on me in a dark parking lot. How did you do that, by the way?" She raised her eyebrow at him, and he grinned, loving her witty yet mature personality.

"Do what?" He asked as he shoved his hands in his pockets. He was afraid that if he didn't keep them hidden, he'd try to touch her. It was like she called to him. Her change of the subject and deflection of his question didn't go unnoticed either.

"Sneak up from behind like that. I'm normally good about sensing that type of stuff. But you're good." She gave him a smile that lit up her face, and damn if he didn't feel a punch in the gut.

If she only knew the half of it, but he just gave his shoulders a shrug and smirked. "It's a force of habit."

They stood there for a few long seconds, just staring at each other. His eyes searched her face, locking in on that bruise again, and he bit the inside of his cheek. Then as if his hand had a mind of its own, he reached out and gently wiped some moisture from her face, right where the bruising was. Her skin was soft and smooth. He heard the slight gasp come from her, but she didn't step away. Her tongue darted out to wet her very kissable lips as if taunting him. He came close to losing all sense of control, but then his head with a brain finally started thinking instead of the little head below. What in the hell was he doing? This wasn't like him at all. He was a one and done kinda guy. He pulled his hand back and took a step back.

"Sorry about that. You are just so beautiful I couldn't resist."

Her cheeks turned pink. "Do you say that to all of the helpless ladies you find needing help changing a flat tire?" She smiled, and her eyes twinkled with mischief.

Damn, she was doing a number on him. That southern accent added to her charm. If he didn't step away now, there was no telling what he'd do next. His conscience said to ask her out, but there laid the problem. He hadn't dated in years. At least since becoming a SEAL. He didn't know how to ask her out. Shit, he needed to think about this. The guy's weekend trip coming up was looking better by the minute. He had some thinking to do. He pulled his car keys from his pocket.

"You'd better get home and get dried off before you do catch a cold." He took a few more steps toward his car, needing to put the distance between them.

"Oh, here, let me give this back to you." She started to pull off the sweatshirt he'd given her to stay warm.

15

He waved her off. "No, keep it. For now, at least."

Her eyebrows furrowed in confusion. "How will I get it to you?"

"I'm sure I'll see you around."

"But I don't even know your name."

"Irish," was all he said and winked then walked to his car, leaving her staring at him with her mouth agape. He would definitely be seeing her again even if he had to turn over every rock in the city, he would find her. As he pulled out of the parking lot, he realized he never got her name. Then a smile formed. If the guys found out about this, he'd never hear the end of it.

CHAPTER TWO

Bailey stood in shock as she stared at the grey corvette as it roared out of the parking lot. She glanced down at the sweatshirt she wore; it was five sizes too big and completely soaked just like the rest of her. She took in the wording on the front, NAVY. She wondered if Irish was in the Navy. He was flirty and sexy but did seem bossy and commanding like someone in the military might be. But what did she know? She brought the material to her nose and inhaled. Whatever cologne the man wore smelled good. Her insides were still quivering from the interaction with "Irish." She wondered what kind of a name that was.

She shook her head; no, this was bad. Very bad. She couldn't consume her thoughts on a man. Not now when she was looking to start her life over here. He was a good Samaritan, helping a woman change a flat tire. A good-looking man at that. Although, Good Samaritans don't offer their personal clothing to strangers and tell them they're beautiful.

She got back into her car and looked at herself in the mirror. Besides being soaked from head to toe, her cheeks were pink and flushed. And she knew why. She placed her hand on the cheek he had touched. The feel of his knuckles against her skin had sent sparks through her body, awakening parts of her that had been dormant. She sighed, thinking about her non-existent sex life. Twenty-six and still a virgin, technically speaking, that is. Her parents and Randy think otherwise.

Ever since Randy came into her life, her mother constantly hounded her about needing to "save" herself for Randy. Like that was going to happen. She hadn't even kissed the man, except for that one time when he forced himself on her during a party. That'd been four years ago, and shortly after she returned home from college. He had duped her, making some bullshit excuse that he needed to talk to her about her father. Being the naïve person she was at the time, she fell for it, and it had almost cost her. Once he had her in a bedroom, he forced her onto the bed. She tried fighting him off, but it was useless. He was stronger and overpowered her. As he started to remove her clothes, she was given a reprieve when his phone rang. Whoever it was must've been important because he leaped from the bed and headed to the door. Not that she complained, but it was odd. It was his parting words to her that still gave her the jitters. He had warned her that if she told anyone about what happened or if she let anyone else take what was his, he would hurt her.

Her life was not so private; she used the same doctors, banks, and anything else as her family did. But after that night, when Randy almost took the one thing most precious to her, she decided to take matters into her own hands, literally. She took her own virginity per se. She ordered a basic vibrator online, and when it arrived, she had a couple of glasses of wine, and as people say, she popped her own cherry. It wasn't the way she had ever imagined her "first" time would be, but there was no way in hell she would ever let Randy touch her.

The real hatred toward her started a few years prior when her grandfather passed away. She had been a freshman in college. At times, he was her shield from her parents' verbal abuse. He was the man behind the fortune of the Anderson family of Birmingham, Alabama. Her family was like royalty in the community, and it was all because of her sweet old pop-pop. He was the reason she was even able to go to the college of her choice. Her father expected her to attend an Ivy League School to carry on family traditions and all that shit. When her father had threatened to withhold her college fund, her grandfather stepped in and paid for it all. She was shocked when she received documents pertaining to her grandfather's will when he passed away. To her surprise, he had already set up an account with enough money to cover the last three years of college, including costs for housing, books, and spending money if she needed it. Whatever was left in the account after she graduated was hers. He hired an attorney who had no ties to the family to handle the account and administer the payouts. That was done to prevent her mother and father from meddling and getting their greedy hands on money that wasn't rightfully theirs. Not knowing who was in charge had drove them insane. They always tried asking, but she honestly didn't know either. And quite frankly, she didn't care. As long as her school bills were paid, it didn't matter who wrote the check. The week following her graduation was when the real bombshell was dropped on her. Her grandfather had intended her to have a hell of a lot more than just a college education. He left her a trust fund, amounting to fifteen million dollars. A twenty-two-year-old with fifteen million dollars to her name could do a whole lot, however, four years later, she had never spent one penny. She took the money left from her college fund, close to ten thousand dollars, and used that to start her life after college. She tried putting some distance between her and her parents, but they always found a way to meddle in her business.

To this day, she was thankful for her grandfather's wisdom in showing her the ropes of adult life. She made a nice little profit off the sale of her home in Birmingham, which she used as the down payment on her new condo here on the beach.

She started to make her way down the road her condo was on. She saw the complex come into view, and made the left turn into the parking lot. She found one of her two assigned parking spots and pulled in, then shut the car off. She took a deep breath. She was home. Exhausted, but home, and that thought made her smile.

She decided she would just take in her overnight bag that had her PJs, toiletries, and a change of clothes for tomorrow. The rest of the bags and boxes could wait until tomorrow.

She punched in her security code on the keypad outside the lobby. Once in, she took the elevator to the sixth floor. She had a corner unit on the top floor. When she entered the condo, she looked around, and although it was completely bare, with stark white walls, she loved it and couldn't help but do a little dance right there in the foyer. It was an open floor plan with a huge island separating the kitchen from the living room. She smiled when she spotted the sliding glass doors. She walked over, pulled the curtains back and slid the door open. She stepped out onto the balcony and felt the cool, damp air as the wind coming off the ocean whipped around. The sky was dark, and the beach was dark, but that didn't stop her from hearing the waves crash along the shoreline. She closed her eyes and smiled as she took in the relaxing atmosphere. Yes, she had found a home and knew this place was going to be a life-changer for her. Although in the back of her mind, a certain sexy stranger loomed.

CHAPTER THREE

"What in the hell do you mean that she left?" Bentley Anderson asked his wife in a low menacing voice as he poured himself a drink from the full bar in the billiards room of his 9,000-square foot mansion. He didn't like surprises, and his daughter had duped everyone today. She would pay one way or another for pulling that shit with him. He would've thought she knew by now that nobody crosses Bentley Anderson and gets away without consequences.

"Like I told you over the phone this morning, dear. Bailey came here and told me she had sold her house and was moving," Annette stated as she sat on the sofa, filing her nails and acting as if the whole situation bored her.

"And she didn't tell you where?" He asked, getting angrier.

"No. How did we not know she had put her house up for sale? We know everyone around town. Someone had to have seen or noticed."

"That's an easy answer. She used a realtor from the next town over," Randy Lamonte replied as he walked into the room. Annette and Bentley both turned toward the doorway and listened. "I've got to hand it to your daughter, Bentley. She's gotten smart over the years. She knew she was being watched. Look what she did with her bank accounts. She moved them to another bank that we had no inside contacts with."

Bentley smirked and took another drink. "Yeah, but all it took was one call, and some money flashed in front of that Manager's face, and we were instantly given information."

"Well, it's not like she's moving today. She told me she just sold the house this morning, so she'll still need to pack everything and close on the sale. That could take weeks," Annette said and looked at her husband as he sat there scowling as he sipped his expensive Scotch. "You will go over there first thing tomorrow morning and stop this nonsense," she told Bentley.

Randy shook his head, "She's already gone, Annette." He got up from his seat on the couch, walked over to the bar and poured himself a drink.

"What?" Annette asked, sounding surprised that her daughter would do something like that.

Randy took a large sip. Bailey's little disappearing act hadn't surprised him. He had a feeling she had been up to something the past few weeks. She hadn't shown her face at the Country Club. She made constant excuses to blow off community functions she would typically attend. He blamed himself for not paying more attention.

"I went by her house when Bentley called me. It's empty. The closing was this morning. Right after she left here, she met the realtor at the closing agency, signed the papers, then left town. I found the realtor's name she used and gave him a call. He told me everything."

"Did you ask him if he knew where she was heading? Surely, she would've said something to him in conversation," Annette asked in that snippy tone of hers that irritated Randy. If it weren't for Bailey's net worth, he'd move on. But knowing she was sitting on a fifteen million trust fund he wasn't bound to give it up. Plus, there were some bonuses, not if, but when Bailey married him. She just wasn't aware of the extras he would be entitled to once they said: "I do."

"He said she mentioned that she was looking forward to being near the beach."

"Well, that leaves a lot of places she could be," Bentley said, looking pissed off.

"Don't worry; I'll find her, Bentley. In fact, I've already got men on it."

Bentley gave Randy a stern look, but Randy didn't let it rattle him. He knew how to handle Bentley. Plus, Bentley needed him to get what Bailey didn't even know she had. "Well, you'd better, or we all are going to be in deep shit. We've got obligations we have to adhere to. We need her here."

"Don't fret it. My guys say they'll find her. She has to register her car, and if she's planning on working, she'll have to file taxes. She can't hide forever. Once we get a hit, I'll take a trip to wherever she may be and convince her it would be in her best interest to come home."

He would convince her any way he needed to, even if it meant getting physical. She wasn't going to ruin his future. He already had too much invested to turn around now.

CHAPTER FOUR

Three Weeks later

Irish sat by Ace and Alex's pool, his feet dangling in the cool refreshing water. It was hot and humid, although not as hot as where he and the team had just come from. They had been living in a South American jungle for the past two and a half weeks. The ladies planned a welcome home barbecue for them. Another few weeks and the season would start to change, bringing the cooler fall temperatures. He was looking forward to it. He could adapt in any type of weather, but there was just something about the fall temperatures that he loved.

He was deep in thought, thinking about the conversation he'd had with the guys a few weeks ago at Stitch's cabin. He caved and told them about "Blue," the blue-eyed goddess he met in the parking lot at Bayside. At first, they teased him, and it was expected, but when they all realized he was serious, they told him that if he truly felt something, he shouldn't ignore the feeling because, in a blink of an eye, it could all be gone. And that couldn't be a more accurate statement after seeing Ace, Potter, and Frost all fall in love and then almost losing their women because of assholes in the world.

But unfortunately, "Blue" was going to have to stay on the back burner for just a little while longer. He needed to make a quick trip home to Michigan to see his mom and dad.

During this last deployment, his dad Ollie had a heart attack. Derek had informed him when he had arrived home. Even though doctors said it was a mild heart attack, Irish would feel better if he saw that his dad was indeed doing okay with his own eyes. The doctor said his dad should be just fine with a proper diet and exercise. Irish's other concern was the farm his family lived on. Over the years, his mom and dad sold off a lot of the livestock. He had a feeling it was getting to be too much for the two of them now that they were getting older. They only kept a few goats around. And that was for the benefit of his young niece Sienna who lived with them.

His thoughts went to Sienna and how she might be dealing with everything going on with his dad. As she was only five years old, she probably didn't really understand. His parents were her legal guardians after his drug addict sister gave her up at birth to continue her life with her drug dealer boyfriend. Neither Irish nor his parents had seen or spoken to his sister, Maggie, since that day.

Damn, he hated being so far away from his parents and niece. He hadn't seen them since Sienna's birthday last October. That little girl was a spitfire, but so adorable, and she knew it too. She had him wrapped around her little finger and was one of the few females who held a place in his heart.

He had plenty of leave accrued, so his Commander told him to take a couple of days to go and spend some time with them. He was actually looking forward to it.

He felt the cool pool water hit his face and then heard a giggle. He wiped the water from his face and grinned as Alex swam over and held onto the ledge next to him.

"You looked so deep in thought; I thought you needed a distraction. Want to talk about what has you acting like a hermit and ignoring your friends? This is supposed to be a fun party, you know." She gave his leg a nudge with her elbow and smiled up at him.

He was silent for a moment as he sat there staring at her. Alex was a beautiful woman and smart as hell. Ace was a lucky son of a bitch to land her. Irish wanted someone like her. Someone beautiful on the inside and out. Someone who could like him for him and not just the SEAL. His mind went back to "Blue," and he wondered if she could be that someone?

Alex's voice broke his train of thought. "Are you thinking about your mystery girl, "Blue?"

Christ, he regretted telling Alex about "Blue." He didn't know the woman's name who had consumed his thoughts for the last couple of weeks. But every time he thought about her, all he saw were those glacier blue eyes that sparkled like diamonds. So, until he found her, he and apparently everyone else referred to her as "Blue."

His lips twitched, and he took a slug of his beer. "Maybe," he replied, and she smiled.

"Well, now that you're back, you can look for her. You said she mentioned she just moved here, right?"

"Yeah, but I'm going home to Michigan for a few days. I don't know if your dad or Ace told you, but my dad had a heart attack while we were deployed. I just want to go home and make sure everything is good with them."

She covered his hand and squeezed it. "No, neither one said anything. I'm so sorry. Please let us know if there is anything we can do." He smiled at her. She was like a mother hen to all the guys, and they all loved her. She took care of them, even though Potter and Frost had their own women now.

"I will. Thanks, honey."

CHAPTER FIVE

Irish turned off the main road in town and onto the long dirt road that led to his parent's farm. With the windows down, the fresh Michigan air infiltrated the car. The radio station was set on country music. He wasn't a huge fan of country, but he was coming around to it more. Mainly because when Alex or Tenley were around, that was all they played. The closer to the farm he got, the more anxious he got. He had to admit he was missing his mom, dad, and Sienna.

He pulled up and parked in front of the old white farmhouse with a wrap-around porch. Noticing some of the paint chipping on the outside, he made a note to re-paint it while he was here. He got out of the car and spotted his mom pushing Sienna on the tire swing that hung from the huge oak tree in the front yard. He smiled, remembering how his mom used to push him on the same tire swing when he was a kid. She was looking over at him, and when she realized who he was, she started running over to him with a big smile on her face, and he was thrilled he was able to surprise her. He had called his dad when he landed to give him the heads up.

"Oh, for heaven's sake! Ky! What are you doing here?" He embraced her and took a deep breath and exhaled. Just the feeling of being able to hug his mom sent some warmth through his body. He gave her an extra squeeze, just because he could.

"Hi, Mom. I've missed you." He kissed her cheek.

"We've missed you too. Your commander said you were out of reach when I called last week about your dad."

"I was, but we got back two days ago. The commander explained everything, but I wanted to come and see for myself that dad was okay and make sure you guys are good and don't need anything."

"Oh, sweetie. You didn't have to. I know how valuable free time is for you." She smiled and winked as she hugged his arm. "But I'm glad you're here."

"Uncle Ky!" He turned at the sound of the little voice and saw his niece, Sienna running across the front yard. Her little blonde pigtails bouncing up and down, and those blue eyes of hers were twinkling. She was wearing a pair of short jean overalls. He bent down and scooped her up in his arms and twirled her around as she giggled. He took notice of how much she'd grown since he last saw her. Damn, he had missed a lot in a year.

He kissed her on the cheek. "And how is my favorite little niece doing?" He asked as they started walking towards the house.

She gave him her little devilish smile and hugged his neck. "I missed you, Uncle Ky." And damn if his heart didn't go pitter-patter at those words.

"I missed you too, peanut. But now that I am here, we can spend some time together, okay?"

"Okay. We can play Barbies and Army men."

Irish looked at his mom for some help. He was all about spending some quality time with Sienna, but damn if he wanted to spend it playing with dolls. But his mom didn't come to his rescue; she just chuckled and shrugged her shoulders, like, "what do you want me to do about it?"

He walked into the house and set Sienna down. "I'll make you a deal. I'll play Barbies with you, but we have to say the men are Navy."

"Huh?" She asked, giving him an odd look, and he had to laugh as he tried to explain the difference between Army and Navy, but defining something like that to a five-year-old was like talking to them in a foreign language. His mom finally decided to step in and distract Sienna with some milk and cookies.

Later that evening, Irish threw on some lounge pants and a t-shirt after getting out of the shower. His thoughts were on his parents. They seemed closed off earlier when he was talking to them. He sensed there was something they weren't telling him. He knew they were still up because the

28

lights were still on downstairs in the kitchen. He had spent about two hours talking with his dad earlier before dinner. He seemed like he was doing well, but Irish could see the exhaustion overtaking him. His dad was in good shape for his age from all the work he does around the farm, but his eating habits weren't so good. Eating a healthy diet was going to be a huge adjustment for him. His dad lived for bacon and eggs, and steak and potatoes every day. That didn't account for all the snacks he consumed during the day.

As he started down the stairs, he heard the two of them talking, and the words he heard come from his dad had him pausing on the stairs to listen. Sure, his parents raised him better not to eavesdrop on someone's conversation, but he was curious.

"I just don't see any other alternative, Natasha. I know it's a hard decision, but what other choices do we have," his dad said, and Irish could hear the stress in his dad's voice.

His mom mumbled something; then he heard her sniffle like she was crying. Not wanting to waste any more time listening and trying to guess what was going on, he walked into the kitchen and stared at his mom and dad, who were sitting at the kitchen table, holding hands and both looking upset.

"Mom, Dad, what's going on?" He walked further into the kitchen and took a seat at the table across from them.

His mom glanced at his dad, and his dad nodded his head. His mom sighed deeply before looking at him. "It's Sienna, Ky. Your father and I are getting older, and it's getting harder to keep up with her, let alone keep up with the farm."

Irish got an uneasy feeling in his gut. "Are you thinking about selling the farm? You guys love this place. You've put so much heart and sweat into it."

"Actually, honey, our main focus right now is Sienna and what's best for her."

"And what exactly would that be? Because from what I can see, she is one happy little girl who loves you both dearly."

29

"We are looking at what options may be right for her."

Irish crossed his arms. "Explain, because I'm not following."

She took a deep breath. "Well, Pastor Nichols, who lives just down the road, offered to have Sienna come and live with him and his family. He and his wife Jillian have a couple of kids, one around Sienna's age."

Irish sat there, staring at his parents. Were they out of their minds? Sure, he understood about them getting up there in age, and he could see how it could be challenging to entertain a five-year-old, soon be six in a month and a half, but how could they even think of placing her with another family. Her biological mother and father had already abandoned her.

Before he could think of other possible options, his mouth started moving before his brain processed the words. "Absolutely not!"

Irish winced when he realized he had shouted at his mom. Her eyes widened, and she looked taken back by his reaction. "Honey, I know this is hard to hear, but your father and I believe this is best for her. We would be just down the road and can see her whenever we want, or she wants."

He shook his head. "No. Look, I understand that it's difficult for you guys, but if she is going to live anywhere else besides here, she's coming to live with me."

His mom's mouth gaped open at that surprise comment. Hell, he surprised himself. "What? How in the world can you take care of a five-year-old girl with the job you have? Think about it, honey. You're gone all the time. Who would watch her?"

That was the least of his worries. He knew his team, plus Alex, Tenley, and Autumn would help when needed. Damn, if he was going to let another family raise Sienna. She was a Daniels and dammit, she was going to be raised in a Daniels home.

"It's final, Mom. There is no reason even to discuss it anymore. Sienna's not going to live with anyone other than her family. I'll make it work. Some of the guys have families; when I'm gone, she can stay with them. We have a great support system in place. Our tight-knit community takes care of their own."

"Irish, she's a handful. This is a huge responsibility. Plus, financially, having a child is an enormous undertaking."

"Money isn't an issue. I don't spend a lot. I've got plenty saved."

"What about the house you just bought? Weren't you fixing it up? Is it livable?"

"It just needs some cosmetic stuff done to it. It will be perfect for Sienna and I."

His mom got up and walked around the table, bent down, and hugged him. She had tears in her eyes, and Irish knew this was a hard decision for her to make. Sienna was the world to his mom and dad. They have been with her since the moment she came into this world.

"You are a good boy, Ky. I love you so much."

He squeezed her back. "Love you too, Mom."

After his mom left the kitchen, it was just Irish and his dad. His dad looked tired, but Irish could tell something else was on his mind. And he had a feeling it had to do with the farm.

Irish went to the refrigerator and got a bottle of water for himself and his dad. "Are you and mom really thinking about selling the farm?"

His dad took a deep breath. "As much as your mother doesn't want to, I don't think we have a choice, son. I can't keep up with the work around here. It's getting to be a lot with all of the land."

Irish understood where his dad was coming from. His parents had about fifteen acres of land, and they probably only used about two acres of it. It was a shame. His parents always said they would grow old here together on the farm. He tapped his fingers on the solid oak table as he thought through some scenarios, then an idea hit him.

"What if you sold off some of the land? Say in two or even three-acre parcels. I noticed on the drive here that more and more new homes were being built on smaller lots. Why not keep the two acres you and mom use for the house and barn, and sell the remaining acres? That way, you guys can stay here where you want to be. Can you handle maintaining the two acres?"

When his dad's eyes lit up, he knew he had hit the jackpot.

His dad slapped his hand down against the table and smiled. "Damn, son. That is a hell of an idea. Jerome Miller, just down the road, did that a few months ago. Damn, I don't know why I didn't think of it."

They spoke for a couple of more minutes. His dad told him that tomorrow morning he would reach out to the realtor that Jerome used. His dad also asked if he was sure about his decision to take Sienna back to Virginia Beach with him. He assured his dad that everything would work out, and his decision was final.

After his dad went to bed, he sat alone in the kitchen. Now that he had taken care of his parents' problems, he needed to take care of his own, starting with a little firecracker named Sienna. He figured he'd start with his commander. After all, he went through something similar when Alex was younger. He would indeed have some words of wisdom for him.

Irish got up from the table and turned the light off and went up to his room. He was tired and ready for a good night's sleep. Tomorrow, he would start making plans—plans that will forever change his life. He laid down on the bed and stared at the ceiling. *Holy shit.... what have I gotten myself into?*

CHAPTER SIX

"Uncle Ky! Stop! Put me down," Sienna yelled, giggling as Irish held her upside down by her ankles. He laughed along with her.

"Are you going to put your stinky little feet in my face again?"

"Noooo! I promise Uncle Ky." Gently, he lowered her to the floor, then started tickling her. Her laughter reverberated through the room.

"What on God's earth is going on in here?" His mom asked, entering the living room with a huge smile on her face.

Irish looked up and smiled. His mom was a beautiful woman. She had the same blonde hair and blue eyes that he had. But beyond looks, she had a heart of gold and would do anything in her power to help someone out— even a perfect stranger.

"I'm just trying to get my point across here to my lovely niece that she needs to keep her stinky feet out of my face." He tickled her again, and she started giggling again, which made his mom start laughing. He missed this type of family time. Just hanging around his parents' house and laughing. It made up for all the shitty places and shitty situations he had been in while deployed. He just wished he had more times like this.

He looked around the room at all the family pictures. There were pictures of him in his Navy uniform, including a picture on the day he graduated and earned his Trident pin. There were some of Sienna's pre-school photos and even pictures of when Irish and Maggie were kids.

Seeing the photos of his sister made him think of the past. Maggie's trouble started about seven years ago when she started hanging around with the wrong crowd and eventually ended up in bed with a drug dealer. A year and a half later, she was pregnant. Her boyfriend didn't want to raise a kid, and apparently neither did Maggie. Thankfully, she carried the baby full-term. Not even an hour after Maggie had given birth to Sienna, she signed all her parental rights away to their mom and dad, making

Sienna their responsibility. The next day, Maggie was discharged from the hospital and disappeared.

Irish's parents treated Sienna as if she were their child. The same rules applied to her as they did when he and Maggie were children. Well, maybe Sienna got away with a few more things as she was also their granddaughter, and you know how grandparents give in a little to their grandkids—especially one as sweet as Sienna. But Irish knew better than to let her use that cuteness of hers to an advantage.

His mom told him and Sienna that lunch would be ready in about twenty minutes. They both needed to get cleaned up. They had been helping his dad move and load yard debris into the back of the truck.

After a quick shower, Irish was walking down the hallway when he passed Sienna's room and saw her standing in front of her closet. She'd already changed into clean clothes. He still hadn't said anything to her about moving with him, but he knew his mom talked with her this morning. He thought maybe now would be a good time for him to speak with her.

He rapped his knuckles on her door. "Hey, peanut, can I come in for a minute?"

She turned and smiled while walking over to her bed. She sat on the edge. This was going to be a considerable change for both of them. He hadn't a clue how to raise a child, let alone a girl. Luckily for him, though, he had a team of people waiting back home to help guide him, starting with his commander. He had called Derek last night after lying in bed and unable to sleep. Derek went through a similar situation years ago when Alex's dad was killed in action, leaving her behind when she was six years old and had no other family to care for her. Between Derek and his other teammates at the time, they all stepped up and took Alex under their wing. The stories he'd heard from those days kind of had him scared and nervous about raising a little girl. But he would never turn his back on his family.

He approached the bed and took a seat next to her. Her blue eyes sparkled as she looked up at him. He swallowed a laugh. With her dirty blonde hair, blue eyes, and facial features, such as the shape of her narrow eyes and her bright smile, she could pass as his kid, hands down.

He picked her up and placed her on his lap sideways so she could see him. She put her hands in her lap and stared up at him with that adorable face of hers.

"I know grandma explained a little to you about you coming back home with me."

He waited, knowing by the way she scrunched up her nose she was thinking. He smiled when she shook her head, yes.

"Uncle Ky? Will grandma and grandpa visit us? Will they still love me?"

"Of course, sweetie. Just because you're coming to live with me doesn't mean they won't visit or stop loving you. You are their world. Grandma and Grandpa are just at an age where they can't keep up with a little pipsqueak like you all the time." He lightly pinched her nose, making her giggle. He loved her laugh. When he would be out on a mission and needed a pick me up, he thought about her and her cute little giggle. It was addicting.

Her eyes got huge like she had an epiphany. "Oh! I get it. Grandma and Grandpa want to do old people things." Irish threw his head back, and outright laughed. He hugged her, squeezing her tight. Her little arms wrapped around his neck, and he buried his nose in her hair and inhaled. She was such a lovable kid, and he knew she would fit in with the others in no time.

She unwound her arms from his neck and looked at him. "Are there other kids where you live? Grandma said I was going to start going to big kids school this year. Will I still get to do that? Will I make friends?"

He smiled; with her outgoing personality, she wouldn't have any issue making friends. "There are lots of kids where I live, plus some of the guys I work with have kids. You will get to meet them once we get there and get settled. And to answer your question about school, yes, you'll start kindergarten this year. And I'm quite sure you'll make new friends there."

She gave him another hug. "I love you, Uncle Ky."

He felt his eyes tear up. She held a big piece of his heart. "I love you too, peanut."

She slid off his lap, walked back over to her closet and started pulling all sorts of stuff out of it, including a large rolling suitcase, and started packing some of her clothes. Well, that went better than he thought it would. Until about ten minutes later over lunch when both Sienna and his mom dropped a bombshell, informing him that he'd also be bringing a cat back with them as well. Mr. Whiskers was an overweight, orange tabby cat who did nothing but sleep, eat and lick his balls. At least that was all Irish seen him do. He didn't have anything against cats. He liked all animals, but this cat didn't like most people, including him. He swore that cat rolled his eyes and growled every time he walked by. Hopefully, Mr. Whiskers adjusted his attitude toward humans soon because damn if he would let a cat rule his house. That shit wasn't happening.

The next day, Irish was taking a break from packing. Sienna had a lot of shit. She probably had enough clothes and toys to fill a small moving truck. Letting her help with the packing seemed to help with the transition. The problem was she had to explain each item to him before she would put it in the box. It was a prolonged process.

Now he found himself sitting on the back porch in one of the rocking chairs, staring out at the woods that surrounded his childhood home. He remembered playing in those woods with his sister and all their friends. Those were the good memories he had of Maggie. He was always asking himself if she would've led a straight and narrow life if he would've stayed here at home instead of enlisting in the Navy. But then he would think of Sienna. If Maggie hadn't gotten involved with that guy, there wouldn't be a Sienna. He was thankful that he and his parents got to experience the joy of that little girl. She was the ray of sunshine they all needed with the dark clouds Maggie brought to them. It was a shame that Maggie chose the life she did because Irish knew she would've made a great mom. But greed and drugs could rule a person's life and make decisions for them. He was just thankful Maggie and her boyfriend gave up their rights to Sienna without a fight. His mom had told him that just recently, Sienna had started asking about her mom and dad. His mom said that Sienna was struggling and thinking that she had done something wrong to make her mom and dad not want her. Shit like that pissed him off and made him want to hunt Maggie down and knock some sense into her. That woman didn't know what she was missing by making the decision she had. But what's done is done. All that mattered now was caring for and loving Sienna to the fullest.

He heard the creak of the screened door and knew it was his mom. He knew the sound of her footsteps and heard her walking toward the door. He turned toward the door and smiled. "Hey, Mom. You want to come and sit with me?" He asked, patting the empty rocking chair next to him.

She walked over and squeezed his shoulder. "That's sweet of you to ask, honey. I miss the days we used to sit out here and just stare at the world around us. She looked out toward the land and woods. "I can sit out here all day," she turned back toward him, "but that's not why I'm here. You have company here to see you." He squinted his eyes at her, wondering what she was up to. Nobody knew he was in town except for his parents, and he hadn't gone anywhere since he arrived. He noticed a slight twinkle in his mom's eyes and saw her lips twitch up almost to a smile but not quite. He could only imagine who in the hell she had invited over. He just wanted to spend the next couple of days getting Sienna's stuff packed up. Even though he had plenty of leave, that didn't mean that the shit wouldn't hit the fan somewhere, and he and the team would be called in, so he wanted to get everything handled quickly and get back to Virginia Beach as soon as possible.

"Who is it?" He asked, dropping his feet from the railing and standing.

She smiled and opened the door. "Well, why don't you just walk your rear-end in the house and see for yourself."

He let out a sigh and followed his mom into the house. From the kitchen, he heard his dad talking to someone in the living room. Then he heard Sienna talking about her Barbie doll collection.

As he made his way into the living room, he was stopped in his tracks when he saw the two individuals sitting on the couch, making small talk with his dad and Sienna.

"What are you guys doing here?" He asked, shocked and surprised to see Ace and Alex.

Alex was the first to approach him and gave him a big hug, and he needed that. "When my dad called Ace and explained everything that was going on with Sienna, Ace and I decided to come up here and help you with the move. I thought that Sienna might feel a little more comfortable if she met a few faces she'd be regularly seeing before she got to town. Plus, I was kind of in her place when I was a kid. Maybe I can help with the transition some."

"What about the Foundation and Clinic? It's crunch time; you only have a little over a month from your opening."

She smiled that gorgeous smile she had, and her green eyes lit up and twinkled. "Family is more important, Irish. I have confidence in the people I hired to keep things running until I get back. Right now, our focus is on Sienna and getting her adapted to the area and military life."

Irish felt his throat tighten from the lump that had formed. He was blown away at the sincerity and generosity that Ace and Alex have shown. He was going to need a lot of help. He hugged her again. "I don't know what to say, except thanks."

Ace slapped him on the back. "That's what friends are for, buddy. We're there for each other no matter what shit life brings us."

Sienna covered her mouth with her hand and giggle. She looked up at Irish. "He said the "s" word. That's a quarter." She got up and walked over to a can that looked like a coffee can that was painted all different colors. She walked back over and stood in front of Ace. "This is a bad word can. You said the "s" word, so you have to put a quarter in the can. Grandma said money from the can will go to my college fund."

Irish snorted a laugh as Ace asked Alex for a quarter and then put it into the can. Ace looked at Irish. "You do know that just from the guys on the team, she'll have college paid for with that damn can."

"You said another bad word. That's another quarter," Sienna stated as she giggled, and all Irish could do was laugh at Ace as he rolled his eyes and asked Alex for another quarter. This was going to be interesting. The first thing Irish was going to do when they got home was buy a bigger can because the can she had now would be filled in a week.

Alex had proven to be a lifesaver over the next two days as she handled organizing all of Sienna's belongings and getting everything packed up. She had the patience of a saint, especially when Sienna wanted to help. She also arranged the moving truck to transport Sienna's things back to Virginia Beach. Autumn, Frost's wife, was gathering all the information he needed to enroll Sienna in school, which starts next Monday. Tenley, Potter's wife, handled getting Sienna set-up with the pediatrician that her daughter, Alejandra, went to. Alex had also called her dad, and he was taking care of all the repairs that needed to be done at the house before they arrived. Irish was still a little skeptical about how they were going to have everything done by the time they arrived in two days. He needed hardwood floors installed, all of the rooms had to be painted, the kitchen was missing half of the cabinets, but Alex assured him it would be accomplished by the time he walked through the door and for him not to sweat over it.

Irish took a seat next to Ace on the back porch. Alex was on the phone with the pilots, getting their flight back home worked out for the day after tomorrow. Her uncle Tink flew them up on one of his security company's private jets.

"I swear when we get home, I'm buying your fiancé a cape."

"Huh?" Ace asked, giving Irish a sideways glance but keeping his eyes on his woman. Rarely did Ace ever take his eyes off Alex when she was near.

"Alex. She's a fucking superwoman." He watched her along with Ace as she talked diligently on the phone while she watched Sienna pick some vegetables in the garden.

Ace nodded his head. "That she is. She's my world. I tell ya, man; I honestly don't know where I'd be right now if she hadn't been sent on that mission with us to Afghanistan last year."

Irish thought it was cool how Ace and Alex had met during a mission. At the time, she had been working for a private firm and was assisting in hunting down a terrorist. The mission had been a shit show from the start and ultimately ended with Alex being kidnapped, beaten, and shot. She survived, barely. Even though he saw the videos of her defending herself and killing her captors, he still wondered how she did it, especially in the condition she was in.

Irish rested his legs on the railing and rocked the chair. "Speaking of Alex, when are you planning to make it official and put a wedding band on her finger? Have you guys talked about setting another date?"

Ace and Alex were supposed to get married months ago, but due to a deployment, their wedding was postponed. They talked about it again, but their careers threw some wrenches in the dates they were looking at.

Irish envied Ace and Alex's relationship. He'd never admit it to the others, but deep down, he wished he could meet a woman who would look at him like Alex looked at Ace. The admiration and love she showed Ace were unbelievable.

He immediately thought about "Blue," the blonde-haired beauty with the glacier blue eyes. She seemed so innocent and delicate, and those traits definitely weren't the type he went for in a woman. Then again, he didn't date. He was all about the quick hook-ups to give him a satisfied and needed release. And the women he took to bed knew that was all they were getting. But "Blue" intrigued him from the moment she looked up at him while she laid in that puddle. He could see himself cuddled up to her after a round of lovemaking.

It couldn't be that hard to hunt her down. She mentioned her condo was near Bayside. Bayside was located on a dead-end street, with only maybe five or six condo complexes on the street. He could ask some friends for help if needed.

Irish was so engrossed thinking about Blue that he almost hadn't heard Ace answer his question. "We were hoping to set a date by the end of the year, but with things going on with the Foundation and Clinic, it's too much right now. When Alex and I last talked about it last month she told me that she didn't need a piece of paper to tell me she's mine." Ace shrugged his shoulders, and he stared at Alex as she continued to speak on the phone. "I told her the same. So, I guess all that matters is that we love each other."

Irish hoped Ace was right, but he had a feeling Alex saw things a little differently and might just be telling Ace that to appease him. He saw how excited she was when she was planning the original wedding. But then again, what did he know about love and marriage? His focus right now was getting back home and settling into becoming a dad and everything that went with it.

CHAPTER SEVEN

A few days had gone by, and Irish still had boxes upon boxes to unpack. His team had come through big time for him. Not only had they painted the entire house inside, laid new wood flooring, installed the rest of the kitchen cabinets, but they also had Sienna's room all decorated. She had mentioned she liked fairies. So, of course, Tenley and Autumn took on the challenge and created a masterpiece that looked like it came right out of one of those HGTV shows. It even had twinkle lights hidden throughout the room, so when the lights were off, it gave the appearance that fairies were hiding. It was absolutely amazing. Not to mention her bed was literally off the ground, and you had to walk over a little suspension type bridge to get to it. He was a bit nervous about that, considering she was still young and could roll-off, but the way the bed was designed, it had sides. Of course, Sienna loved it. It had been hard to drag her from the room.

The biggest challenge so far had been hair maintenance. Sienna had long hair, and the nightly washing and detangling process was killing him, especially the first time he made her cry when he yanked too hard. He still felt terrible. Thankfully, Tenley being the sweetheart she is, had stopped by and dropped off some kind of spray that would help with the detangling process. While there, she also gave him a crash course in ponytails and pigtails. But whatever it took to make sure his little peanut was cared for, he'd make sure it happened, even if she did step out in public with uneven pigtails.

For him personally, the hardest adjustment was when he traded his Corvette in for a more family friendly vehicle. Diego took him to a dealership that a friend of his owned and he traded the sports car in for a red Lincoln Navigator. He'd admit, the Navigator was pretty cool.

Sienna's first day of school was in two days. They had missed the meet the teacher day because they were traveling back to Virginia Beach, but when Autumn swung by the school to get everything he needed to get Sienna enrolled, she was able to meet Sienna's teacher. Autumn seemed impressed with her, so he felt good about that.

The next couple of weeks were going to be hectic and possibly a little difficult for Sienna, and that had him worried. Because of the schedule at work, he wasn't going to be able to drop her off or pick her up from school, which he wanted to do, to start getting into a routine. It would be good for both of them. For now, Tenley offered to pick-up and drop-off since Alejandra attended the same school.

The first night he and Sienna got home, he'd had "the talk" with her. The talk meaning there were times he would need to leave for work. He assured her she would be taken care of. He'd already made arrangements with Alex. She would be Sienna's guardian any time he was out of town. If it weren't for his team and the women, he was pretty sure he would be up shit creek without a paddle. They'd all been nothing but supportive since they heard Sienna was coming to live with him. In just the couple of days they've been home, Sienna had already become close with Alejandra, Potter, and Tenley's daughter, as well as Cody, Frost, and Autumn's son. Irish had a lot of respect for Cody. He was already a little alpha male as he watched over Alejandra and Sienna. He had a protective streak in him. He proved that when he took it upon himself to paddle his surfboard out into the Atlantic Ocean to save his mother from an evil man.

Then there was Mr. Whiskers. Irish still wasn't completely sold on the cat yet. That damn cat still gave him an attitude, even though he was one who fed him, gave him water, and cleaned his shit out of the litter box every single day. To top it off, the damn thing decided to make himself at home in his bed. Every night, he had to chase him out, but every morning he'd wake up, and the bastard was back in the bed. This morning, he decided it was a battle he didn't want to fight. In his career, he'd learned there are times when to pick your battles, and this was not one of those times.

43

Overall, all was well in the Daniel's household.

CHAPTER EIGHT

Irish and Sienna walked into her school. It was "Back to School" night, and Sienna was practically bouncing as she walked, holding his large hand. She'd been so excited the last few days. He had to admit he was somewhat curious to meet her teacher, Ms. Anderson, that she'd been talking non-stop about for the past three weeks since school started. She also mentioned several times how pretty she is. Not that he would ever hit on one of Sienna's teachers. No way. Plus, now that things were settling at home, he was determined to start his hunt for "Blue."

The last few weeks had gone by in a blur. Keeping up with Sienna had been an eye-opener, but he wouldn't trade spending time with her for the world. He felt he had taken on the role of fatherhood well. He'd even received compliments from the guys. That's not to say there had been times where he'd had to call up one of the women and ask for advice.

Sienna had adjusted to the move and new living arrangements quickly. She was also doing well in school based on the assignments she had been bringing home in her daily folder. He enjoyed their nightly routine. After he would pick her up from Tenley's, they would come home, and he would fix them dinner. After dinner, they would go through her daily folder together, and he would ask her questions and sometimes even quiz her on things she was learning in class. Then it was bath time, and if time allowed a little TV time together on the couch with Disney Jr., then off to bed with a bedtime story. Irish loved every minute of it.

They were running late getting to the school. The one night that he needed to leave work on time, a situation occurred. He was worried they wouldn't even make it, but they did, although from the looks of the empty room, they were the last ones.

As Sienna steered him into the classroom talking a mile a minute, she paused, then squealed before she took off running. "Ms. Anderson!"

Irish scanned the set-up of the room. There were four tables with four chairs at each in the middle of the room. To one side was a play area, and the other side was arranged like a reading library with shelves of books surrounding a couple of bean bags for the children to sit in while they read their favorite book. It was pretty cool.

His eyes zeroed in on the petite woman who was bent over hugging Sienna. As he made his way over to the two of them, the woman stood and met his gaze. Irish felt his knees buckle, and he almost lost his ability to stand. It was her…

"Irish?" That sweet, soulful, southern voice rang in the air with a gasp. All Irish could do was stare. He swallowed hard; his throat was dry as a desert. He looked into those eyes and the face he had memorized over a month ago. Shit, he had it ingrained in his head. "B-Blue?" He said, finally able to speak. He shook his head. Did he just stutter?

She quirked an eyebrow. "Blue?"

His eyes grew large when he realized he said that out loud, and he felt his cheeks warm. "I'm sorry. Ever since that night we met, I haven't been able to stop thinking about you. Your eyes. They are so unique." Her eyes widened, and her cheeks turned pink. Then like a freight train, it hit him. *Blue, the woman who had caused many sleepless nights as he fantasized about her, is Sienna's teacher!* This was so not a good thing. "I am so sorry. I sound like some whack job." He ran his hand through his hair. He was a mess. She just stood there, and finally, she smiled and held her hand out.

"Why don't we start over? I'm Bailey Anderson, Sienna's teacher."

He grinned and shook her hand, still in denial that Blue was standing in front of him. "Ky…Ky Daniels, Sienna's uncle."

She scrunched her eyebrows together and gave him an odd look. "I thought you said your name was Irish."

He shrugged his shoulders. "It's a nickname." She nodded her head. Christ, this was awkward.

She cleared her throat and grinned. "Why don't we have a seat while Sienna plays a little, and I can tell you about what she's learning now, and

46

I can go over what the curriculum is for the remainder of the year since I didn't get a chance to talk to you before now." She gestured toward a larger table off to the side of the room that he assumed was her desk.

They both sat down, and when she started talking, all he could do was stare and get lost in her beauty and voice. She was dressed in a pair of form-fitting stylish black pants, a brown cowl neck sweater, paired with dark brown boots that came up just below the knee. She was absolutely stunning. Her blonde hair was straight and hung below her shoulders. She had the sides tucked behind her cute little ears. Her face looked natural, not much make-up, but it glowed like she had gotten a little sun. He couldn't get over the fact that "Blue" was literally sitting in front of him. Was this fate? He wondered to himself.

"Ky?" That sweet southern angelic voice pulled him out of his head.

He cleared his throat. "I'm sorry, can you repeat what you just said?"

She smiled, and Jesus if that didn't make his dick harder. By the time he got through with this meeting, he was going to have a permanent tattoo of his zipper on his dick.

"I asked you if you were okay. You seemed to really zone out there for a minute."

"Sorry, I was just thinking about something." He wanted to tell her it was her he was thinking about.

She smiled and pulled her bottom lip between her teeth, and he wanted to moan. She probably had no clue how seductive she appeared right now. She tried inconspicuously not to look over his body, but Irish caught her, and he smiled to himself. *Oh yeah, could the pretty little teacher be having some of the same naughty thoughts I am?*

Thank God she asked a question because if she hadn't, there was no telling what his next course of action or words would have been toward her. She was that appealing.

"If you don't mind me asking, what is it that you do? The last week we've been talking about careers. The other day we went around the room, and each student had an opportunity to say something about what their parents or guardian, as in your case, did for a living. And well, Sienna

47

seemed a little flustered, I guess you could call it. I mean, she jumped right away at the opportunity and even raised her hand to go first and has no issues speaking in front of people, but as she started, she couldn't really say what you did other than you help people."

Irish wanted to laugh. God, he loved Sienna. She still couldn't comprehend the military stuff and the difference between Navy and Army, and he definitely was not getting into the things he did with her. But she absolutely said what he told her to say if anyone ever inquired about what he did for a living. And that was that he helped people. That statement left a plethora of things he could be. However, saying that would only last for another year or two as she started getting older and understanding more.

He held Bailey's gaze but noticed a slight twinkle or sparkle to her eyes. "I'm in the Navy," he said gruffly, and when he saw her eyes light up, his stomach formed a knot. Could this little pixie have a thing for military men? God, he prayed not because that would devastate him. He had enough of the women who wanted him only for the uniform he wore. He didn't want another one.

Her lips quirked up just slightly, and he had a feeling he was missing something. "Well, that explains a lot about Sienna's family drawing," she said, and Irish was now utterly confused.

"What drawing? I didn't see anything in the folder she brings home," he stated.

Bailey smiled again, then got up and walked over to the wall that had a bunch of drawings tacked up on it. He couldn't help to take a quick glance at her ass as she stood on her tiptoes to remove a piece of paper.

"We hung them up to show tonight. But I am happy to hear that you look at her folder." She walked back to the desk and sat back down. "You'd be surprised at how many parents don't."

She handed him the piece of paper, and he looked at it. There were eight stick people in blue, three stick people in pink, and three stick people in green. Under the blue ones, Sienna had written the names of Irish and each of his team members. Under the pink ones, she wrote, Alex, Tenley, and Autumn, and under the green were Cody, Alejandra, and Sienna.

Irish was in awe. He was so caught up in his emotions; he hadn't realized a tear had slipped out of his eye. He went to wipe it away and locked gazes with Bailey. She, too, looked emotional. He couldn't believe a five-year-old understood who her family really was. All the people she drew were her family.

Realizing he must have looked like a dork, he set the paper on the desk. "I'm sorry." He said, still staring at it.

She gave him a sympathetic smile and patted his hand. Her touch sent jolts of electricity up his entire arm.

"It happens all of the time and trust me; it won't be the last time she does something that gets you emotional. Autumn, the woman who I met and gave Sienna's enrollment papers to, explained a little about Sienna's situation. Mainly that you were taking over guardianship of her."

"Yeah, my parents are at that age where they should be settling down more, and having a rambunctious, full of life five-year-old was hindering that," he stated with a grin.

"I completely get what you're saying. I just have them for a couple of hours a day, and they wear me out. But I come back every day because it's what I love to do. And it gives me a greater pleasure when I can give something like this," she motioned toward the picture, "to a parent and really see the love and proudness in their eyes."

"I'm sure all parents, some time or another, get that emotional feeling when they see something extraordinary their kids do or accomplish," he said, and suddenly, he wished he hadn't because a look of sadness crossed her beautiful face. It happened quickly, but then it was gone, and a slight smile appeared. "I'm sorry if I said something that upset you," he told her, as he studied her. But she waved him off.

"Please, don't be sorry." She glanced over to the table where Sienna was building something out of playdough and smiled, then looked back at Irish, pausing almost as if she were considering her words carefully. "Let's just say my childhood wasn't filled with warm and happy memories." She gave him a soft smile, then cleared her throat. And just like that, she was back focused on what was in front of her; whatever thoughts or memories that had saddened her just moments ago were gone. "Anyway, Sienna talks very highly of everyone in the picture. She seems really happy and is very social in class. You're doing a wonderful job with her."

Before Irish could explain the picture, Bailey continued and tapped her finger on the picture. "I'm going out on a limb here. I know men and women in the service like to keep a low profile, but from the little gold symbol above the eight blue stick figures, I'm guessing you and the rest of her 'uncles' are SEALs or the proper name I believe is Navy Special Warfare Operator."

His eyebrows shot up with surprise. Not many people realized that. To the general population, they were just SEALs.

Irish took a deep breath. He, along with the rest of his team, weren't the type to boast about being Special Forces. But he couldn't lie to her, especially since she was Sienna's teacher. He nodded his head. "You would be correct."

She followed up quickly. "Don't worry; I know you guys like your privacy. Your secret is safe with me."

For some reason, he didn't doubt it. She seemed like an honest to goodness person, and the way she spoke about her students, he knew she loved her job and genuinely cared for the kids.

More relaxed, for the next fifteen minutes, they spoke about upcoming projects the students would be working on. She even convinced him to help out with the fall festival the school was hosting next month. He didn't want to stop talking, but Sienna had made it clear she was hungry, so they said goodnight to Ms. Anderson.

As Irish walked out of the school, Sienna took his large hand into her tiny one and looked up at him. "I really like Ms. Anderson. And she's real pretty too. I want to be pretty like her when I grow up."

Irish smiled. "I like Ms. Anderson too. And yes, she is very pretty just like you." He winked, and she giggled.

Even though he knew he shouldn't even think about getting involved with Bailey because she was Sienna's teacher, he couldn't let the feelings go. There was definitely a connection. The attraction to her made his blood surge. He wanted to ask her for her number but felt it just wasn't the right time or place. But now he knew where to find her, and eventually, he would ask.

Bailey sat at her desk. She took another glance toward the doorway that Irish and Sienna walked out of. She couldn't believe that Irish had been under her nose this whole time. Well, at least since school started. What were the odds that her mystery man was connected to one of her students?

Ever since their encounter in the parking lot a little over a month ago, she hadn't been able to shake him from her thoughts. Every night, she would sit out on her balcony, using his sweatshirt he had lent to her to keep warm. Then she remembered what he said. He'd been thinking about her as well. Was this fate telling her to take a chance?

She had moved away to get out from under the hold of one man, and here she was practically lusting over another one. But this one was definitely different. He was just a man. Not trying to be something that he wasn't. But one thing that did intimidate her was he was a warrior; he was a Navy SEAL. Those men were powerful. They were trained to kill. They were one of the country's elite Special Forces group. That alone had put a little doubt in her mind. Randy wasn't nearly as fit as Irish was, and Randy could control her physically. What would someone with Irish's power do to someone like her?

She felt her stomach growl, reminding her that she'd skimped on lunch. Her meeting with Principal Pega during her free period took longer than expected, giving her just enough time to scarf down a banana. Deciding she would grab something on the way home, she quickly arranged her desk so everything would be ready in the morning, then grabbed her bags and headed to her car. Maybe she'd stop at the place where she had gotten her flat tire and try the food. Some of the other teachers told her she had to go. So why not since it was just down the street from her condo and on her way home.

CHAPTER NINE

Irish and Sienna walked into Bayside. Sienna was craving chicken fingers. Irish didn't have any objections since he had missed lunch today and could go for a big bacon and cheddar burger and cheese fries. The place wasn't crowded, and they were able to get the usual table he and the team normally sat at near the back exit that led out to the patio overlooking the beach.

They had just placed their order when Sienna blurted out, "Uncle Ky, look...Ms. Anderson is here."

Irish's head snapped up immediately, and he looked toward the front entrance where Sienna was pointing, and sure as shit, there she stood—looking just as beautiful as when he'd left her just twenty minutes ago. The way she scanned the place, he wondered if she was meeting someone here. His gut clenched. Was she meeting a guy? He watched as she stopped a waitress and asked her something. The waitress smiled and waved her hand in the air, and then Bailey started zigzagging through the throng of tables. She was getting closer to their table, and his heart rate started to pick up. She spotted an empty table three down from his and Sienna's. When she went to sit, she turned her head and locked gazes with him. Her eyes widened in surprise, and she smiled wide. He smiled back and waved. A waitress stopped at her table, and Irish heard her order an iced tea. When the waitress left, Bailey walked over. He felt nervous yet excited at seeing her twice in the same day.

"Ms. Anderson! See Uncle Ky; I told you it was her," Sienna exclaimed as she waved to Bailey.

Bailey laughed, then looked at Irish. "Looks like we both had the same idea."

He smiled. "Yeah, it seems that way. This place has the best food."

"Well, that's good to know, considering this will be the first time I've eaten here."

Irish knew he must have had a shocked look on his face because she followed up her statement. "If you remember, I was scared to come in here when I got my flat tire. However, my co-workers said I had to try it, and well, I don't have much to eat at home, so I thought what the heck. It was on my way home; I might as well stop."

"Uncle Ky, can Ms. Anderson sit with us? She doesn't have anyone to sit with?" Sienna asked him with a pout in her lip. He had planned on inviting her to sit with them anyway. Before he could answer, Bailey did.

"Oh, I don't want to interrupt your dinner time together. I just didn't want to be rude and not come over and say hello, again." She gave him a shy look. It made his dick stir instantly.

He reached out his hand and touched her arm. He heard her short intake of breath as his hand made contact with her soft skin.

"You wouldn't be interrupting. It would make both of us happy if you could join us. I give Sienna another five minutes, and she'll be playing games over there," he motioned to the two video arcade games up against the wall, "and it'd be nice to have someone to talk to. Plus, I can help you decide what you want to eat, considering I've tried everything on the menu." He winked, and she blushed. Damn, her shyness was a turn on. She nibbled on her lip as she thought about it. He didn't realize he was holding his breath or still touching her arm until she finally agreed, and he exhaled. He smiled and signaled to the waitress, happy that he was going to get some more time to talk with her.

"So, if you don't mind me asking, what is the story with Sienna," Bailey asked Irish as she bit into her French dip sandwich. The best French dip sandwich she had ever eaten. Who knew a place like this would have such awesome food? This would serve as a lesson to never judge a book by its cover.

He set his burger down. "What do you mean?" He kind of asked on the defensive. He was very protective of Sienna.

53

Bailey must have realized because she quickly reached across the table and touched his hand.

"I'm sorry. That didn't quite come out right. I'm sorry if I offended you. What I meant to say was, where are her mom and dad?" She quickly glanced over at Sienna playing the games. "I mean, look at her, she is the spitting image of you with the blonde hair and blue eyes, but she calls you uncle." He looked into her translucent blue eyes and could see the sincerity, compassion, and honesty be stilled in her. This woman was different on so many levels than the women he hooked up with.

He shook his head, feeling like a buffoon. "No, I'm the one who should apologize. I didn't mean to come across as a jerk. It's just when it comes to Sienna; I'm very protective and cautious."

She nodded. "I understand. And you don't have to apologize. She's lucky to have you and has someone who cares about her the way you do."

He thought about her words for a second. Yeah, Sienna was lucky, but he also was lucky himself. In just the few weeks that Sienna had been living with him, she'd brought so much joy and happiness to his world. With the shit he deals with at work, and how it can sometimes be a downer, it's nice to be able to come home to a house filled with laughter and fun.

He started explaining about Maggie and her boyfriend. As he rambled on, he snorted a laugh and ran his hand down his face.

"What?" She asked so innocently.

"You." He stared at her for a few seconds. "The only people that even know about Sienna are my teammates and their significant others. But with you, words just seem to fall out of my mouth. There's something about you that makes me open up and want to spill my life story."

She gave him a genuine smile. "Please know that everything you've told me tonight will not go beyond this table. Trust me; I'm fully aware that sometimes there is that one person you feel comfortable opening up to." It seemed to Irish that Bailey was a person who kept her emotions hidden from others so that she wouldn't have to talk about herself. It had him curious to know what lied beneath her facade. He remembered her mentioning earlier that she didn't have a great childhood and how she looked sad.

"Ky, I know we kinda, sorta, just met tonight, but please know if you ever need to talk to anyone, you can call me. I know you probably have your friends and teammates you can call, but I just wanted to throw that out there. If it's about Sienna or if your neighbor pisses you off, know I'd be there. My number is in the packet of information I gave you at the school."

Well, damn, earlier, he was chastising himself for not getting her number, and here she had already given it to him. He smiled and could feel his attraction growing for her by the second. "I appreciate that. I may just take you up on it," he said, trying to see the direction this conversation would go.

"I'd be disappointed if you didn't," she replied, holding his gaze, and Irish couldn't help but think she was insinuating something else. So, he decided to dig a little deeper.

"You would? And how would your boyfriend feel?" He asked, still not taking his eyes off her.

She played with her straw and grinned. "Yeah, I would. And there is no boyfriend." They stared into each other's eyes, and Irish was mesmerized by her demeanor. She was gorgeous and seemed so kind and caring. Plus, she loved kids. Fuck! What was he thinking here? He was a master at flirting, especially when he needed and wanted some action. But whatever was happening between the two of them was unknown territory. *You want her. You want an actual relationship with her.*

The sound of Sienna's squeal interrupted their moment. They both looked toward the game machine Sienna was playing and saw Ace. He was walking towards them with Sienna in his arms, hanging upside down. Then he spotted Alex right behind him, and when he saw her eyes lock on the beauty sitting across from him, he knew he was fucked. He could see the little twinkle already in her green eyes. Alex loved trying to play matchmaker with him. She called it her life project to find him a woman capable of making him happy and satisfied. Alex knew sex for him would be very important to him in a relationship. But it wasn't just sex; he wanted someone he could make love to and feel the connection of something more. He was tired of the meaningless one-night hook-ups. He glanced back at Bailey and took one look at the innocent look on her face. Oh yeah, he could so see himself making love to her. He would worship every inch of her body and soul.

Alex reached the table and gave him a hug and kiss on the cheek. "I thought you were at Open House tonight at Sienna's school?" She asked as she made herself comfortable in the chair next to Bailey.

"We were, Sienna got hungry, so we stopped in here on the way home." Irish looked at Bailey. She sat there smiling, watching Sienna trying to climb up Ace's large body like a monkey.

"I see," Alex said with a smirk on her face. She glanced over at Bailey, then back at Irish and raised her eyebrows in question. Irish wanted to laugh because he knew it was eating at Alex to know who the woman she was sitting next to. Just to be a wise-ass, he thought about not introducing Bailey to her right away. But then, he thought better of it because that wouldn't be fair to Bailey and might make her uncomfortable.

Bailey turned his way and smiled at him. He grinned back and then heard a throat clear. When he glanced back at Alex, she was practically squirming in her seat. Ace was just standing next to the table, holding Sienna against his hip. Talk about an awkward few seconds of silence.

"I'm sorry. Ace, Alex, this is Bailey Anderson."

Alex stuck her hand out, and Bailey shook it without any hesitation, which made Irish's smile grow. "It's nice to meet you, Bailey. How do you two know each other?" Alex asked, waving her hand between Irish and Bailey.

Irish went to speak, but Sienna beat him to it. "She's my teacher, and Uncle Ky likes her, and he says she pretty like me." Irish saw Bailey's cheeks turn a light shade of pink as she grinned and lowered her head. Alex, on the other hand, was biting the inside of her cheek to keep from laughing, and Ace, of course, stood there with a shit-eating grin on his face. Yep, he was definitely fucked.

56

Bailey cleared her throat and then looked at Ace. "Are you guys staying for dinner?"

Ace smiled. "Yep. Alex was craving a chicken sandwich."

"Would the two of you like to join us?" Bailey asked before Irish could, and he smiled, sensing Bailey was completely comfortable around his friends, even though she'd just met them.

"Oh, we don't want to impose on your date," Alex exclaimed, and Irish didn't know if Alex's smile could get any bigger.

Bailey looked to Irish and then back to Alex. "Oh, we're not on a date. And you wouldn't be imposing. I didn't even know Ky and Sienna were going to be here. I just stopped in on my way home. It just so happens we were all thinking the same." She smiled, and Alex smiled. Ace snorted a laugh, and slapped Irish on his back and took the seat next to him with Sienna on his lap. This was going to be hell.

Bailey liked Alex immediately. She didn't come across as fake like the women she was used to back in Birmingham. She was so down to earth and absolutely gorgeous, especially with her dark hair, green eyes, and her olive complexion. Her fiancé, Ace, wasn't hard on the eyes either. He was kind of the opposite of Irish except for the eyes. They both had blue eyes. Ace had jet black hair and was stockier in his build, whereas Irish had dirty blonde hair and a leaner build. Neither one looked like they had an ounce of fat on them. But that was to be expected, considering all the training they must do.

Alex's voice brought Bailey back to the table. "Your eyes are gorgeous. They are so.... blue. And not just any blue. The color is unique. I don't think I've ever seen anything like them before." Bailey was going to respond, but suddenly, Alex's eyes widened, and her mouth gaped open.

"Oh, my God! You're Blue!" Alex looked over at Irish and was practically jumping in her seat. Bailey wasn't sure what to think. But considering that Irish had called her the same name earlier tonight when he first saw her, he must have told his friends about her. She then wondered how many people might know about her.

"For Christ's sake, Alex. Will you calm down? Can't you see you're frightening her?" Irish scolded his friend, but Bailey knew he was joking.

Alex touched her arm, making her look at her. Bailey couldn't comprehend why Alex seemed so happy. Was she this "Blue" that Irish had been telling his friends about?

"I'm so sorry. I don't mean to scare you. You don't realize how bad Mr. Broody over there has been wanting to find you since the night he helped you in the parking lot." Bailey didn't miss the warning glare that Irish sent Alex's way. Then Ace intervened. "Alex, how many times do I have to remind you to mind your own business sometimes. This being one of those times."

"Oh, my God!" Alex clapped her hands together and bounced in her seat. "This is awesome! We are going to get along great! Just wait until you meet Tenley. Oh! And you already met Autumn." Alex followed up completely, ignoring her fiancé's warning, which Bailey found a little funny. She heard Irish sigh as he rubbed his hand down his face, and Ace just laughed at him.

As the evening went on and everyone finished their dinners, Irish was surprised but thrilled by how well Alex and Bailey got along. The way they were talking and laughing with each other was like watching two old friends catch up.

Alex had spent a lot of time telling Bailey about her Foundation and how excited she was about the grand opening next month. Bailey seemed intrigued and asked a lot of questions, like how it was funded, how its operation was run, and the history behind it.

What also surprised Irish was Bailey's knowledge of the U.S. military. She was quite resourceful and knew a great deal about all the different branches of service.

"You are like a little data bank of history. How do you know so much about the military?" Ace asked her as he took a drink of his beer, and Irish wondered the same. God, he really hoped she wasn't a military groupie. That would be such a disappointment.

"Oh, I love all aspects of the military." She answered Ace and Irish's eyebrows shot up. Ace gave him a look, but then she quickly followed up on her comment. "I studied a lot of military history in high school and college. I still do. It all fascinates me. I swear I'm not a crazy person who stalks military men. I support and respect all the branches of our nation's armed forces, and I think they should be given a lot more respect and credit from our government for everything they do. I mean, take you guys, for example, going off on missions and leaving your loved ones behind. Putting your lives on the line to protect all of us here at home."

Ace was taken back by her comment, and he looked over at Irish and quirked one of his eyebrows.

Irish shrugged his shoulders. "Don't look at me; I didn't let the cat of the bag. Your lovely, adorable niece drew a picture at school and tried to recreate the Trident Pin. And knowing her military attributes, Bailey here picked up on it and asked. I wasn't going to lie."

Irish sat there and listened to Bailey as she tried to put Ace at ease at the knowledge of her knowing they were SEALs. The more she spoke, the more his respect for her grew.

"Ace, you have nothing to worry about," she told him in that rich southern accent of hers. "I promise, what I know about my student's personal and family lives are sacred to me, and I don't share any information with anybody unless a child is endangered, and only then would I divulge any information I'm privy to with school officials or law enforcement. I understand you guys keep a low profile, and I respect that. You have jobs to do and don't need any type of interference."

Irish wasn't sure what Ace thought until he saw Ace's lips twitch. His team leader loved this, and Irish knew he was going to hear so much shit about it. He gave Alex five seconds when she got outside tonight to call Tenley and tell her about Bailey. By the time he arrived for PT tomorrow morning, the entire team would know. They were like a little dysfunctional family, and everybody had to be up in everyone's shit. But in the end, everyone loved, cared, and looked after each other.

As the night went on, with Alex's help, Irish was able to keep the other women in the bar vying for his attention to a minimum; however, there were a few that were able to get through and make it over to their table. Although Bailey hadn't seemed fazed by the women's advances, Irish knew they didn't go unnoticed, and that bothered him. In no way did he want Bailey to think he was interested in the other women. There was only one woman he was captivated by, and that was the Southern angel sitting across from him.

Bear and the entire Bravo team had shown up. They were celebrating Duke's promotion in rank. Duke was a combat medic for Bravo Team. Irish and Ace excused themselves for a few minutes and went over to congratulate the man of the hour. Even though Irish was across the room, his eyes were always on Bailey. She and Alex continued to talk. If Bailey passed Alex's assessment, that was great because Alex had a way to sniff out the fakes.

A few minutes had passed when he noticed Bailey stand swing her purse onto her shoulder, and it looked like she had paid the waitress. Damn, he wanted to buy her dinner. He excused himself from the guys and walked over to the table.

"Are you leaving?" He asked as he gently touched her arm and turned her toward him. He saw her eyes widen when he touched her, and he couldn't help the excitement he felt. She was definitely showing signs of the attraction.

She tucked a strand of her silky blonde hair behind her ear, an ear that he would love to nibble on.

"Yeah, I need to head home. I need to finish planning my lessons for next week. Thank you for letting me join you and Sienna. I enjoyed it. Your friends seem like really nice people."

"That they are. You and Alex seemed to enjoy yourselves."

Her eyes lit up. "We did. We exchanged numbers and talked about getting together sometime. Plus, I want to know more about her Foundation."

"Listen, we have training this week and next week, and I'm not sure what my schedule will look like, but once things settle down, I'd like to see you again."

Bailey felt her heart rate increase. She definitely wanted to see Irish again. She found it funny that he was looking for her, while she was hopeful that she would run into him again.

"That might be doable," she replied with a smirk, and he chuckled.

"Might?" He asked, cocking his head sideways as if he enjoyed the back and forth flirting, they were doing as much as she was.

She laughed. "When things at work settle, and if you still want to see me, you know where to find me." She had no clue where this brazenness was coming from. Normally, she shied away when guys would come on to her.

He grinned. "Yeah, I do."

She smiled.

"Let me at least walk you to your car."

"Oh, you don't have to. Go back and enjoy the celebration with your friends. I'm parked in the spot right next to the door." He gave her a once over like he was torn on what to do. "Go, I promise I'll be fine."

She went to give him a little playful shove, but he surprised her when he stepped forward, placed his hands on her hips and leaned down and kissed her cheek.

She closed her eyes as she felt a flutter sensation in her belly. His lips felt so soft and warm and again her skin. So bad, she wanted to turn her head so their lips would meet. But all too soon, he stepped back and slid his hands in the front pockets of his jeans. Jeans that molded to his thighs and other areas that caught her eye.

"Bye, Ky."

"Bye, Blue." She widened her eyes and laughed again, shaking her head. She needed to get out of here before she did or said something that would embarrass her.

As she made her way to the door, she took one last glance over her shoulder, and in a blink of an eye those flutters she felt in her stomach disappeared when she saw two women approach Irish as he made his way back to his friends. It appeared the women knew Irish by the way they had their hands on. She wondered if he had a past with them. They were both beautiful and seemed confident. One of them turned, and she recognized her from when she had approached the table while they were eating. They hadn't even seemed to notice that she was sitting at the table with him when they'd rudely had interrupted their dinner. Maybe since she was conversing with Alex, they assumed she was Alex's friend.

Why was she even getting herself worked up about it? It wasn't like they were an item, though he did say he wanted to see her again. She got into her car and drove out of the parking lot. The first order of business when she got home was to pour herself a glass of wine. She had some thinking to do as this had the potential to be a disaster.

CHAPTER TEN

"I found her! It took a little longer, but I fucking found her," Leonard, Randy's private investigator, boasted as he entered Bentley's office at the law firm. It was late in the evening, and most of the staff had already left for the day. Leonard had been searching twenty-four-seven for any clue that would lead them to where Bailey had disappeared to, and it looked like the long hours paid off.

"Where is she?" Bentley asked, beating Randy to the question, and asking not nicely as he sat forward in his oversized leather chair and pulled his glasses off.

Randy sat back and waited patiently for Leonard to speak. Though he should be pissed at Bentley for acting like a bully and the one in charge. If it weren't for Randy hiring Leonard, they would all still be sitting around with their thumbs up their asses, waiting for Bailey to call or something, which she would never do. She left, was gone, and it appeared she had no intention of ever coming back. He'd been waiting for a break. Bailey had been off the grid for a little over a month now, and he knew it was just a matter of time.

"Virginia Beach," Leonard said, taking a seat in the other chair and handing a folder to Randy.

Randy thumbed through the pile of papers in the folder and then turned his nose up in the air. "Virginia? What in the hell is in Virginia Beach?" Randy scanned the papers. She owned a condo on the beach and was a teacher at an elementary school. Her car was still registered in Alabama. He figured she was smart enough to know that would be the first place they'd look. He read a little more. The title to her condo was filed under the name Virginia Anderson. Her grandmother. Clever, very clever.

Randy closed the file and laid it on the desk. He was already forming a plan in his head.

Bentley picked up his glass of scotch and turned toward Randy. "You are going there and will talk some sense into that dense daughter of mine. She should be here in Birmingham, where she belongs. Representing our family. Not in some beach bum town doing God knows what."

"Rest assured, Bentley. I'll have her back here in due time. I need to make a few arrangements first. I'll plan a trip for next week. In the meantime, I'll make a few calls to some associates around that area and get some information."

"Well, once you get her back here, you need to keep her on a tight leash. Maybe a firm hand would help teach her who she belongs to."

"Oh, don't worry. I've got big plans for Bailey."

"Good, because her disappearing act has caused me major problems. The two of you should be married by now, and our plan should be in motion. We're behind schedule, and I've got some heavy hitters breathing down my neck."

Randy thought to himself, "*Well, you shouldn't have borrowed a large sum of money from a loan shark to pay for some investments until you knew for sure you would have the money to repay the loan with interest.*"

Randy wasn't worried about getting Bailey back to Alabama. If a firm hand, as her father says, is needed, then so be it. He had no qualms in dishing out some discipline. Because once he got her back here with him, he would see to it that she would never leave him again, at least if she knew what was best for her.

CHAPTER ELEVEN

Bailey sat at one of the outside patio tables at Bayside. Ever since she had dinner with Irish last week, it had become a favorite for her. The food was so good, plus it was a beautiful late September night. The temperature hovered right around seventy degrees with a gentle breeze blowing in off the water. It was cool enough for jeans and a light sweater. The sky was clear, and the large full moon illuminated the earth below it. Bailey took a deep breath and exhaled. She'd come to love the smell of the salt air brought in from the ocean. Other than the soft music playing through the outside speakers and two tables on the opposite side of the patio seated with guys drinking and eating, it was peaceful.

She chuckled to herself as she sat at a table nestled in the corner of the deck, sipping her white wine. A couple of large potted plants obscured this table from the public view. She felt hidden and in her own little world as she sat back and thought about the night she arrived in town. A place that she had been scared to enter because of what it looked like on the outside, had now become her go-to place to eat. Tonight, she brought some work with her. She needed to get out of her condo for a little while, so she thought it was a great idea to have dinner and do a little work while she enjoyed the relaxing atmosphere.

Her mind drifted to Irish. She'd seen him a few times in the past week when he'd picked up Sienna from school but was bummed she couldn't talk to him since she was on bus duty. The last time they spoke was the night of "Back to School." She smiled, thinking about that night. Irish was so open about himself and seemed like a really sweet guy. She, on the other hand, felt guilty for not sharing much about herself. She would rather keep her past to herself and spare anyone the details of hearing how her childhood was so screwed up, which continued into her teens and early adulthood. She felt herself getting angry, and she didn't want the past to ruin her evening. She turned and looked toward the water and listened as the waves rolled ashore. One of the guys on the other side of the patio barked out a loud laugh, which made her smile. That group seemed to be having a good time.

She was so in tuned with the ambiance around her that she hadn't heard someone approach from behind her until she heard a voice that made her heart stop and her blood turn to ice.

"Hello Bailey."

She slowly turned around and standing there, looking smug, was the last person she ever wanted to see again.

"What are you doing here, Randy?" She asked him as she signaled to the waitress for her check. She had no clue how she was going to leave considering he blocked the only path to the exit. She could jump over the railing but after taking another look at how high up she was from the sand below; she nixed that idea.

He gave her a body a once over and just his look alone made her nervous. "Why else would I be here, sweetheart. I'm here to bring you home where you belong."

She shook her head. "Don't call me that. I don't have anything to say to you. And for the record, this is my home now."

His eyes took on an evil glare. "That is where you're wrong. Your home is with me back in Birmingham. Your parents have demanded your return."

"Well, you can tell my parents to go to hell." She signed the credit card slip the waitress had left, then started to pack up her papers. So much for an enjoyable evening she thought to herself.

She stood, completely dismissing him. He grabbed her shoulder and spun her around, backing her further into the corner. Her hip caught one of the chairs and it fell over. Her back was pressed up against the wood railing and she looked up at him. Randy was much taller than her five-foot-two frame. He shocked her when he grabbed her throat and pressed his body against hers. Fear engulfed her as he tightened his grip on her throat.

66

"Please, don't." She whispered. Between the tall plants, the low lighting and the way Randy had his body positioned, even if someone could see them, they wouldn't be able to see his hands on her. From a quick glance it would appear as if they were engaged in an intimate moment.

She grabbed the wrist of the hand on her throat. He applied just enough pressure to limit the amount of air she could breathe in.

"Where is this feisty temper coming from?" He was trying to intimidate her and was doing a damn good job as tears formed in her eyes. "You know better than to fight me. You will never win." He pressed his body closer, and she could feel how aroused he was. "You had to have known I would find you. I always do." He leaned down and buried his nose in her hair and inhaled. The act sent a shiver down her spine. "God, I've missed you. You smell delicious. I cannot wait to finally make you mine."

She started shaking and knew deep down that he would force himself on her with or without her consent. She needed to be smart and tough. She got away from him once; she could do it again. She had a new life here where she was happy, and she wasn't going to let him, or her parents take that away from her. She was done being their doormat.

She looked up at him. "You and my parents are the reason I left," she spat at him.

The cocky bastard just grinned and ran the back of his other hand down her cheek. His touch was sickening. She managed to get her hands up and she pressed against his chest.

"Quit fighting me, Bailey. You know I always win."

Suddenly, Randy was yanked backward, freeing her from his hold. She started coughing and trying to catch her breath. When she looked back at Randy a man had him pinned face down against the table. The guy looked over at her. He looked angry.

"Are you okay?" He asked her.

She nodded, though she knew she wasn't okay. Now that Randy knew where she was, neither he nor her parents would let her be. She reached for her throat feeling the soreness. Another guy appeared in front of her.

"Let me take a look, honey." He said in a soothing voice as he moved her hands from her neck and tilted her head so he could get a better look. She heard him take a deep breath as he gently touched her skin. She heard Randy raise his voice. The other guy said something back to him, but she had so much noise inside her head she couldn't focus. The thought that Randy could have killed her scared her and made her body tremble.

She wasn't sure how much time had gone by when the other guy reappeared.

"Is she okay?" He asked the guy looking at her neck.

"I think so, but it's going to bruise."

She looked up at both men. They were very tall. Taller than Randy. The one guy who had pulled Randy off her, took a defensive stance, and crossed his arms over his chest. His expression alone should've been a warning. She owed him for saving her.

"Thank you." She said looking at him.

"We wouldn't have known you were in trouble had that chair not of fallen over."

"We?" She asked and he nodded his head toward the two tables on the other side of the patio. When she glanced over all the guys were standing and looking in her direction. One guy was in a dead stare with her as he spoke on his cell phone. They all looked very intimidating but also familiar.

She turned back to the two men in front of her. Now that she got a good look at them, they too looked familiar.

"Have we met before?" She asked and the guy who had handled Randy grinned, and the light hit his unique grey eyes just right, and that was when it hit her. He was with the group that Irish and Ace had joined the night she had dinner with Irish and Sienna.

"You're Ky's friend. I saw you talking to him the other night. You guys were celebrating someone's promotion or something like that. Alex told me your name. Give me a minute, and it will come to me." She tapped her index finger against her chin, and the guy stood there patiently. She looked up at him again. "You're an animal," she blurted out and

68

immediately covered her mouth in shock as she felt her cheeks warm. "Shoot! That didn't come out right, sorry."

But the guy apparently thought it was funny as hell because he threw his head back and laughed. It was a loud, deep laugh. Then she remembered and pointed. "Bear! Your name is Bear. You work with Ky and Alex's fiancé, Ace."

Bear had seen the woman take the table in the corner of the patio. It was one of the best spots to sit when someone just wanted to relax and be left alone.

When he saw the man walk out onto the patio and approach the secluded area where the woman sat, he got a bad vibe. There was just something about the guy's body language that seemed off. He almost chalked it up as a mistake, but then he heard the chair hit the ground and just knew something was wrong.

He had no idea that it was the same woman who had caught Irish's attention. It wasn't until his teammate Joker recognized her.

He wasn't normally one to get involved in other people's drama; however, when a person is being assaulted, then all bets were off. In her case, when Joker told him who the woman was, it became more of an urgency to diffuse the situation. He didn't hear most of the conversation, but he had heard enough to know the situation could have taken a turn for the worse if he hadn't intervened.

As he looked her over, he had to admit she was cute. Knowing Irish had his sights set on her, he wasn't interested in her that way. Although Irish better shit or get off the pot because the pretty lady wasn't going to stay single for too long. Not with the way men had been looking at her all night. She had an innocence about her, and that made Bear laugh. She was totally not Irish's type.

He stuck his hand out. "I'm Bear, and that's the rest of my team over there," he said, pointing to the table.

She shook his hand. "I'm Bailey," she replied shyly.

"And I'm Duke." The other guy said then grabbed her bag off the table.

Bear took her elbow and started to lead her toward their table. "Come on, I'll introduce you to everyone, and then you can tell me what all that was about."

Bear had a feeling that they hadn't seen the last of that guy, and if Irish was interested in her, then he needed to know what he was dealing with. Plus, who knew if the guy wasn't sitting outside in his car, waiting for her to leave. She definitely wouldn't be traveling back to her home alone.

Bailey gave him an unsure look as she nibbled her lip. It was like she needed to be persuaded. He turned toward her and put his hand on her shoulder, and she looked up into his eyes. Being in the military, especially Special Forces, you acquire the skills to read body language, and her eyes told him she was unsure. "Bailey, I would feel a lot better if you hung out with us and waited a little while before you left."

Her eyes widened. "You think Randy could be waiting for me in the parking lot or something?"

She was smart too, again, not like the women Irish fucked around with. "Yeah, honey. I'd be much more comfortable if you sat with us for a little bit, and then one of us can walk you to your car and follow you home."

"Oh, I didn't drive here," she told him, and he raised his eyebrows in question. "I live about a mile and a half down the road. I walked here on the beach."

There was no way in hell that he was letting her walk home. "Okay, would you object if I drove you home?" He knew for a fact that he wouldn't be the one escorting her home. Joker was on the phone with Irish already, and he was pretty sure Irish was already on his way.

He watched as she pondered his question. Then she looked at him. "Would you feel offended if I called Alex just to make sure you really are who say you are? I mean, a girl does have to be careful, right?"

He chuckled. "It wouldn't offend me in the least. Actually, it makes me happy to know you take your safety seriously. There are too many people in the world that don't take the necessary precautions and then end up in big trouble."

She smiled. "Okay then, lead the way. I think I need a drink anyway after dealing with that prick." He laughed again and guided her over to the table. Irish was a damn lucky man.

Bailey was enjoying the conversation with Bear and his team even though she couldn't stop thinking what Randy's next move was going to be. There was no doubt in her mind that he wasn't already planning his revenge.

She looked around the table at the guys. Aussie, who was freakishly tall, and Bugs were in the middle of a debate about which one of them was a better grill master. Some of the recipes they were describing had sounded delicious. All eight men were unique in their own way. They asked questions about her job and how she liked the town and made some suggestions on some of the sights she needed to see. They even offered her a tour of the base. The conversation flowed, although it seemed to be a little one-sided as they didn't really leave much room in-between the questions they threw at her.

She glanced down at her watch and saw how late it was. She hadn't realized it had been a little over an hour since the ordeal with Randy. She'd tried to leave several times already, but then one of the guys would ask her a question, which led to another conversation. She got the feeling that they were purposely stalling her. She really needed to go home. She was tired and her neck was really sore.

"Hey, are you okay?" Bear asked, setting his beer down on the table.

She covered her neck with her hand. She would be surprised if it weren't already bruising as she tended to bruise easily.

"It's a little sore. But I'll be fine." She told him.

"Bastard...I should've done more than just throw his ass out of here."

She gave him a soft smile. Bear was a nice guy and very protective. "It's okay. I'll survive. I've done it before."

Duke, who sat next to her, brushed her hair back over her shoulder so he could get a better look. One of the guys mentioned he was a Combat Medic. "Son of a bitch," he said out loud, and now he looked pissed off.

"Is it bad?"

"Not too bad, but it's noticeable," he told her with a scowl on his face.

"Shoot."

"Who was that asshole anyway?" He asked her.

She nibbled on her lip. She had managed to avoid that topic up until now. "Just my past." But then she jumped when she heard the angry voice behind her.

"That isn't a good enough explanation?"

Irish stood there with his arms crossed, looking mighty fine in a pair of casual black track pants and a long-sleeve t-shirt. His angry expression only added to his sexiness. She looked at Bear and glared at him. "You called him!"

Bear gave her a fierce look, a look that made her think twice about raising her voice at him again. But he just shrugged his shoulders and calmly replied before taking another sip of his beer. "When one of our own is in trouble, we make sure they're taken care of."

She took a step back and wondered what he meant by that statement. She didn't need or want babysitters. She had dealt with enough of that shit from her parents. She didn't need to be controlled by a bunch of domineering alpha-males.

"What does that mean?"

Irish stepped close to her. He turned Bailey toward him. She knew the moment when his eyes settled on the bruising on her neck because his eyes turned cold. The blue darkened, and his expression became hard.

"He did this to you?" He asked, lowering his voice to almost a whisper as his fingers gently touched her skin, causing a slight shiver.

"She should ice it," Duke stated from her other side. He was still looking at her neck.

"I'll be right back," Irish told her. She watched him through the window as he went to the bar and spoke with the bartender. A brunette approached Irish, and he smiled wide at the woman before hugging her. She kissed him on the cheek. From Bailey's view, the woman was strikingly beautiful with long wavy chestnut hair that fell to the middle of her back. It wasn't one of the women she encountered last week. Jesus, did he have a different woman for every night of the week. She felt like a fool. She wasn't going to stick around and be his flavor of the week or, in Irish's case, the flavor of the night. She wasn't into playing the damsel in distress and have the hot military guy come and rescue her for a reward of a night of fun. She wanted someone who would be faithful, compassionate, and loving.

She felt sick to her stomach. She grabbed her bag and purse from the table and started to walk inside when a hand landed on her arm. When she turned, she met Bear's curious gaze.

"Where are you going? Irish will be back in a minute. He went to get you some ice. He said to wait here."

She raised one of her eyebrows at him. "Well, Irish isn't my handler, and I need to use the ladies' room," she stated with an attitude and shook herself from his hold and made her way inside. Irish was still engrossed in the brunette and had his back to her. She saw the sign for the restrooms and headed down the short hallway. When she got to the ladies' room, she noticed a side door a little further down that led to a pathway to the beach. She could easily slip out, and nobody would ever notice until it was too late. Although she felt a little guilty for sneaking around, she also wasn't going to sit around and be someone's puppet. She headed outside and walked toward the water, where it was darker and harder for anyone to notice her. With it being such a beautiful night, there were other people out for an evening stroll.

She pulled her hoodie tighter against her as a chill swept through her body. The entire walk home, she never let her guard down. Not knowing if Randy had left the area made her feel vulnerable. Once she was safely home behind her locked door with the alarm set, she would give her cousin a call and see if he could offer any advice on how to deal with her family.

As far as Irish went, it was a pity because she thought there could be something there. She felt a connection with him but seeing him with the other women had her wondering what type of a man he really was.

Irish quickly made his way back outside to the table. He hadn't meant to take so long, but when Lauren, an old friend, spotted him and started talking, he didn't want to be rude.

When he reached the table, he looked around for Bailey. "Where'd she go?" He asked Bear, who was talking to Joker and Duke.

Bear looked around and grimaced before banging his fist on the table. "Son-of-a-bitch! She said she was going to the bathroom."

"Okay, what is wrong with that?"

"Because that was like fifteen minutes ago. What in the hell took you so long?"

"I ran into Lauren. Remember the Marine with the K9 who saved our asses last year in Iraq when he sniffed out that IED?"

"Fuck...don't remind me. That was too close of a call. Shit, it would have wiped out both of our teams." Bear gave Irish a look. "Wait, didn't you hook up with her shortly after that?

Irish winced. "Yeah, but I haven't seen her since. We left that next day."

"Is she stationed here?"

"No, she left the Corps a few months after she returned home from that deployment. She's married now to a Colonel. He's stationed at the Pentagon. She's here in town visiting a few friends."

Bear rubbed his chin. "I see...well, I think your reunion with Lauren is the reason your little pixie gave us all the slip. She watched you the entire time and saw Lauren hug you. She made us all look like fools, too, if she left the same way she got here. She had to have walked past this deck."

"Walked?"

"Yeah, she walked from her condo."

Irish then remembered her mentioning she didn't live far from here. "She shouldn't be out walking in the dark alone. Not when some man comes here threatening and touching her. What the fuck was she thinking?"

"No, it wasn't smart. But she was pretty adamant that she wanted her independence. When I told her, you wanted her to wait, she commented that you weren't her handler."

Irish wondered about that. Then he remembered the night he met her and the faint bruise on her cheek. He grew angry.

"Whoa, what's with the killer face?"

Irish explained. "Shit, do you think this guy is the one who hit her, and she's been running from?"

Irish shook his head and ran his hand through his hair. "I don't know. But I intend to find out."

Bear took a swig from his beer. "She's cute. But I'm having a hard time understanding why you of all people are so hung up on her."

"What's that supposed to mean?" Irish asked, wondering why Bear would say something like that.

"She is far different from the women you associate with. And when I say different, I mean that in a good way. She's shy, almost innocent like. Shit, wait until word gets around here that you're off the market."

"Well, I don't have her yet. But you're right; she is different. That's what I find so attractive about her. Plus, she's easy to talk to. She could care less about my status as a SEAL. She is someone that I actually feel comfortable around besides you guys."

Bear tipped his bottle Irish's way. "Well, just a friendly suggestion. You'd better claim her soon; otherwise, some other guy is going to swoop in and carry her off into the sunset."

Irish took a seat at the table. That's twice now his past had come in-between him and Bailey. He needed to make it right and convince her it was her that he wanted.

CHAPTER TWELVE

Randy watched from afar as the group of men cared and catered to Bailey. She was gorgeous and being the new girl in town, Randy knew men would be all over her, especially with her sweet, bubbly personality. But she was naïve and inexperienced.

He was almost positive the men who were fawning over her were in the military. They just had that demeanor and vibe about them. But the one he was the most curious about was the blonde guy who had shown up a few minutes ago. He seemed awfully in-tune with her, especially the way he touched her neck. The beautiful, slender neck that he could have broken if he wanted to. He wondered if she was dating him, which led to the thought of her fucking him. He snapped the pen he was holding between his fingers. For her sake, he'd better be just a friend.

She was meant to be with him. At least long enough for him to get his hands on the main prize, then he couldn't give a rat's ass what she did and even what happened to her. He wrote down the license plate from the Lincoln Navigator the guy showed up in. He would send it to Leonard back in Alabama to see what kind of information he could pull up on the guy. He needed to know who he was dealing with.

As much as he wanted to stick around and continue this cat and mouse game with Bailey, he had obligations to get back to in Alabama. He was hoping that by threatening her, she would cower to his demands, but his girl seemed to have grown a backbone.

Bentley had called him to get an update on the situation and to let him know that Ralph, the loan shark Bentley borrowed money from, had paid a visit. He gave Bentley a couple of more weeks to come up with the money. There was plenty of money to cover Bentley's loan; however, all the assets, stocks, and cash held by the Andersons could only be liquidated by one person, and that was Bailey. She had no clue that she held the family fortune in her hands. Between Bentley and his shrewd team of lawyers, they'd buried everything and made it look like that Bentley and Annette controlled it all. Of course, Bentley was given some cash and stocks when his father died, but that money was long gone, and now he needed Bailey's money, and that included her trust fund. She thought nobody knew about that, but people talk, and eventually, gossip gets around.

By marrying Bailey, Randy was promised a large chunk of the assets. As soon as they said I do, he would start the process of moving assets into his name and then splitting them with Bentley. Bentley despised Bailey, and Randy believed it was because she was the apple of her grandfather's eye.

Randy put the car in gear. He had a flight to catch. He would let her think she had won the battle for now. But soon, very soon, he'd have her.

CHAPTER THIRTEEN

Bailey entered the chic day spa near the boardwalk. She had been looking forward to this treat for herself for a couple of days. She had booked a ninety-minute massage. Believe it or not, in her twenty-six years, she had never had a massage but had always heard how relaxing they were.

When she brought up wanting to get one, the ladies at school gave her the name and number of this place. They all raved about it. She swore she saw one of the ladies blush as she talked about it. Apparently, they weren't the only ones who thought that because when she made the appointment, she only got in because they had a cancellation. If it weren't for that, she would have had to wait over a month for an appointment.

The interior of the establishment reminded her of a hotel she'd stayed at in South Beach. It had an art deco vibe with a modern, crisp look, a lot of white with red as a contrast color that popped in some of the décor.

She approached the front desk, and the gentleman behind the desk stood and greeted her. When he smiled, she thought she was staring at a life-size Ken doll. He looked almost fake. His teeth were super white teeth, he had an incredible tan, and his light brown hair didn't have a single strand out of place. Not to mention that he too was dressed in white slacks and a red polo that matched the décor.

"Hi, sweetheart. How can I help you?" *Smooth...*

She smiled. "I have an appointment for a massage."

"Your name?"

"Bailey...Bailey Anderson. I called this morning."

The guy smiled again. "Oh yes, that was me you spoke with. I assume this is your first visit here?" He gave her a sideways smile as his eyes roamed over her body, making her briefly think maybe she'd made a mistake in coming.

But she quickly blew it off as the guy just being arrogant and cocky.

"Yes."

He handed her an iPad and asked her to complete the questionnaire, which she did quickly and returned the iPad to him.

"Is it possible to request a female massage therapist?" She asked. As this was her first massage, she would feel a little more comfortable having a female masseuse. But Jock's sly smile told her that answer was going to be no.

"All of our massage therapists are male. I can tell you're nervous, but I promise every member of our staff is professional and highly trained. You'll be in good hands with Manny," he winked, and she gulped. She could do this. Her body was craving the stress release. She nodded her head.

She removed her clothes and slipped under the sheet on the massage table. The sheets alone felt wonderful against her skin. They were so soft.

She buried her face in the cradle on the table and waited anxiously. The soft rainforest music playing, coupled with the low lighting, already had her feeling relaxed.

She faintly heard the door open, and light footsteps followed. A few minutes later, the sheet was lowered to the top of her ass. She tensed up, but seconds later, strong hands began to move across her back in sweeping motions. Her eyelids started getting heavy, and she fell further and further into a relaxing state.

Suddenly, her eyes popped open. Something didn't feel right; someone was on top of her. She felt something long, hard, and thick between her butt cheeks. She lifted her head and looked over her shoulder to find Manny completely naked and straddling her legs.

She flipped over, throwing the guy off onto the floor. She almost exposed her boobs when the sheet started to fall. He got up quickly as she pulled the sheet higher, covering her body.

"Whoa, sweetie. Are you okay?" He asked her, standing there in his birthday suit like it was a choice of work attire.

He was asking her if she was okay? No, she was far from okay. There was a naked man on top of her. *Oh my god. What if I would've fallen asleep. Was he going to molest me?* She took a deep breath and swallowed.

"What are you doing?" She asked.

Manny smirked and crossed his arms in front of his chest, and his manhood stood at attention.

"I don't know why you're in a tizzy. I'm giving you exactly what you asked and paid for. Do you not like it? Because I got other moves I could try out on you," he said calmly but in a cocky and arrogant way—kind of like the man out at the front desk.

She shook her head. Was this person for real? "Umm...I don't remember paying or even asking for a prostitute." Then she realized she'd been staring at his crotch the entire conversation and slapped her hand over her eyes.

"Oh, my God...Can you please put that thing away?"

She heard him laugh, then the rustling of clothes. She was so embarrassed and beside herself; she didn't know whether she wanted to cry or kick the guy in the balls.

"We don't promote prostitution here. We use other methods to help women relax, like what I was doing with you. We use our entire bodies. Which is what you paid for. Rest assured, there is absolutely no type of sex going on here whatsoever."

Thank God for that because she wasn't sure what she'd do if anyone found out about this. That lasted about two hours when Alex called her, and she agreed to meet her and her friend Tenley for lunch at Bayside.

"So, let me get this straight, your friends at work recommended Deep Waters and didn't tell you about their method of relaxation?" Alex asked, using air quotes.

"No! If they did, I sure as hell wouldn't have gone. Oh, my God, it was so embarrassing. I hadn't realized anything was different until the man climbed up on to the table and mounted me. His penis was cradled between my butt cheeks."

Bailey put her hand over her mouth, still completely shocked and worked up over the incident. However, that only made Alex and Tenley laugh more.

"And then, I sat there having a conversation with the man, realizing that I was talking to his penis because I was staring at it. How could I not? It was so big and kept twitching every time he uttered a word. It looked so angry and mean."

"My God, Bailey. That is the funniest thing I've heard in weeks," Tenley said, wiping her eyes. "Next time you want to get a massage, let me know, and I'll set you up with my man Lei. He's the bomb. And I promise he won't try to molest you. You don't have the right anatomy parts for Lei's taste." She winked, then explained that Lei was gay, but a great massage therapist and a great listener.

"Bailey, what are you going to do when you have sex for the first time? You can't scream and run from the man when he whips out Richard and the twins."

Bailey looked at Tenley. "Who the hell is Richard?"

"Oh, Jesus!" Alex said, trying not to laugh at the serious expression on Bailey's face.

Tenley was now laughing so hard she sounded like she was wheezing. Her little pregnant belly was shaking so much Bailey swore the babies in there had to feel like they were in the middle of a spin cycle.

"Richard isn't an actual person. I'm talking about a man's sex pistol, womb raider. You know, his dick."

"Oh…." Bailey replied, now completely embarrassed. She could feel how hot her cheeks were. She'd bet any amount of money her face was bright as a shiny new red fire engine. She had admitted earlier in the conversation with the two women that she was a virgin. Both Alex and Tenley found that hard to believe.

"I think you frightened her, Tenley," Alex told her friend between her bites of food. Then as if knowing Bailey was mortified, Alex shifted gears. "You should come to the dojo with me. It's right by the base. They have an awesome kickboxing class that I take twice a week." She hooked a thumb

81

over at Tenley. "Preggo here used to go with me, but the only thing she's been kicking up lately is her feet."

Tenley gave Alex an evil eye as she shoved another gooey cheese fry in her mouth, and Bailey giggled. She loved the comradery between the two best friends. She'd wished all her life for friends like these ladies.

She looked at Alex and thought about it. Kickboxing just might be a good stress reliever. "I'd love to. What days and times are the sessions?"

"I take the evening class on Tuesday and Thursday. The instructors are all former military. Ace knows them. They even offer other self-defense classes if you're interested in that as well. But don't be surprised if Irish tries to talk you out of going." Alex gave her a grin, and Bailey scrunched her eyebrows together.

"Why would he do that?" She asked.

"Because most of the instructors and men who work out there are single, and you are cute as a button. I wouldn't be surprised if you walked out of the first class with several offers of dates."

Bailey's eyes widened. Okay, maybe kickboxing class wasn't such a good idea after all.

"Will you stop, you're scaring the poor girl," Tenley told Alex.

Bailey looked at Alex. "What does me going to a kickboxing class have to do with Irish?"

"Honey, I'm just going to lay this out there for you. Irish wants you."

"Ah. I don't think so."

"Nope, that man has been a completely different person since the night you two met."

Bailey shook her head. "No, you have it wrong. I'm way out of his league. I don't fit into the demographic of the type of women that he is obviously into. I've seen them."

"And that is why. You aren't like the rest of those women."

"But why would he want me? I'm just a boring kindergarten teacher. The women I've seen hanging on him and lusting over him are beautiful and confident. Plus, I'm not into just being a notch on somebody's bedpost." Bailey glanced out the window and pondered the what-ifs.

"Trust me, Bailey, we've been in your shoes."

"I don't know. I mean, I'm Sienna's teacher. Then there are some personal issues I need to address before I'd consider dating anyone. Nobody needs to be brought into that mess."

"Does that mess have anything to do with the guy that Bear was ready to rip apart? At least that's what I heard."

"How do you know about that?"

"Like I said, when one of the guys sets his sights on a woman, the entire team watches after said woman. News travels fast in our tight-knit community. Plus, Irish was at my house when Joker called him as the shit was going down. I don't think I've ever seen Irish move as fast as he did."

So, that was who Joker was on the phone with. But she still didn't understand why he came when he was flirting with that woman at the bar.

"Who was the guy? Joker said he got physical with you."

She blew out a breath and touched her neck, where the small bruise was. She really didn't want to air all her dirty laundry. Instead, she opted for the condensed version. "Randy is the guy my parents believe I should marry. If they had their way, I'd have been married probably before I even graduated college."

"Why was he here if he knows you don't want to be with him?"

"Because he can't get it through his stubborn head. His family is just like mine, rich, and a bunch of assholes. All that matters to them is money and prestige. Hell, they probably all had a hand in finding me." She shrugged her shoulders and shoved a fry in her mouth. "I just want to be left alone and live my life."

"Wow...I would've never guessed you came from a family like that. You're so down to earth, caring, friendly, and you love children."

"That's because I made a promise to myself. I swore I wouldn't let money and greed run my life like it does my parents. I hated living in that lifestyle. After high school, I went to college and got my teaching degree. But it still wasn't enough. My parents still hounded me and tried to control every waking minute of my life. It took a couple of years until I finally had enough of their shit. I applied for several teaching positions in various states. I got offered a job in each one, but in the end, I chose this town. I sold my house, packed up my belongings, and drove away with a smile on my face."

"Well, we're certainly glad you did. And I'm almost certain that a certain SEAL is too." Bailey went to protest, but Tenley held her hand up and smiled. "Sweetie, you really have no idea how lucky you are. You can deny it all you want, but I'm telling you, you've captured the eye of the most popular SEAL. Believe me, hearts are going to be breaking when the ladies find out Irish is taken."

Bailey went to respond, but a series of loud cheers rang out through the bar, and when she turned around to see what all the ruckus was about, her smile quickly faded.

What she saw contradicted what Tenley and Alex were just telling her. Irish stood there, looking just as scrumptious as he always does. But that wasn't what drove the smile from her face. It was the gorgeous, tall dirty blonde dressed in a form-fitting black dress paired with black stilettos. She had her arm looped through his as she hugged it to her chest and smiled up at him.

Bailey quickly turned away, her heart breaking, again as she did. Then she snorted a laugh. At least what Tenley said was true. Hearts were breaking. But she never expected it would be hers shattering into a million pieces.

She tried to shake off the feeling of being betrayed because in all honesty, she hadn't been. She and Irish weren't in a relationship.

She grabbed the check the waitress left and fished out enough cash to cover the tab plus the tip. It was time to leave. She couldn't sit back and watch him frolic with the ladies. She would go back to her lonely condo on the beach and dwell on the what-ifs.

She slid her windbreaker on and prepared to leave. As she stood, she looked at Alex and Tenley, two women who had quickly become her friends. She then wondered if they would still even want to hang out with her. Hell, she honestly didn't know if she could or even want to hang with them knowing that he would be around. And it's not like she would ever ask them to choose between her and Irish. Irish was a part of their family. She, on the other hand, was an outsider. It was best if she removed herself from the entire equation. There were approximately 450,000 people in Virginia Beach; surely, she could make other friends. Maybe?

A hand came down on her arm, stopping her from turning to leave, and she looked down and locked gazes with Alex.

"Honey, whatever is going through your head right now, you need to shake it off." She motioned with her head in the direction of the bar. "Look, he's pushing her away. Believe me, Bailey, you are who he wants."

Bailey looked over, and the woman in question was sticking her bottom lip out in a pout as Irish ignored her while he spoke with Ace. Yeah, it was nice to see, but she realized that no matter what, she would always be competing with other women. That was even if he was truly interested in her. He'd made a few comments to her that gave her the impression he was interested, but there was still that nagging feeling she couldn't shake. She needed to think, and now was the perfect time to make her exit before he saw her and made her feel even more awkward and confused.

She looked back at Alex and shook her head. "I'm sorry, Alex, but I don't think it will work. I need to get home, it's getting dark, and I walked here."

Alex didn't look happy but nodded her head, then patted Bailey's hand. "Will you still meet me at the dojo tomorrow for kickboxing?"

She was about ready to say no, but then she considered the incident the other night. If she knew a little self-defense, she could fight off Randy if he came sniffing around again.

"Yeah, I'll be there. We have some storm preparations we need to do at the school after the kids leave. I'll meet you there around four?"

Alex smiled. "That's perfect. The class starts at 4:30. So that gives you time to fill out the paperwork they have all the newbies fill out."

She gave Alex a half-smile, took one last look toward the bar, and slipped out the side door. That seemed to be becoming a habit, but damn, was that door convenient.

85

Irish stood at the bar, talking with Ace and Potter. He'd only decided to make the drive to Bayside because Potter had texted a picture of Bailey sitting at the table with Alex and Tenley having dinner. Luckily, Sienna was at Juliet and Derek's house, having dinner with them and Alejandra. He had a good hour before he needed to pick her up.

Irish owed Potter for looking out for him. He hadn't seen or spoken to Bailey since the other night when she gave him and Bear the slip. At first, he hadn't understood why she left, but then the more he thought about it, he saw it from her point of view. But still, to sneak out, especially considering Bear explained to her that the guy who had been bothering her could've easily been waiting for her outside hadn't been the brightest idea.

Unfortunately, things couldn't have gone any better this evening. It was like fucking deja vu. The first person he ran into on his way in tonight was no other than Zoey. Zoey was beautiful and someone he had slept with. But Zoey's problem was she didn't seem to understand when he told her before they had sex that sex was all that was going to happen between them. Although she agreed, she still wanted more afterward, and every time he showed up, and she was here, she would make a beeline for him, hoping he had changed his mind.

After spending about ten minutes trying to be nice and not sound like an asshole, she finally got the message and moved on to another group of men across the room. Good riddance.

"Dude, I think you missed your window of opportunity." Potter lifted his beer in the direction toward the side door, and when Irish turned, he saw Bailey slip out the door. *Dammit!*

Irish turned back to Ace and Potter. "What the hell? I know she saw me. She was looking right at me. Why would she leave?"

"That's just it. She did see you—with Zoey."

He squinted his eyes at Potter and then looked back toward the door his little pixie snuck out of. Son-of-a-bitch! His entire life, he'd never had to chase after a woman. But there was a first for everything. However, when he caught up with this one, he planned to never let her go.

His past had come back to haunt him. So far, the three times he'd been here at Bayside with Bailey, he'd had to deal with overly aggressive women. He didn't want those women. The only woman he wanted attention from was the one who kept slipping from his grasp.

Quickly telling Ace and Potter he'd see them tomorrow; he ran out the same side door Bailey did. He made his way down to the beach and realized that there wasn't very much lighting down here. His eyes adjusted to the darkness after a few seconds, and he scanned the shoreline. Thankfully, the moon was bright because if it hadn't been, he probably would have missed the short person walking about a hundred yards ahead of him. Damn, she walked fast. But then he thought that was a good thing, considering she fucking walked here, knowing it would be dark by the time she left. He definitely needed to have a talk with her about placing herself in dangerous situations.

Bailey was deep in thought about what happened back at the bar. Alex and Tenley were right; Irish did have a past. Though they both said he only had eyes for her, she was finding that hard to believe. She adjusted the volume on her phone. She had her earbuds in, listening to her torture playlist. The one full of sappy love songs she created. It was like being reminded of something she would never have. Love. She didn't know why she put herself through that, but one thing she did know was as soon as she got home, she would take a nice hot shower, put on her PJs, pour a glass of white wine, and cuddle up with her soft blanket on her balcony. It was becoming a nightly routine. Except her thoughts would be on the one man that she could not get out of her head. It didn't help matters that she wore his sweatshirt every night.

She had the music so loud she hadn't heard Irish calling her name as he jogged toward her. When his large firm hand landed on her shoulder and pulled her backward, it was no surprise that she screamed and threw a punch. Which did nothing but hurt her hand when she connected with Irish's steel abs.

"Goddammit, Bailey! Stop hitting me. It's me, Ky!"

Once her mind registered the face, her heart began to settle, she squinted her eyes at him, then unleashed a fury of hell on him.

"What the hell? Do you realize that you could have given me a freaking heart attack? Hasn't anyone taught you that you shouldn't sneak up on people?" She shouted, poking him in the chest.

All he did was plaster that gorgeous smile on his face, and she was ready to retract her claws and forgive him. *My God, what in the hell am I thinking?*

She looked around, feeling a little off kilter. Here she stood on the beach with a man she was attracted to, the moon reflecting off the water. It had romance written all over it, but whatever was going on between her and the sexy as sin man standing in front of her with his hands on his hips was anything but romance. What it was, was fucked up.

"What do you want?" She asked him.

Expecting to hear some lame excuse, she was jolted when he reached out and grabbed the front of her hoodie and pulled her against him. Their chests collided, and she found herself wrapped up in his warm arms. She tilted her head back and looked up at him. His blue eyes were like ice but seemed to darken a smidge. He appeared calm. She, on the other hand, was a basket of nerves. She felt herself trembling, but she wasn't sure if it was from the chill outside or from being in the confinement of Irish's strong, muscular arms. He pressed his warm body against her.

"Ky, you're confusing me. I don't know what you want?" She asked in a pleading voice. She couldn't go on playing the "does he like me" game.

She got her answer when she saw his nostrils flare before he leaned down and whispered in a raspy, deep voice, "This." His lips came crashing down on hers.

Irish didn't know what had come over him. One minute, he was ready to explain what had happened, and the next, he was watching her lick her lips, though she probably didn't mean anything sexual by it, but dammit, he needed her to know that he wanted her. So, he did the first thing that popped into his head. He kissed her. And she was what he was expecting and then some. So sweet and giving as she opened right up for him, letting his tongue slip in for a quick taste. Not wanting to overwhelm her, he slowed it down and pulled back. He wasn't going to fuck this up.

He smiled as her eyes fluttered open. They were filled with lust and desire, and he felt he'd accomplished what he'd set out to do.

"I've wanted to kiss you since those eyes of yours looked up at me as you laid in that damn puddle," he told her, pulling her into a hug and squeezing her tight. He could feel the rapid beat of her heart against his chest. She was special, and he knew his life was about to change.

He took her hand and started walking down the beach toward her condo. He wasn't sure which one was hers, but he wasn't going to let her walk alone.

Bailey was still in amazement from her mini rendezvous with Irish on the beach. He had walked her to her condo, kissed her one more time on the lips, and told her he would call tomorrow. He even waited until she was safely in the building and saw her get into the elevator. He was a total gentleman, and that impressed her.

She reached her floor and quickly let herself into the condo, shutting the door behind her. The first thing she did was open the slider to the balcony, letting in the brisk air. Her body was on fire. She heard her phone vibrate against the table by the front door. Looking at it, she saw she had a voicemail. Not bothering to see who it was from, she hit the button and put the phone on speaker to listen. Just as she turned to head into the kitchen to grab a glass of wine, she froze when she heard her mother's voice.

"Bailey, this is your mother." Bailey rolled her eyes. "I just saw Randy at the club, and he was very upset. Something about a friend of yours threatened him. He went out of his way to come and see you to talk some sense into you. You need to get your head out of the clouds and come to your senses. You are an Anderson, for God's sake. What would your grandfather think of your behavior? Running around with thugs and hoodlums."

Bailey grinned. Her beloved Pop would probably be cheering her on. After all, he was the one person who'd encouraged her to follow her dreams and do what made her happy. He would have loved her new friends.

She heard the phone beep, ending the message. She had missed the last part of her mother's rant. It was probably another demand to call her. Yeah, fat chance of that happening.

Her phone beeped again, and she looked down and saw it was a message from Alex.

"Everything okay? I saw Irish run out after you?"

She smiled. That was nice of Alex to check on her.

"All good."

"Is Irish still there?"

"No, he walked me to my condo, then left."

"Are you still going to meet me at kickboxing tomorrow?"

"Yes, I'll be there."

"Awesome! You can fill me in then. Later!"

Bailey shook her head and laughed. She needed to get a shower, then get some sleep. Tomorrow was going to be a long day. There was a hurricane spinning out in the Atlantic, and the forecast had it coming extremely close to the Virginia coastline. The meteorologists were saying the storm could go either way. It could skirt the coastline and take a sharp right turn out to sea, or if the jet stream lifted, there was the potential of a direct hit. The city wasn't taking any chances. After tomorrow, they were going to close the schools. Being from Alabama, she'd experienced hurricanes. Some were bad, but she believed she would be okay to ride the storm out in her condo. She hadn't heard anything about any mandatory evacuations, so as of now, she would hunker down and hope the storm went out to sea.

Her mind then steered toward Irish, and she wondered if he had to report to base as the storm hit or would they have to leave the area. She hadn't a clue how the military stuff worked when it came to that. Reading and studying it was completely different from seeing and living it.

CHAPTER FOURTEEN

Irish and Ace were walking out to their cars when Irish turned toward Ace. "Is Alex home?

Ace raised one of his eyebrows up. "No, why?"

Irish chuckled to himself. "I wanted to see if she could give me one of those massages of hers. I'm feeling kinda tight in my shoulders, and her hands are amazing." Irish looked over and knew his friend was seconds away from punching him. Irish had a habit of messing with Ace, Potter, and Frost. He'd playfully flirt with Alex, Tenley, and Autumn just to get a rile out of them. They all knew he was joking; however, they were also very protective of their women.

He shot Ace a grin. "I'm just messing with you. It's too fun and too easy not to. But all joking aside, I do need to talk to her. I'm kind of in a bind tomorrow with Sienna."

With the hurricane approaching closer to the US mainland, the base, along with the rest of the town, were preparing and bracing for the worst. Though it was only a category one storm, it still had the potential to do damage. Flooding was the main concern. The front of the storm is expected to hit the area late Tuesday night, and then it is predicted to take a turn to the northeast and skirt the coast before heading back out to sea.

Ace stopped walking and crossed his arms across his chest. "What's going on?"

"Well, since we have to report to base tomorrow and finish preparations, I need someone to watch Sienna."

"Derek thinks we should be done by the time school lets out. Unless the guys tonight don't get their shit done, then we could be later."

"Nope, the county already announced this morning that they are closing schools tomorrow and Wednesday."

Ace furrowed his eyebrows and crossed his arms across his chest. "I don't know what she had planned for tomorrow. She did mention she had to go by the office to make sure the staff of volunteers took care of the preparations there. She's at her kickboxing class right now at Murphy's place. Why don't we drive over there now and ask her?" He glanced down at his watch. "She should be finishing up in a few minutes, and it's on our way home."

Irish pulled into the parking lot of the gym and dojo that their buddy Murphy owned. Murphy was a former SEAL himself, but a bullet to the lung forced him into early retirement. After about a year and a half of battling depression and PTSD, Murphy found the best way to keep himself grounded was to help people. He taught people to defend themselves as well as keeping healthy and fit. When in the SEALs, Murphy was one of the best when it came to hand-to-hand combat. He knew several variations of martial arts. When a storefront just outside of the base became available, he scooped it up and opened his own gym and dojo. He taught most of the classes himself.

Irish got out and started walking toward the building when Ace waved him over. He was looking into the front window.

"You got to check this out. Typical Murph, he's got a woman on the ground. But this one seems to be putting up a decent fight."

Irish wasn't surprised to see Murphy rolling around on the mat with a woman. He was lying on top of her, covering her body. The woman looked tiny under him. Murphy was a beast and a mean motherfucker when he wanted to be. But he also had a way with the ladies.

He watched as Murphy lifted the woman up in his arms as he stood. The woman struggled, but she didn't give up, which Irish had to give her some credit for. From the look on Murph's face, he was having a bit of difficulty. The woman wiggled her body and somehow ended up over Murph's shoulder, then slinked down his back like a snake winding its body around its prey. Her sneaky but cool move surprised Murph because before he realized what she was doing, she was on the ground and did a leg sweep move, taking out Murph's legs, sending him onto his ass.

"Holy shit! That was awesome," Ace exclaimed as he seemed to be enjoying the show as much as Irish. And Irish had to agree with him. That was a sweet move.

Alex stood to the side, laughing, which then made Murph laugh. Murphy pushed himself up and helped the woman stand. When she was on her feet, she spun around to grab her water bottle, and all the air rushed out of Irish's body.

"Oh shit!" Ace stated. Oh, shit was right, Irish thought. That was his woman.

Bailey was having a blast. This evening had actually worked out great because of the impending storm; nobody but Alex and she had shown up, so the two of them got a private one-on-one class with Murphy. It was an awesome work-out, and she even learned a few self-defense moves. She'd definitely be returning.

At first, she was a little intimidated by Murphy, but after spending time with him, she realized under all those frowns and muscles, there was a big teddy bear hidden there. Not that she would ever tell him that. The man was huge. His arms were the size of her thigh.

At the moment, she was in a predicament. She was on her back with Murphy on top of her and in-between her legs. He was showing her another self-defense move. She couldn't remember the name of it, but she was having some difficulty getting out of his hold.

"Move your legs higher against my ribs and squeeze," he told her, but she was afraid she might hurt him, so she released her legs and sighed.

"I can't do this. I'm afraid I might hurt you."

"Sweetheart, you aren't going to hurt me. Let's do this; imagine me as someone who you despise." Her mind immediately went to Randy. Murphy smiled. "Good, I can see you already have someone in mind by that look in your eyes. Now imagine that I am that person."

93

As soon as Murphy's gorgeous face morphed into Randy's cruel and angry face, her instincts kicked in. She raised her legs and squeezed with all her might. The weight from his body pressed into her made it difficult to breathe, but she was determined. No way in hell would she let Randy overtake her.

As she was squeezing her legs against his ribs, he made a move that had him standing and lifting her off the ground. She was still wound around him as he squeezed her. As he adjusted his body, his hold on her loosened just a smidge and gave her enough wiggle room to maneuver her body. She used her leg muscles to push herself up and over his shoulder, then slithered down his back and between his legs. When she found herself on her back on the floor, she took out Murph's legs, and now they were both on the floor.

Murphy was breathing hard and looked at her. "What in the hell was that?" He barked out.

She shrugged her shoulders and laughed, still trying to catch her breath. "I honestly don't know. You told me to think of someone that I despised and wanted to get away from, so I did. I'll admit I panicked and completely forgot the moves you showed me, but I wasn't going to give up, so I improvised."

"Well, whatever the hell it was, it was fucking awesome." He stood up and helped her to her feet, and Alex walked over to them.

"Damn, Bailey, where in the world did you think of that move?"

"I don't know."

"I need to remember that one." Alex high-fived her.

Murph looked at Bailey. "So, will I see you back for classes?"

If she felt this pumped after every class, then hell yeah, she would be coming back, and she grinned. "Absolutely."

Murphy let out a bark of laughter and wrapped her up in a hug and kissed the top of her head. Even though she knew it was a friendly gesture, Alex had already warned her about Murphy and some of the other men that worked out there. She looked up at Murphy. His eyes looked over her body, and she wondered if he was interested in her.

94

Murphy motioned toward the big window in the front. "I believe you ladies have an audience."

Confused, Bailey spun around and met a pair of eyes that looked to be burning a hole in Murphy. She swallowed.... hard. *Oh shit!*

Irish waited patiently while Alex and Bailey finished up inside. It looked like they were registering for some classes. He was happy that Bailey was interested in some self-defense classes. But he wasn't thrilled about Murphy and some of the other guys who taught the classes. They were worse than him when it came to women. He would make time very soon to talk with Murph and let him know that Bailey was his and off-limits.

"Hey Irish, what brings you here?" Alex said as she walked over to Ace.

"Irish said he needed to talk to you," Ace told her as he wrapped his arm around her waist and kissed her.

"Me? I thought you came by for another reason." She smiled and glanced over at Bailey. Irish almost laughed out loud when Bailey's cheeks turned bright red, and her eyes went wide.

"Well, that was a bonus seeing that Bailey was here because I actually needed to talk to her too." Well, that wasn't exactly true, but it sounded good.

"Well, what did you need to talk about?"

"We have to be at the base tomorrow, and I don't have anybody who can watch Sienna until I get home from work."

"Oh, yeah. Bailey mentioned that the schools were closed tomorrow. Any other time you know, I'd take her in a heartbeat, but I have the inspector coming tomorrow to look over the equipment at the clinic. I wanted to get it in before the storm."

"No, it's fine. I'm sure I can find someone else." He ran his hand through his hair. Shit, he didn't know what to do now.

"Ky, I don't have anything pressing, and since the schools are closed, that means I'm off. I can keep her for the day if you want. I don't mind. I don't have much planned except to grab a few boxes from my storage unit in the basement of the building. Then maybe run to the store and pick up a couple of things."

He looked at her. "Really? You wouldn't mind?"

She smiled. "I wouldn't have offered if I minded. She's a good kid. She can be my helper. I have some coloring books and stuff I can keep her occupied with."

"How about this? Why don't I give you a key to my place, and when you are finished up at your condo, you can take Sienna back to the house. That way, she'll have her toys and stuff there that will keep her occupied. Shit...."

"What?"

"Sorry, nothing for you to worry about. I just have a couple of things I wanted to get done before the storm, but I don't know if I'll be able to."

"Like what? Depending on what it is, maybe Sienna and I can help after we're done at my place."

He must have had a funny look on his face because Bailey laughed. "Look, why don't you make a list of things that she and I can take care of while you're at work. You can drop her off on your way to the base. I'll fix us breakfast, and she and I can get the stuff done around my condo, and then we can run any errands you need, then we'll go back to your house until you get home."

"I don't know when we'll be done, though. It could be late by the time I can get home."

"Speaking of the storm, where are you staying?" Alex asked Bailey. Shit, Irish felt like a tool for not asking her that.

Bailey scrunched her eyebrows together. "What do you mean...I'm staying at my condo."

Alex shook her head. "You can't stay there. It's right on the beach. If the storm hits the way the forecasters think it will, your street will flood. It floods just from heavy rains. The tidal surge will flood that area. Though your condo should be okay since you are high enough, you, on the other hand, will be stuck until the water recedes. These storms can be so

96

unpredictable, and the slightest movement could be good or could spell disaster for the area.

"She's right, Bailey. You can stay with us. We have plenty of room," Ace told her, but Irish didn't miss the look he was giving him—kind of like wake up and get with the show. Ace was literally giving Irish an opportunity here.

"Well, you guys know the area, so I'll take your word for it. I definitely do not want to be stuck in my condo." She looked over at Irish. "How far is your place from theirs?" She asked.

"About five to ten minutes, depending on traffic," he told her.

"Well, since your place isn't that far, once you get home, I'll drive over to their house since it seems I'm staying there." She grinned at Alex, who gave her a wink.

"Or you could just stay at our place." Holy shit, he couldn't believe he just blurted that out. He heard Alex snicker, and Ace grinned.

He could tell he had shocked her. She was nibbling on her lower lip and was looking to Alex for her to give her some help. He needed to sell her on it. "Come on; Sienna would love if you stayed over. I'll even be a gentleman and give up my bed and sleep on the couch."

She grinned. "Boy, you really know how to pull out the big guns to get what you want, don't you?"

Ace and Alex snickered, then made their exit, saying they needed to get home. That left Irish alone with Bailey.

Yeah, he knew it was a dick move to bring up Sienna, but he knew she wouldn't be able to say no to that. He would do anything to get her to stay at his place because they needed to talk, and it would give him plenty of time.

She pulled her bottom lip between her teeth, and he knew she was considering it.

"I guess so. But I'll take the couch. I don't want to put you out of your own bed," she said after several seconds of silence.

"Good, now that's settled, there is one more thing I need."

"There is?" She asked cautiously, and he took a step closer to her and placed his hands on her hips. Her eyes grew wid.

He bent his head and pressed his lips gently against hers, then pulled back. It was quick, but he needed it. Last night had been a tease, and he needed to feel that connection again. He smiled. "You pack one hell of a punch, woman." He moved his hands and squeezed her hand. "I have to be at the base at o-seven-hundred. I'll drop Sienna off around quarter to. Is that okay?"

He had to laugh. She was still in a state of shock from his kiss that all she could do was nod her head. He kissed her forehead and opened her car door for her. She went to say something, but he just lifted a finger to her lips.

"Shh…we'll talk more tomorrow when I get home."

"Okay," was all she said and got into her car and pulled out of the parking lot. He watched as she drove down the road, then shook his head in disbelief. Holy shit, this was really happening.

Bailey didn't even know if she was driving in the right direction. She was still trying to process what in the hell had just happened. Irish kissed her again. That's twice now that he had kissed her. She lifted her fingers to her lips. And what was she thinking, agreeing to stay at his house? Oh God, now she didn't know if she could go through with it. What if things didn't go as planned. Then she'd be stuck in his house and no way to leave because of the storm. She didn't know what to do, so she called Alex.

"Did he scare you off already?" Alex said with a laugh, but Bailey couldn't respond. She couldn't get her brain to function properly. "Bailey? Are you there?"

She shook her head to get her mind on the right track. "He kissed me."

"Huh?"

"Ky…he kissed me right before I got into my car."

"Oh my God! Yes! This is great!" Alex may have been happy, but Bailey was panicking.

"No, this is not great."

"Why not? You like him, and he likes you. What's stopping you."

"Alex, we talked about his. He is so more experienced than me. What if I mess everything up?"

"Oh, honey. You will be fine. Irish is a great guy and very understanding. Just be honest with him."

"You mean, tell him everything, including my virginity?"

"You are going to have to tell him some time or another. If the subject comes up, just be upfront with him."

"I'm scared, Alex."

"What are you scared of?"

"Rejection. Alex, Ky is the first guy that I've really liked. I've never had a boyfriend and never had sex. And I'm afraid that my experience or lack thereof will scare him away."

"If my gut is right, I don't think you have anything to worry about. Plus, he's a SEAL. Nothing scares him." Bailey thought about it for a second. "Look, if you need anything and need to talk, just call me, okay?"

"Okay. And Alex?

"Yeah?"

"Thank you."

"Anytime. Us women need to stick together. Just relax and let things go at their pace. It will all be good. Enjoy the time together."

"I will. Thanks again."

"You bet. I'll talk to you later."

"Bye."

She got out of her car and headed upstairs. It looked like she would need to pack an overnight bag. She still wasn't sold on the idea, but she would do what Alex said. She would take the time to talk to him and get to know him. If it didn't work out, then so be it. At least there wouldn't be any regrets.

CHAPTER FIFTEEN

Irish pulled into his driveway. He turned the ignition off and sighed as he rubbed the back of his neck. He was glad to be home. Forecasters now believed that the storm was going to turn eastward, causing it to just skim the coast. The state had already declared a state of emergency, and flood watches had already been issued for coastal areas. Winds were predicted to gust as high as 90 mph. They didn't have to report back to base until tomorrow afternoon unless an emergency or crisis occurred. And even then, it would have to be something major, considering they have a full staff on base to ride the storm out.

He got out and pulled his bag from the back and slung it over his shoulder. He saw his neighbors Will and Nicole outside, putting their outdoor furniture inside the garage. He wished he could use his garage to pull his car in but unfortunately, it was full of boxes. When he bought the two-bedroom, two-bath house, he wasn't expecting anyone other than himself to be living there. With Sienna living here now, he needed the spare room for her—not that he minded being put out because it was for her.

As he climbed the steps to the front porch, he noticed the front door was open, but the screen door was locked. An enticing smell caught his attention, and his mouth instantly watered. It smelled so good. "Bailey!" He called through the screen door. He heard a sound from the kitchen, then a few seconds later, she appeared, and his chest tightened at the thought that if he played his cards right, he could home to this every night. The baby blue lounge pants and matching tank top gave her a casual look. Her long hair was down, and her face was free of make-up. She looked fresh and comfortable. She smiled wide, unlocked the door, and opened it for him.

"Hey! Sorry about the door. It is so nice outside, and with the breeze, I thought it would be nice to let some fresh air in before the storm hits, and we have to close up the house."

He grinned and entered right behind her. His eyes immediately went to her ass. Although the lounge pants she wore were loose through the legs, they fit perfectly around her ass. Her tank top was snug and showed just how well-endowed she was. His dick was instantly hard.

She turned toward him. "Oh! I wasn't sure where your uniforms from the cleaners needed to go, so I hung them on the hook on the back of your door. Sienna showed me."

"So, you were in my bedroom?" He teased.

"I promise I didn't snoop, but I do have to say I was quite impressed by the neatness," she smiled, although her cheeks turned a little pink, and he thought it was cute she was blushing.

"I can thank the Navy for that." He turned his nose in the air and sniffed. "What smells so great?"

"Oh, crap!" She squealed and ran toward the kitchen, her little bare feet barely making a sound on the wood floors as she ran through the house. Yeah, he noticed her little sexy feet as well. Her toes were painted fire engine red.

He took his boots off by the front door, then followed her into the kitchen. As soon as he entered, he stopped and leaned against the doorway. He watched Bailey ease around the kitchen like it was her own domain. He saw the table had been set for three. The new colorful flower arrangement in the middle of the table didn't go unnoticed either. She must have picked that up while she and Sienna were running errands. It made him smile. It was like she belonged here in his home. His heart stopped momentarily when the thought hit him. Holy shit! He could actually see himself coming home to this, to her every night. She stopped in front of the stove and stirred whatever was in one of the two pots. Her back was to him and he hadn't realized she had been talking to him. Christ, he had been so engrossed in her he hadn't heard a damn word she said.

He pushed himself from the wall, walked up behind her and pressed his body against her back and let his hands rest on her hips. The light and sweet perfume she wore tickled his nose. She stopped stirring and stood still. Her body was tense. He wanted her to feel relaxed. He moved her hair, exposing the side of her neck, then bent his head so his mouth was right next to her ear, and he smiled when he felt a slight shiver wrack her body.

"What are you making?" He asked in a low voice, using his thumbs to caress her hips. Her tank top stopped just short above the waistband of her pants. As he kept rubbing her hips every now and then, his thumb would hit her bare skin, enticing him to explore more. She was taking deep breaths, and he could see how fast her heart was beating by the pulse in her neck.

She took a shaky breath before she spoke.

"I made macaroni and cheese, and broccoli to go with the roasted chicken. Do you want to taste?"

She turned in his arms with a spoon in her hand, making his hands fall from her body. She held the spoon of mac-n-cheese out, offering it to him. Instead of taking the spoon himself, he gently grabbed her wrist. Her eyes held his as he leaned forward and took the spoon into his mouth. As he licked the spoon, he heard her gasp, and her lips parted. She looked at his lips, then back at his eyes. Her pupils were slightly dilated. He still had a hold of her wrist, and he watched as her chest rose with every breath. Oh, yeah, she was feeling the attraction as much as he was.

"Ky…"

"Shh…That was really good, but I want a taste of something else." He released her wrist and cupped her cheek with his large hand. Just as he leaned down and was going in for something a little tastier, he heard Sienna squeal. Instantly, he dropped his hand, and Bailey turned back toward the stove. He knew the moment was over, but he still had all night.

"Uncle Ky! You're home!"

Bailey was thankful for Sienna's intrusion. Jesus, what was she thinking? They were in the kitchen for God's sake, and honestly, if Sienna hadn't made her appearance when she did, it was quite possible she and Irish would have taken the moment a little too far. She felt really hot and aroused. She wanted him, and damn did the man look hot in his uniform.

She reached over and turned the stove off, then smiled as she watched Irish squat down as Sienna barreled toward him. When she got to him, he scooped her up and held her with one arm. Bailey could only imagine what it might feel like snuggle with him with all those muscles he could wrap around her.

"We are going to make a huamongous fort tonight," Sienna told him.

"Oh, a huamongous fort?" He asked amusingly at her pronunciation of humongous.

Sienna shook her head up and down. "Uh-huh. Ms. Bailey got the blankets and sheets down from the closet, and she said, when you got home, we can make it."

"She did, did she?" He looked over at Bailey and grinned, and she smiled back. The man's smile alone made her belly do somersaults.

"Yep, and I was a big helper today. After we did our work at her house, we did everything on your worklist. And I even got to check off the things on the paper." She looked at Bailey and whispered, "What's the name of the paper again?"

Bailey smiled, loving Sienna's personality. She whispered back, "To-do list."

She looked back at Irish. "I got to check off the things on the to-do list."

"You were a big helper, and I'm sure Ms. Bailey appreciated your help." Again, he smiled and winked.

"And I already got my bath. See...smell." She lifted her leg and stuck her foot in his face.

He pretended to sniff her feet and made her giggle, which made Bailey smile. "Well, they do smell clean," he told her.

"Ms. Bailey said we should get our baths now before the storm comes. She said it's not safe to take baths when it's storming out. The latricity can hurt you.

"Do you mean the electricity?"

"Yeah, the latricity." Sienna gave him a look. "Don't you know what latricity is, Uncle Ky? It's dangerous." Irish chuckled. "Yes, peanut. I know what *electricity* is."

They continued to talk. Sienna told him everything they had done today, from cleaning up her condo to going to the store to get hurricane supplies, then picking up his clothes from the cleaners. The interaction between the two of them warmed Bailey's heart. It was amazing to see this giant of a man give a little girl his complete attention. How she wished she could've had even an ounce of that type of love from her parents. Even if it were just a small hug or hell, even a smile would've been better than what she got. Her parents hadn't loved her, and they never would. She was just a type of business transaction for them. A tax write-off, and someone that her mother could show off at Junior League and beauty pageants. She felt the tears start to fill her eyes, thinking about her fucked up childhood. She turned back toward the stove to make herself look busy and not draw attention.

A few minutes later, Irish set Sienna down and sent her to wash her hands. Bailey sensed him approaching and turned around.

"Is everything okay?" He asked, and he cupped her cheek. She closed her eyes and leaned into his palm, loving how his large hand felt pressed against her skin. It was soothing and comforting—something she'd never experienced before.

When she opened her eyes, his concerned blue eyes held hers. She smiled, wanting to assure him that everything was okay.

"Everything is fine," she told him. He caressed her cheek with his thumb. "We didn't know what time you'd be home. I was going to wait until about seven, and then I was going to feed her."

He smiled. "That's fine. Thank you again for everything today. You didn't have to cook, but it is a really nice surprise to come home to."

"It's no problem, and I actually like cooking. I don't get to do it often."

"Why is that?"

"Well, for starters, I live alone, and I'm not going to cook a big meal for just myself."

His eyes held a sparkle to them. "Well, then I guess we need to have you over more often, and we can cook together."

Sienna came back in, ending their conversation. She stood in-between Irish and Bailey and looked up him. "Uncle Ky, Ms. Bailey made my favorite, macaroni and cheese, and it didn't come from a box. She said her grandma taught her. Do you think she can teach me how to cook dinner?"

"I think we could persuade her," he said, smiling and ushering Sienna into a chair at the table. He looked over at Bailey. "Do I have time to take a quick shower? It'll only take a couple of minutes. Another thing I can thank the Navy for," he uttered as he unbuttoned his uniform blouse, revealing a tan t-shirt that molded to his chest and biceps. Her tongue nearly rolled out of her mouth.

Thankfully, she hadn't made a complete ass out of herself and was able to speak. "Sure. I hope you don't mind, but I got a shower myself. Sienna showed me where you keep the towels. The food is just warming, so take your time, and I'll start dishing everything out." She tried to look away, but he took a step toward her, took her chin between his thumb and index finger, and held her gaze.

"I don't mind one bit; you make yourself at home. I'm really glad you're here."

She was glad too, even if she was a nervous and emotional wreck right now. Then, she thought back to what Alex told her. Everything would work out.

She smiled up at him. "Me too." She was looking forward to the rest of the night and getting to know more about Irish.

He leaned down and gently pressed his lips to hers. It was quick, and he released her and walked toward his room, pulling off his t-shirt and revealing an upper body she had only seen on the covers of romance novels. He was lean but muscular with a waist that dipped in. And his back…oh, how she just wanted to run her hands up and down all the muscles. Just as she turned to dish the mac-n-cheese into the bowl, she heard Irish shout from his bedroom. *Did he just call the cat a nasty fucker?*

Irish was grinning as he pushed open the door to his bedroom. He was looking forward to spending the evening with Bailey, especially after Sienna went to bed. There were so many questions he wanted to ask her so he could get to know her better.

He went to grab his lounge pants he'd left on the bed this morning but saw they weren't there. He looked around the room, then walked into the bathroom, thinking maybe he put them in there. Suddenly, he heard a growling noise come from the other side of the bed.

Slowly, as he wasn't sure what he would find, he made his way around the bed, and the growling grew louder. When his eyes landed on the cat, he had to do a double-take. The damn cat was humping a piece of clothing. And not just any clothing, he was playing "bury the bone" with his lounge pants!

"Oh, you nasty fucker!" Irish yelled and tried grabbing the pants, but the cat hissed and growled, trying to take a swipe at him. Okay…so Mr. Whiskers gets angry when you interrupt his sex romp. But then again, wouldn't any male act that way?

"Ky…Is everything okay?" Bailey asked, entering the room with Sienna right behind her.

Irish looked at Bailey, who was looking at the cat and gaining an understanding of the situation. When her eyes grew wide, and she covered her mouth, he couldn't help but laugh.

Sienna stood between him and Bailey and asked, "Uncle Ky, what is Mr. Whiskers doing with your pants?"

"Umm…" He looked at Bailey, hoping she might know what to say, but the sparkle in her eye told him he was on his own. He cleared his throat. "He's just playing or maybe exercising." Bailey tried unsuccessfully to cover her snort of laughter.

"But he has toys to play with. Why does he want to play with your pants?"

Thank God Bailey put him out of his misery. "That's a very good question, Sienna. Why don't you and I go and gather some of Mr. Whiskers' toys? Maybe he couldn't find them. That will give your uncle a few minutes to jump in the shower, and then we can eat."

When Sienna agreed and left the room with Bailey, Irish felt relieved. He tried one last time to grab the pants, but Mr. Whiskers wasn't budging. Finally, he just said fuck it; if the cat wanted those pants that bad, he could have them. Damn, if he was ever going to wear them again, knowing the cat had his way with them.

CHAPTER SIXTEEN

After the incredible dinner, Irish helped with the dishes until Sienna was ready to build her fortress. Bailey assured him that she was capable of finishing things up and that she would join them when she was done. It wasn't that he didn't think she was capable of cleaning a kitchen; he just didn't want to leave her side. Plus, with everything she did for him today, including cooking, he felt bad for not helping more.

He could tell something had upset her right before they were getting ready to eat dinner. She seemed to perk up during dinner, but he could tell she was starting to revert to her quiet self.

He didn't want to push, but he also wanted to make sure he hadn't done or said something to upset her. God, this relationship stuff was stressful. He wasn't used to it, the feelings, emotions, and all that went with it. When he wanted a woman, all he had to do was walk into a bar, and women threw themselves at him.

He had a strong feeling that Bailey had been hurt or betrayed by someone in her past. He wondered if the guy who showed up at Bayside the other night was an ex-boyfriend. That was on his list of questions he planned on asking her.

Once the fort was built, the three of them sat in it, playing Candyland with battery-operated lanterns for light. The storm had started to move in, and the wind started to blow. He looked over and saw Sienna was practically asleep against Bailey. Bailey looked down and smiled as she ran her hand over Sienna's hair. She was a natural with kids, and he could see that Sienna was already attached to her.

"Uncle Ky...I'm sleepy," Sienna told him, barely able to keep her eyes open.

"Okay, peanut. Do you want to sleep here in your sleeping bag?"

She yawned, "No. I want to sleep in my bed. This floor is hard." He laughed to himself. If she only knew all the places and conditions he'd had to sleep in. The sleeping bag under him made a lot of his nights in the field feel like a thousand-dollar mattress.

"You know, the power might go out, which means your fairy lights won't work."

Sienna scrunched her nose up in thought. Then Bailey spoke up. "Actually, Sienna, you could borrow my magic lantern. It has magic powers that keep out all the scary creatures that like to come out at night."

Irish watched as Sienna's eyes widened. "Really? But what about you. I don't want the scary monsters to come after you."

Bailey smirked and glanced at Irish. "I think I'll be fine tonight."

"Uncle Ky can keep you safe. That's what he does at work. He keeps people safe." Sienna looked at him. He was amazed at what Sienna understood. Sure, she didn't know exactly what he did for a living but to hear what she said actually made him feel proud. And he would do exactly what Sienna said. He would protect Bailey. And not just tonight; he wanted to protect her forever. "Uncle Ky, can Ms. Bailey tuck me in tonight?"

"If she wants to, it's fine with me. But I still want my kiss, hug, and nuzzes."

As Bailey went to crawl out of the fort, Irish reached out and grabbed her hand. "You don't have to. I can do it."

She gave him a warm smile that he felt all the way to his heart. "You've had a busy day. Stay put and relax. I don't mind."

"You are coming back?"

"Do you want me to?"

"Yeah," he smiled, feeling giddy inside. Shit, he'd never gotten giddy over a woman.

"Then, yes. Give me a few minutes to get Sienna situated in her room."

After getting Sienna tucked into bed and putting new batteries into the "magic" lantern, so it would stay lit through the night, Bailey made her way back out into the living room. She stood there, looking at the fortress that Sienna called it and smiled. It was huge and took up a good portion of the living room, but considering Ky had built it, she shouldn't be surprised. Those guys seem to go all out in whatever they did. They all lived by that motto, go big or go home.

She followed the light coming from the small lantern inside the fort, and crawled back in. Irish was lying on his back with his hands tucked behind his head, looking relaxed and comfortable. The way his arms were bent made his biceps flex. He had his eyes closed, but she knew he was awake. She could feel a shift in the atmosphere. There was like this strange pull of energy between the two of them. She laid down in the spot next to him, mimicking his pose. It was silent except for the howling winds and rain outside. She should have felt a little on edge considering they were getting hammered with some of the outer bands of the hurricane, but instead it felt peaceful with Irish by her side.

"Is Sienna all settled?" He said, breaking the silence but keeping his eyes closed.

"Yep. No dragons or trolls will enter her room with the magic lantern lit." She smiled, thinking about the magic lantern that her grandfather had given her when she was a little girl. He promised her that as long as she had it lit, nothing bad would bother her at night. Too bad that didn't include her parents because they were monsters.

Irish's voice pulled her from her thoughts. "You're really good with kids. What made you become a teacher?"

That was a loaded question, and she thought about how to answer without opening herself up to more questioning, but the more she thought about it, there was really only one answer. "Probably because of my childhood."

"What do you mean?" He rolled onto his side and leaned on his elbow, looking down at her. She kept her eyes glued to the ceiling of the fort. "Sometimes, I think I'm trying to relive my childhood through the kids I teach. My childhood isn't a time that I like to remember nor talk about. I enjoy seeing my students learn new things and experiencing new challenges and conquering them. It gives me satisfaction that I'm doing what I was meant to do."

He placed his hand over her clasped hands that rested on her stomach.

"Was your childhood really that bad?"

She chuckled, but not in a happy way. "Oh, it was bad. Believe me." She felt a little self-conscious, but then Alex's words came to mind. She needed to be open and honest. Let him learn about her just as she wanted to know about him. Nobody really knew what she underwent as a child and into her early adulthood. Well, except for Ms. Kay. Ms. Kay was the family's housekeeper. But to Bailey, Ms. Kay was her only true friend at the time.

"It's so bad; you may want to throw me out and let the wind carry me back home."

Irish squeezed her hands and said, "If it's too much, you don't have to."

She let out a sigh. "No, it's not that; it's just I've really never have spoken to anyone about it before. I've never had to."

She rolled onto her side, facing Irish. She too had her elbow propped up, with her head resting in her palm.

"Lay it on me," he said, and oh, how she wished she could just forget about the whole conversation piece and just lay one on him. She wanted to feel those lips of his again.

She smiled at him. "Okay, but don't say I didn't warn you." And so, she began. "I was born into a very wealthy and controlling family. I'm an only child to the world's most ungrateful parents. I did, though, have an amazing and loving set of grandparents on my dad's side.

"I attended boarding school at a very young age, where I only came home during holidays, and even then, I didn't have much interaction with my parents. When I was home, I mostly stayed with my grandparents while my parents jetted all over the world. My grandparents weren't happy about the situation, but there was nothing they could really do."

111

She closed her eyes for a minute, thinking about how she was going to explain the next chapter in her life. She felt his hand slide to her hip, and her eyes popped open. His touch was comforting.

He ran his hand up and down her bare arm. "We can talk about something else if this upsets you. I would be just as happy if we just lay here quietly. I'm a patient man."

He was so sweet and caring, and she wondered again how she was so lucky or, in her case, unlucky to meet him. But she'd already started down the path, so she may as well get it all out. And quite frankly, it felt good talking about it. It was like she was able to rid herself of all the demons and emotions she'd been hoarding over the years.

"That's funny because you don't seem to come across as patient. I thought you guys were the get in there and got it done type."

He laughed. "We are, but we can also be very patient when the need arises. Trust me, with my specialty; patience is key."

"What exactly is your specialty Mr. G.I. Joe? Or is that something you can't tell me?" She teased.

He playfully poked her in the side, making her giggle. "First of all, I'm Navy, G.I. Joe is Army," he grinned, and she laughed. "My bad. I'll be sure to remember that, Sailor." She gave him a grin and wink.

"I'm a sniper."

"Oh, wow, I guess being patient is a key skill."

"Do you know how to shoot?" He asked her, still stroking her arm.

"No. But it's something I've always wanted to learn but never got around to it." She wrinkled her nose and looked at him. "Can you teach me?"

She watched as a smile took over his face. "I'd love to. And considering I'm an expert marksman, I'm the best teacher you could have."

He stared into her eyes, and then he got serious again. "So, now that we can add teaching you to shoot to your 'to-do list,' do you want to continue telling me what happened with your folks?"

Okay, he may be patient, but he was a pushy sexy man, although he acted in a subtle way.

"Things only got worse, especially when my grandma died, and then my grandfather became ill. I was fourteen when grandma passed away. Pop only made it to the end of my junior year." She blinked away the tears in her eyes. She had been devastated when Pop died. They had been her lifeline, the only family she could turn to for guidance or confide in. She had an aunt from her mother's side, along with her husband and son, Jonathan, who she kept in contact with regularly. But aside from them, she had no one else. Nobody to spend holidays with, nobody to just talk to.

Irish brought her hand to his lips. "I'm sorry. You must miss them a lot."

She sniffled but managed a slight smile, knowing they would want to see her happy and with someone like Irish who seemed to care about her. "I miss them very much. I think they would've liked you."

"Yeah?" He said, grinning and his eyes twinkling.

"Yeah," she replied, smiling back at him. "Anyway, after Pop passed, my parents became even more distant, almost to the point of non-existent. Their behavior had worsened, and they became more controlling. I know it had to do with money. My grandfather built the Anderson empire. So, when he died, everything, of course, went to my father. Businesses, the mansion, bank accounts, you name it." Everything except for the secret trust fund he had left her. But she wasn't ready to bring that up. At least not right now.

"After high school, my parents expected me to follow in my father's footsteps and attend an Ivy League school. But unbeknownst to them, I had applied and was accepted to the University of Central Florida." She smiled, remembering when she told her dad. "Man, was my father pissed when he found out. He threatened to pull my college tuition money."

"What did you do?"

She grinned. "I was eighteen, a legal adult, so I did what I wanted to do, I left for UCF at the end of the summer. I was going, come hell or high water."

113

"You were such a rebel," he teased her. "If you don't mind me asking, how were you able to afford to go? That is, assuming your dad made good on his threat. I mean, any college is expensive nowadays."

Her lips twitched upward. "Ah, yes. Well, my dear old dad wasn't aware that Pop had set up a college fund to cover my undergraduate degree. Everything from tuition, housing, books and even spending money was included. I got to keep whatever was left in the account after I graduated." She couldn't stop a tear from escaping as she remembered the day she graduated from college. The only people in attendance were her Aunt, Uncle, and cousin. Her parents hadn't even called to congratulate her. She wished her grandparents could've been there. But she knew deep down in her soul that they were both watching from above, smiling and cheering as she walked that stage and accepted her diploma.

Irish used his thumb to wipe away the tears from her cheeks. He spoke in such a caring and compassionate voice while looking deep into her eyes. "Your Pop sounds like he was a really special man and obviously, cared for you deeply. I wish I could've gotten the chance to meet him."

"My dad was so angry. My grandfather had hired an attorney from out of state to handle my college account. That was done to prevent my mother and father from meddling and getting their hands on the money. After college, I made a grave mistake and moved back to Birmingham. I did, though, purchase a nice little ranch style house and got a job teaching at the local elementary school. That only added to the feud with my parents. They were embarrassed because I chose to work instead of pretending I was some rich, spoiled debutante. If you weren't kissing my parents' asses, then they would turn their noses up at you. That just isn't me; I actually have to remind myself that I'm related to them."

Irish was flabbergasted as he laid there and listened to Bailey tell her story. To have gone through such a shitty childhood as she had but then to come out on top and be who she was today was astonishing. He could already see that she was nothing like her parents. So many emotions swept over him. On one end, he was furious and angry at her parents. But then he was feeling excited because the situation had brought her here.

His mind was working overtime, trying to listen and figure out if there was ever any boyfriend anywhere in there because she hadn't mentioned one. Then he thought of the incident the other night with the asshole. Why not just come right out and ask?

"The guy who showed up the other night, was he an ex-boyfriend or something?"

When her eyes widened in surprise, Irish knew there was definitely a past of some sort between them. He wondered if she even planned on bringing up that ordeal. He squeezed her hand. When she swallowed hard and paused before saying anything, he had a feeling that whatever she was going to say wasn't going to be good. He was still pissed off at seeing those marks on her neck.

"Yes, but not an ex-boyfriend. He's someone who I wish I had never met." He moved his hand to her hip, and his thumb grazed her exposed skin where her shirt had ridden up. Her skin was soft and smooth. "I knew it wouldn't take him and my parents long to find me. They probably had their private investigators looking for me the moment they realized I was gone."

His hands stilled, and he stared at her. "Are you saying that your parents didn't know you had moved? You didn't tell them?"

She looked up at him with those blue eyes of hers and grinned in an adorable way. "Nope. I managed to sell my house under the radar. Then I informed my mother I was moving the day I signed the closing papers. I don't even think the ink was dry before I was in the car and on my way here."

He released her hand and ran his hand through his hair. Jesus! What kind of people were her parents to make her take that kind of action? Then he became worried. If they were as controlling and conniving as she portrayed them to be, would they cause trouble for her here? He placed his hand back on her. He needed for her to feel the connection and know he was here for her.

"Are your parents and this guy going to be a problem? I mean, the guy already showed up once, and honestly, I'm concerned, considering how aggressive he was. Do you even know if he is still around?" He reached out and ran his fingers along her neck, where the guy had held her.

She looked him in the eye and swallowed hard, and he could sense her fear. "I can't say for sure, but they are a relentless group, so I wouldn't be surprised if they try to stir up trouble. Part of me wonders if there is something else driving their aggressive ways. And to answer the second part, no, according to a voicemail my mother left the other day, Randy is back in Birmingham."

She took a deep breath and exhaled. "Randy. The guy who Bear saved me from is the son of my parent's best friends. He's eight years older than me. The first summer I was home from college, he was around a lot. He was always wanting to take me out, always coming over to the house. Showing up at places where I was. At first, I wasn't sure what his deal was, but then one night, when my parents thought I was out, I overheard a conversation between them and Randy."

He lifted her chin for her to look at him. When he saw the fear and tears in her eyes, he wanted to take her into his arms and shield her from everything and everyone.

She covered her mouth, and tears cascaded down her cheeks. "Oh God, Ky. It was awful. They were laying out plans for the rest of my life. How I would belong to Randy, and once that happened, how our family's assets would merge. Basically, they were going to sell me out to gain more power and money."

Son of a bitch! He pulled her into his arms and hugged her close to him. "I'm so sorry, baby," he said, kissing her temple.

She shook her head and pulled away but kept her hand on him, which he was thankful for. It was like she was reaching out and finding that strength she could grab hold of. He wanted to be here for her.

"That's not the worst. This is so embarrassing. I'm so sorry. This is probably too much drama for you to worry about."

She started to pull away, but damn if he was going to let her do that. There were no side doors here that she could easily slip out of. She was his, and he was going to protect her no matter what.

"Slow down there, sweetness." The poor thing was shaking like a leaf, and he wiped her tears again. "Sweetheart, there is no reason to be sorry or embarrassed. You have no control over your family's doings. But look at you. You didn't let them win. You went on to live your life like your grandparents wanted you to do."

He saw the faint smile on her face, and that made him smile. He wiped the remaining tears from her face, leaving her with a red nose.

"Now, if you think for one minute that everything you've shared with me will make me want to drop you, you've got another thing coming, baby. Your honesty and willingness to share your experiences humble me. I'm here now and promise you I will be here tomorrow when you wake up next to me." He leaned forward and gave her a quick kiss on the lips. "Now, I want you to finish telling me the rest, and you'd better not leave anything out." He saw her gulp, and he wondered how much worse it could get.

He sat and listened as she explained how she overheard them, discussing plans for an arranged marriage. The more he heard, the more he realized that all Bailey had been was a pawn for her parents and their wealth. These people were sick. They never loved her. They were in love with money. She was a means as a tax-write off until she turned eighteen-years-old, then she became a means for a wealthier future.

When she finished, she curled into his body, and he just held her as the storm rolled on outside. She cried, and he let her weep. He had a feeling she'd never really had a good cry, and sometimes, people just needed one. This was twenty-six years of pent up feelings and emotions. He couldn't imagine what it must have felt like to be that alone growing up.

He spoke against her head. "Sweetness, I want you to promise me something." She lifted her head to look at him, and because of the tears, her eyes reminded him of sparkling ice glaciers. God, she was beautiful and so trusting. "I want you to promise me that if your parents or Randy

117

ever make any contact with you, whether it be text, phone call, or making an appearance like Randy did the other night, that you tell me. If I'm deployed, I want you to promise me that you'll call my commander."

She started to shake her head. "Ky, I don't think that's necessary. I don't want to---" He cut her off.

"No exceptions. With what you've told me, I don't trust them not to show up here and try to take you away, or worse, do you harm. Promise me. Please."

"I just don't want to be a burden. I mean, come on. Calling your commander? Isn't that a little over the top?"

"You aren't a burden. Your being with me means you are now a part of our unit. You are family. We all take care of one another. When the team is deployed, there are plans and protocols in place to protect the ones here at home. I won't go into detail now, but Alex, Tenley, and Autumn all went through traumatic experiences, serious enough that we could have lost them. But they survived because we worked together to bring them home safe.

His persistence paid off. "Okay, Ky. I promise. I kinda got the same lecture from Bear before you showed up that night. You can check my phone; he actually put his number in there."

He reached out and tucked a stray hair behind her ear. "That's a start. But I would hope I would be the one you would call first." His large palm cupped her cheek.

"Of course, you'd be."

They stared at each other, both of their blue eyes holding one another's gaze. He gripped her hip tighter and pulled her toward him. His touch sent electricity zapping through her body.

"I want to kiss you right now," he told her.

She licked her lips as she glanced at his lips. She wanted him to kiss her. "What's stopping you?" She asked, sounding seductive to her own ears.

He closed the distance, and she closed her eyes, anticipating the feel of his lips. When she felt his firm but gentle lips, she scooted closer. He tightened his grip while she slid her free arm around his waist. Her hands wanted to explore his taut body. His lips gently brushed against hers a few times. She opened her eyes for just a moment, and her eyes locked on his. They were nose to nose, mouth to mouth. She could feel the warm puff of air with every breath he took. He grinned, and this time, he swiped his tongue against her lips, and she opened. He invaded her mouth, leaving no area unexplored. He nibbled, sucked, and stroked with experience and ease. As he let up, he nibbled her bottom lip, eliciting a feminine moan from her.

Irish was a great kisser. Not that she had many experiences to compare to. She thought back to the conversation she'd had with Alex and Tenley. Of course, he was a great kisser. He'd had a lot of practice. He was very experienced if what Alex and Tenley had told her was true. Then she wondered, was this what this was right now? Would he want to sleep with her tonight and then be done with her? She was confused and upset that now of all times, her mind decided it wanted to sit and process things. She abruptly pulled back. They were both breathing heavily.

"Everything okay?" He asked, not letting his hold on her go.

She shook her head. "I don't know. I need to ask you something, but I don't want to come across as sounding like a jealous bitch."

"Bailey, you can ask me anything you'd like. I'm an open book. That is unless it pertains to my job, then I can't guarantee I'll be able to give you an answer."

"No, it has nothing to do about your job. That's not what worries me. Well, I mean, your job worries me. You put your life in danger every day, but..." She looked away from him as she contemplated asking what had been on her mind.

"Hey, what is it?" He asked, turning her face back towards his.

"I've heard...." As embarrassing as it was to ask, she needed to, so she could have peace of mind. *Just ask!* "How many women have you slept with?"

119

He closed his eyes and grimaced as if her question caused him pain. "Can I plead the fifth?"

Her stomach sunk, and she lowered her eyes. "That many, huh?"

He was quick to respond. "Let me explain. With my career, I never thought about settling down. The burden of having someone waiting here at home for me and worrying if I'll make it back alive was something I couldn't live with. Then there was the thought of my partner being unfaithful to me while I was gone. It was better for me not to have those worries. Any woman in the past who I've had sex with was just that, just sex. There were no commitments. And I'm ashamed to even to say this, but I never even stayed the night with a woman. When the sex was over, I was gone. They understood that before anything even got started."

Bailey felt sick to her stomach. She'd never been with a man before, and Irish was beyond experienced. He seemed like he should have a title of Master or something. She was jealous. How was she going to tell him she was a virgin? Would he laugh at her? Would he run? Oh, Lord help her.

"What are you thinking about right now, sweetness?" He asked, twirling a strand of her hair around his finger as he watched her.

"What exactly sets me apart from your other conquests of women? How do I know that you're not in this for just the sex? That I'm not just another easy lay for you?" There, she said it. And judging by his fierce expression, she thought she may have overstepped.

He pulled her closer and looked into her eyes. His eyes were so expressive.

"First of all, don't ever think of yourself as an easy lay. That thought never even crossed my mind. So, get that shit out of your head right now. If I just wanted sex, you wouldn't be here at my house. I wouldn't have left Sienna with you all day. And most importantly, you sure as hell wouldn't be here in my arms while we have a heart-to-heart talk."

"Do I want you? Absolutely! I don't think you realize how hard it is for me to lay here with you and not get lost in this fine body of yours. Those other women meant nothing to me. I've never wanted to get to know them. But you…I want to learn everything about you; your favorite color, your favorite song, you name it, I want to know."

He held her chin. "I haven't been in a committed relationship in a long time. But you have to believe me when I tell you that night we met; something changed in me. Nobody else since that night has occupied my mind but you. I mentioned you to the guys, and they even gave you that nickname 'Blue.' For your beautiful blue eyes. And then, when I saw you in that classroom, I just knew it was fate. I want you and only you."

She wanted to believe every word he was telling her, but she couldn't shake that little bit of doubt she held on to. Before she could really get inside her head, she was being lifted, and he placed her on his lap. She didn't know where to put her hands, so she looped them over his shoulders.

"What are you afraid of? The truth." He asked her.

She wet her lips and took a deep breath. "If we move forward with this relationship, I'd be giving you something that I haven't given any other man. Something I have fought hard to keep because it is my gift to give and not for others to take."

She watched his face carefully as he contemplated her words. She knew when it clicked, and he realized what she was trying to tell him. His eyebrows shot upward, and his eyes widened, before they darkened. He gripped her waist. Not in a violently but a possessive tight hold that had her body reacting.

"Sweetness…are you telling me that you're a virgin?"

She bit her bottom lip and could feel how flush her face was right now. "What if I told you I was?"

"If I weren't sitting here looking at you, I'd call you a liar."

She tilted her head. "Why?"

"Why what?"

"Why would you think I was lying?"

He ran his knuckles down her cheek to her neck before he clasped his large hand behind her neck. His possessive hold aroused her. He smiled, and his eyes crinkled in the corners. He was a gorgeous man.

121

"Because you're beautiful, smart, sexy, and no guy in their right mind who dated you would be able to resist keeping his hands off you. But your eyes are so expressive when you speak. They speak the truth."

She lowered her head shyly and tried to look away, but his long thick fingers held her in place.

"Don't you for one second feel embarrassed for telling me," he told her firmly. "Look at me." He nudged her chin up, so she looked him in the eye. "I, for one, am damn thankful that fate put us together that night. I can't explain it, and this is going to sound corny, but the moment my eyes locked on yours, I got this feeling deep inside my chest. I don't know what it was, but I've never experienced something so powerful and deep." He leaned forward and pressed his forehead against hers. "You are special, Bailey Anderson. I don't know how or even why you've remained pure, but I respect the hell out of you, and you have my word that I will never break your heart. We go at your pace." She closed her eyes as he kissed her forehead, her eyes, and her nose until he finally found her lips. His words and actions were sweet and caring. Jesus, she was in love with him already.

"Can I ask you a question?"

She snorted an un-ladylike laugh, one that her mother would've reprimanded her for. "After what I just told you, I don't think there is anything that you couldn't ask me."

"How have you managed to stay celibate all these years?"

"Well, that is an entirely different story. One that will surely have you hating my parents."

"I already hate your parents. Anyone who treats their child like your parents treated you don't deserve to be called a parent in the first place."

"From the first meeting I had with Randy, my mother made it clear that my virginity belonged to him. She knew I was still a virgin. That's what happens when your mother is best friends with your gynecologist. Talk about major HIPPA violations. Anyway, over the years, I was getting tired of her holding that over my head. Part of me wanted just to go out, and have sex with the first man I ran into to throw it in my mother's face."

"But you didn't?"

She shook her head. "I couldn't go through with it. Before my grandma died, she and I had talked one day, and she told me that the man who I chose to give my *gift* to is the man whom I'm destined to marry. I know that sounds so fairytale-like, but that's the honest to god truth why I couldn't do it. Every time I came close, and believe me, there were a couple of times that I came very close; it was her words that prevented me from going through with it. It's something I didn't want to look back on and regret."

He smiled and kissed her nose. "Well, I, for one, am glad you didn't go through with it."

"Why is that? Knowing your past, I thought you would prefer someone with more experience in the bedroom."

He gave her a soft smile and brought her hand up to his lips and kissed it. "Because I know that I'll be the only man to ever make love to you. The only man who will ever give you the pleasure you deserve and the only man to love you."

She swallowed the enormous lump in her throat and did everything to hold back her tears. But now she had to tell him the rest of the story. This part was a little more embarrassing, but she made Alex a promise. She would be honest with Irish.

She took a deep breath. "There's something else I need to tell you. Though I have never been with a man, technically speaking, I'm not a virgin."

He scrunched his forehead up. "I don't understand. Either you've had sex, or you haven't."

She covered her face with her hands. "Geeze, I can't believe I'm having this conversation with you."

"Hey...look at me. There is nothing you say that could scare me off or think anything less of you."

"I sort of took my own virginity," she blurted out.

"You what?" He asked, looking confused at that revelation.

She didn't know if she should be embarrassed or laugh at the expression on Irish's face. "I was so pissed at my mother one night when

123

she started on me about not spreading my legs for any other man but Randy, and I was just so tired of it. I felt as if that tiny thin barrier inside of me was a controlling factor in my life. So, I ordered myself a vibrator online, and the day it was delivered, I had a couple of glasses of wine, and I think you get the gist of what happened next."

He gave her a sideways glance. "You didn't?"

She buried her face in her hands. "I did, and the next day I, of course, had to call my mother."

"What exactly did you tell her?" Irish asked, looking amused that she actually bought a vibrator and devirginized herself just to piss her mother off.

"I told her I met a guy; we got drunk, and we had wild sex."

"And what was her reaction?"

With a roll of her eyes, she said, "She flipped out and called me a whore and along with other colorful names that popped into her callous mind."

"Damn." He wrapped his arm around her and pulled her down, so she laid on top of him. They laid there in silence. Chest to chest, both of their hearts beating together as one. She wondered what was going through his mind right now. Did she have too much baggage? But the thought of him stepping away from her caused her to tear up again. She tried everything to hold back the dam threatening to break. She took a deep breath and sat up, bringing him up with her.

She reached out and cupped his cheek, and he gave her a sweet, sultry smile. "Are you sure that you're okay with everything I've told you tonight? Because if you're not, I understand completely, and I'll walk away with no hard feelings." She had to know because she needed to walk away before she became any more invested in him. She was falling fast and hard for him. If he told her everything was fine now, but then a month from now decided he couldn't handle her past and walked away from her, she didn't think she'd be able to survive that heartbreak.

No sooner did she get those words out, he was pulling her back onto his lap. His strong arms embraced her, and he wiped her eyes, something he seemed to be doing a lot of tonight.

"I don't know what you have going through that pretty little mind of yours, sweetheart, but I'll be damned if I'm letting you go." He brushed her hair from her face. "You are a brave and courageous woman, Bailey. I'll admit, what you've been through pisses me off immensely, and if I ever come face-to-face with your parents, I'll tell them exactly what I think of them. Then I would tell them that you are mine, and if they ever hurt you again, they would have to deal with me." And on that note, he leaned forward and kissed her. And boy, did he kiss her. It was a toe-curling, melt her panties type of kiss.

As she eased back, she gazed into his eyes. "I'm yours?"

He grinned but stated in a serious and commanding tone, "Damn straight, you're mine, woman. You belong to me, and nobody fucks with what is mine."

Holy freaking shit. Irish was intense. He was fierce. And the best part of it all, he was hers.

"Now come here. You taste too good. I need more," he told her in a sexy, commanding tone before his mouth descended upon hers once again. There was no opposition from her; she opened immediately, wanting and needing his mouth on her. Neither one of them held back. He plunged his warm, velvety tongue into the depths of her mouth. He took possession and led a full-on assault, nibbling, sucking, and stroking. His fingers slid into her hair while his other hand rested just under her breast. He gave her tresses a slight tug that sent sparks from her head to her core, causing a moan to escape. He was lethal. He was wild, and she felt on fire. The feel of his hands on her body drove her insane. She could only imagine how it would feel to be skin-to-skin with him. She wanted so much more, but she needed to slow this down before she ended up losing her virginity right here and now. She pulled back, ending the euphoric kiss, and just stared at him. His eyes glistened, but she sensed some concern. "I'm sorry, I need to slow things down a little."

He chuckled and dropped a light kiss to her nose. "No worries, sweetness, and I should apologize. Your body is just too tempting, and I can't help myself."

He grinned, and she looked at that sexy scar of his. She reached out and rubbed her thumb along the faint white line, wondering how he got it. Probably some super-secret mission that he couldn't talk about. Not that it bothered her. She'd read enough to know how things worked with these men. She leaned forward and placed her lips against the scar and felt his breath shudder, and she leaned back.

"Did this happen on a mission?" She decided to ask.

He chuckled and rubbed the scar. "No, I got this in high school. One winter, I slipped on a patch of ice on our farm and came down face first on a barbed wire fence." She winced, thinking how bad that had to have hurt. She reached up and ran her finger along the scar again. "Do you have scars from your job?" She felt him tense and instantly regretted asking. "I'm sorry. That isn't any of my business."

He squeezed her hand and gave her an assuring smile. "No, it's okay. You are bound to see some eventually. We all have scars. Some are visible, others are not, but we don't talk about them. It's just part of the job."

She nodded her head in understanding. What these men go through are both physical and mentally challenging. "I get it. I may not know everything about your job, but I know enough not to ask questions."

He rolled her onto her back and hovered above her. His lean muscular build was snuggled between her legs. So snuggly, she could feel his hard length against her belly, causing her to suck in a breath. He grinned, then lowered his face until his lips were just inches from hers. "That is what you do to me." She felt her cheeks warm. He was very well endowed. "All that is for you. When you're ready, of course." He lowered his lips the rest of the way onto hers. This time, she was prepared for the kiss, but to her surprise, he was gentle and passionate. He made love to her mouth. Almost as if he were giving her a preview of what was to come. Gentle strokes of his tongue explored every inch of her mouth. His hands came up and cupped her cheeks as she placed her arms around his neck, pulling him

126

closer. He pulled her bottom lip between his teeth, tugging at it before letting go. Her body felt so hot right now as he trailed his nose down her cheek to her neck, where he nuzzled the skin just below her ear. Apparently, it was a very sensitive area as the sensation sent her skin broke out with goosebumps and sending eruption signals down to a place that was dormant on the way to extinction. He took a deep breath before he lifted his head.

"When I pulled out of the parking lot that first night we met and watched you in my rearview mirror as you stood there staring at the back of my car, I knew I had to see you again. I just wish it hadn't taken as long as it did. However, life got in the way. But I can't complain because I love Sienna like she's my own. Plus, if it wasn't for her, I'll never know if I would've found you. You deserve so much happiness, care, protection, and love. And I want to give you those things: me, my team, their women, and my family.

She smiled and lifted her head and kissed him. He rolled off her but pulled her close against him, and she snuggled in, taking in the scent of his aftershave and his soap. She could get used to this very easily as they both lay there. She placed her hand on his chest and traced her fingers with his. This man, a warrior who fought, protecting their country, was truly a gentle giant.

Bailey's phone vibrated, alerting her that she had a text. She knew it wasn't her parents, checking to make sure she was okay. They never showed an inkling they cared, so why would they start now? She reached up behind Irish's head and lifted it to see the screen and was surprised to see Alex's name.

"It's Alex," she told Irish as she read the message. "She wants to know how we are holding up and since the storm isn't too bad if we want to go to their house tomorrow morning for breakfast."

Irish snorted. "She couldn't wait until tomorrow morning to either call or text?"

"What do you mean?"

He had a wicked grin on his face and pulled her back next to him.

"I know Alex and her tactics. She's fishing for information. What she really wants to know is how things are between the two of us. Trust me."

"Okay…how should I respond?"

"Give me your phone." She handed it over. "Now, come here." He squeezed her even closer to him, and he held up the phone. "Smile." He took the picture, then hit a few buttons.

"Wow!" He said, staring at the phone.

"What?"

He turned the phone towards her, and when she saw the picture, her throated tightened. "Wow is right."

It was a beautiful picture of the two of them looking comfortable in one another's arms. He pressed a few more buttons, then handed it back to her.

"What did you do?"

He grinned and shrugged his shoulders. "Just giving her the answer she really wants to know. Oh, and letting her know the three of us will be at breakfast."

Her phone vibrated, and they both looked at the message.

"Holy shit, girlfriend! Tenley, Autumn, and I want details! I'll have mimosas ready for us."

Irish laughed, then looked at Bailey. "I told you," she giggled and then laid her head back down against his body, and for the first time in her life, she felt happy and protected. And she was thankful that fate had led her here and into the arms of this amazing man. She let out a little giggle.

"What's so funny?"

"It only took me twenty-six years to have my first boyfriend."

She felt his body shake with laughter. Then she felt his lips against her cheek, and then what he whispered in her ear gave her goosebumps. "Your first and your last." With those words, she snuggled closer and found herself falling fast asleep.

CHAPTER SEVENTEEN

Irish blinked his eyes open and knew it was morning because of the sunlight coming in through the window. He was trained to be a light sleeper; his body and mind always seemed to be on alert, even in a state of sleep. He glanced over at the pixie who lay curled up beside him. She was so beautiful and seemed so full of life, and damn, it made him happy that she was his woman. Yes, he would admit it to anyone, Bailey Anderson was his woman, and that brought a big smile to his face.

Amazing couldn't even begin to explain the woman Bailey was. The woman who lay sleeping and snoring was a rock star. He knew it had to have been difficult for her to share what she had with him last night. Though from everything she told him, he was pretty sure her life growing up had been a hell of a lot worse. He felt honored that she trusted him enough to share those years of agony with him. And he meant what he told her when he said he would be by her side when she woke up this morning and that nothing she told him would make him turn away from her.

To hear her speak about how her mother and father treated her ate at him. And that fucker Randy. He actually hoped the asshole came back again because that would give him the excuse to beat the shit out of him. From the sounds of it, when her grandfather died, she lost the only family who loved her. But what impressed him was how strong she was on the inside. She obviously had a good head on her shoulders to see what they were doing and escaped from their stronghold, even when money was thrown in her face. Nowadays, people are so money hungry, they would sell their souls to make a quick buck. Not Bailey, though, she went against her parents, even when they threatened to take away money. She hadn't mentioned any other family besides an aunt, uncle, and cousin, and he wondered if she truly was alone and on her own. But that didn't really matter because she wasn't alone anymore. She had him now, and he would

129

show her what family love really was. Hell, she already held his heart in her hands.

Suddenly, he got an odd feeling in his chest. Almost like the one he got the night he met her. He rubbed his hand down his face. *Well, fuck me. I have her in my arms for one night, and I'm fucking in love.*

He heard Sienna's little giggle, a sound he has grown to love. He looked down, and there she sat staring at them with a huge smile on her face. Her presence must have been what woke him up. And, of course, Mr. Whiskers was right there with her with his motor running as she petted him. He swore that the cat's purr was louder than a damn Harley.

"Hey, peanut. You sleep, okay?" She nodded her head. "No creatures got into your bedroom?"

She grinned, "No, Ms. Bailey was right. Her lantern is magic."

At that moment, Bailey snuggled closer to him, and he felt her smile against his neck. The little minx was playing opossum.

Sienna cocked her head sideways and looked between him and Bailey. "Uncle Ky...are you and Ms. Bailey going to get married?"

His head swung back to his niece. *Where the fuck did that question come from?*

"My friend Sara Jane said when her mommy fell asleep with her new daddy that they got married. Can I be in the wedding? I want to be a flower girl like Sara Jane was in her mommy's wedding. Ooo... Can I wear a pretty poufy dress? Like my *Wedding Day Barbie*. I want to look pretty like her. Will we be a family too? That means she can move into our house. Will she share your room?"

As worried as Irish should be at what else little Sara Jane had told Sienna about mommies and daddies, he couldn't hold back his laughter. And apparently, neither could Bailey. He could feel her body shaking, trying to hold in her laughter, but he could hear her little snickers. Shit, now he had to answer the question.

He put his mouth against Bailey's ear so only she would be able to hear him. "I'm glad you find this so funny, sweetness. Any input would be much appreciated," then gently bit down on her earlobe. He smiled when he heard her emit a faint gasp. God, how he wished he could nibble her entire body, but the thought of his audience had his growing erection slowly deflating.

He looked back at Sienna, who was shockingly patient, waiting for an answer.

This was not a conversation he had anticipated this morning. He cleared his throat. "Well, sometimes when mommies and daddies, whether they are new or old..." At that, Bailey laughed out loud, and he looked at her. "What? What did I say wrong?"

She sat up, brushing her hair that had fallen out of her ponytail off her face, and she looked at him. "You can't say mommies and daddies are new and old." Irish knew she wasn't scolding him because her voice held some laughter to it.

She gestured to Sienna. "Come here, sweetie." Sienna crawled over, and Bailey positioned her so she sat between Irish and her. "You see, marriage happens when two people fall in love."

"Like the prince and princesses in my Disney movies," Sienna asked with her nose scrunched up.

"Yes, that is a good example. Some people can fall in love over the years, and then some people fall in love the moment they meet someone."

"Like you and Uncle Ky. Uncle Ky said he met you in a parking lot and helped you. Do you love Uncle Ky?"

"Well, there are times when people can fall in love at first sight." Irish listened to every word Bailey said. He looked into her morning eyes as she held his gaze, and he swallowed hard. Was she insinuating that fate was real?

"Isn't that right, Ky?" She asked, holding his stare, and all he could do was shake his head yes. He was afraid to speak for fear of the words he might spew because deep down in his heart, he knew he had fallen in love with Bailey the moment he looked in her eyes.

Bailey sat back in the chair, looking at her new friends. Autumn, Alex, and Tenley had been trying to get her alone since she, Irish, and Sienna arrived for breakfast about an hour ago. The guys were all inside doing their thing before they had to leave to report to base. She took a sip of her mimosa, then set it down on the table. She was still giddy from waking up this morning next to Irish. She was also still a little embarrassed about everything she had shared with him last night. But he assured her with a scorching kiss that everything he told her last night hadn't changed. She was Ky Daniels' woman.

"I don't know what you want me to spill?" She said, looking at the overzealous women. Alex had cooked up a breakfast buffet for everyone. Tenley was the lone person still eating. But she had an excuse. She was eating for three people: herself and the two little babies inside her tummy.

"Oh, come on. Alex showed us the picture of you and Irish. You two were all cuddled together. Irish doesn't cuddle."

Tenley scrunched her nose up. "Where were you anyway? It looked like you were in a tent. Oh, please tell me he didn't make you guys sleep outside in the storm, so you could get a full experience of what the team has to endure on missions."

Alex started laughing and pointed at Tenley. "Remember when you and Potter went on that camping trip a couple of months ago, and you thought he was taking you to Stitch's cabin for a romantic weekend."

Tenley rolled her eyes. "Ugh! I still give him shit about that trip."

"What happened? A trip to a cabin in the mountains sounds very romantic," Bailey asked, happy that her night with Irish wasn't the center of attention anymore. Not that she was ashamed or anything.

Autumn laughed as she chimed in. "Oh, they went to the mountains, but Potter 'accidentally' forgot to tell her about their accommodations."

"Lack of is a more suitable term," Tenley huffed out as she rubbed her pregnant belly. "Oh, and I came home with a souvenir too."

"From the woods?"

"Yeah, poison ivy on my ass. Apparently, my husband didn't do a good enough recon, or he would've seen the patch of poison ivy I had been peeing in all weekend. Anyway, we weren't talking about me. Let's get back to your night."

"I don't know what you guys want me to tell you. Mostly, we just talked. Well, I guess it was just me that did most of the talking. I kind of spewed everything. Honestly, I thought I was going to scare him off."

"What exactly did you tell him?" Alex asked.

"I told him about my childhood and how awful my parents were and still are. Then he told me I could ask him any question I wanted, and I made the mistake of asking him how many women he's slept with."

"Oh boy…and how did that go over."

"He pleaded the fifth. But it wasn't like you guys didn't warn me. I knew about his past going into this. I understand he had a life before me."

"That's a good outlook to have, so what happened next?"

"Well, as the conversation moved along, we got on the subject of my sexual experiences."

"So, you told him you were a virgin?"

"I did."

"And? You can't leave us hanging," Tenley exclaimed around a mouth full of cinnamon bun that she had just shoved into her mouth.

"At first, he didn't believe me."

"Why the hell not?"

"I believe his exact words were, there was no way in hell that any man I dated would be able to keep his hands off me. Anyways, I explained a little more in-depth about my mother's expectations of me to save myself for Randy. You know, the guy who showed up the other night. And how I got drunk one night and decided to take my own virginity, so to speak."

She hadn't explained that part to the girls, so she proceeded to tell them about the night she took her virginity and the part about her mother dragging her to the doctors to confirm it.

"Holy shit, Bailey. Your mother is a bitch," Autumn, the quieter one of the three women, stated.

"Yeah, she is, and unfortunately, my father isn't any better. Actually, he's much worse."

"So how was Irish after you told him all of that?" Alex asked.

"Surprisingly, he was very understanding. He hates my parents, and God help them if their paths ever cross."

Alex reached out and covered her hand. "He's a good guy, Bailey, and he will treat you well."

"So, did anything happen between you two last night? Because that picture of you two cuddling doesn't explain a whole lot," Tenley asked.

"We kissed a little, but that was the extent of it. He knows my past and reservations, but he promised we'd take things at my pace."

"There's nothing wrong with that."

Bailey gave her shoulder a shrug. "I don't know. I guess it's my inexperience wreaking havoc on my mind. I just don't know how I'll know I'm ready. I mean, the women who I've seen at Bayside and have obviously slept with him are beautiful and experienced. In the back of my mind, I keep asking why he would choose me over them."

"Oh, you'll know, sweetie. And as far as why he chose you over the others is simple. You stand out from the others. Trust me, it just happens. Ask Alex and Autumn. It happened to them, and it happened to me. You meet that one person, and you know instantly you are meant to be with them. Plus, as soon as you and Irish bump uglies, you'll be thanking the heavens from above for his experience. And you'll be able to confirm the rumor."

"Rumor? What rumor?" Bailey asked, very confused.

"Oh, Jesus, Tenley. Now you're going to scare the poor girl," Autumn scolded her friend, then took a sip of her drink.

Tenley leaned forward and spoke in a low voice, so the guys couldn't hear with their super-sonic hearing. "Rumor has it that Irish has a tattoo in a certain *special* place. From what I've gathered through hearsay, this tattoo is how he got his call-sign." Tenley waggled her eyebrows up and down. "None of the guys will tell us, so it looks like you're going to take one for the team."

Bailey absorbed Tenley's words, and then it sunk in. "He has a tattoo on his penis?"

Tenley sat back and sipped her sparkling cider. She shrugged her shoulders. "Don't know for sure, but Alex and I have overheard some conversations that have led us to believe he could."

Oh shit.... Bailey picked up her mimosa and downed it as the women laughed.

§

The guys were all kicked back around the kitchen table, where they could still keep an eye on the women outside. The kids were in the game room down the hall, watching tv and playing air hockey. The good news was the storm had just skirted the coast leaving minimal damage in its wake.

"So, you and Bailey looked cozy last night?"

Irish looked at Ace and grinned. "Alex showed you the picture, huh?"

"Yep. And hopefully, now she'll stop talking about you and Bailey and how the two of you need to communicate and shit. No offense to either one of you, but I was starting to feel as if the two of you were going to join us in bed," Ace stated, taking a drink of his coffee as the others snickered. That's when Irish noticed the words on Ace's coffee cup, and he busted out laughing.

Ace raised an eyebrow in his direction, and Irish pointed at the coffee mug. The others around the table started laughing as Ace turned the mug around and frowned.

In big, bold black letters, the cup read, *"Busier than a cucumber in a women's prison."*

"Fucking Alex and her damn coffee mugs," Ace mumbled, getting up to get a new mug. Alex had a fetish for collecting inappropriate coffee mugs. You never knew what a mug might say. This one he'd never seen before, but it was hilarious, especially seeing Ace with it.

Ace cleared his throat as he sat back down. "We were talking about you."

"And your point? What, do you want to sit around and gossip like girls while we paint each other's nails?"

"No, smart-ass. I want to know if you were able to get any more information about that guy who showed up."

"We talked about a lot last night. She has a past, and I have some concerns."

"What kind of concerns?"

"Not what you are thinking. She had a rough childhood. Her parents are assholes who only appear to care about their lifestyle and money. Her grandparents had tried to protect her the best they could, but they passed away when she was in high school. After their death, her life spiraled." He explained a little of her past, including the asshole who showed up at Bayside the other night and put the bruises on her neck.

Potter asked. "Is he going to be an issue? It already pisses me off that he touched her."

"I asked her the same thing. She said she wouldn't put it past them to make a move. I mean, this guy, Randy already made one appearance, and according to Bear, he heard him threatened her. He also wasn't happy with Bear for intervening."

"Well, from the looks of it, she took her grandfather's words of advice to heart and got away from the stronghold her parents thought they had on her."

"That she did. She didn't even blink an eye when they threatened to cut her out of the will."

"They are that wealthy?"

"From the sounds of it, they are very wealthy."

"Money comes with a lot of connections. In your opinion, do you think her parents and this Randy guy could show up again?"

"I honestly don't know."

"Well, if anything should arise, just let us know. Alex, Tenley, and Autumn have already formed a tight friendship with her."

Irish looked at his teammates. Specifically, Ace, Potter, and Frost. "Is it normal to already have that possessive and protective feel over her?"

Ace laughed. "Yeah, man, it is. Once you find the one, you just know. But it's a great feeling to have." Frost and Potter agreed with their own words.

"Oh, on a side note, do any of you know anyone who might want a cat?" They all looked at him strangely, and he proceeded to detail Mr. Whiskers' night of passion with his pants. Then regretted it because he knew that conversation would come back to bite him in the ass.

CHAPTER EIGHTEEN

The ladies had just placed their drink order and were looking over the menu at the restaurant they'd stopped into after a day of shopping for dresses and shoes to wear to Alex's Foundation's grand opening gala when Tenley looked at Bailey.

"Umm, Bailey, the guy sitting three tables down from us keeps looking over here. Well, looking at you specifically," Tenley told her.

Bailey tensed up, and fear took over. Her first thought was Randy.

"What does he look like?" She asked, not wanting to look in case it was him. She had already pulled her phone out and had her finger on Irish's name to call.

"I'm not going to lie; he's hot," Alex and Autumn shook their heads in agreement.

Randy was handsome, but not hot, so she took a quick glance, and her eyes widened when she saw who Tenley was referring to. Bailey gasped and covered her mouth as she looked away quickly.

"We need to go now!"

"What? Why? We just got here. The guys are already on their way and should be here any minute," Alex told her.

Bailey tried to shield her eyes with her hand. She probably looked ridiculous. She took a peek and saw the guy get up and make his way over to their table. Her heart started to beat even faster. This had disaster written all over it.

"Oh, God!" She tried to get up.

"Whoa, honey. You look like you're going to be sick." Yeah, well, she felt like she was going to be sick.

"I need to get out of here," she pleaded with her friends.

"Why? What's wrong? Oh, look, there are the guys now," Tenley said, waving at them. Bailey looked toward the entrance and was getting to make a run for it when she locked eyes with Irish.

Bailey turned toward Alex and Tenley. "Remember my massage day?"

"Who could forget that. What does that have to do with this guy?" Alex looked up at the guy approaching quickly, then looked back at Bailey. And Bailey knew the moment Alex realized who this guy was. "Oh shit! Tell me that is not the guy who practically molested you on the massage table."

All Bailey could do was nod as her stomach turned into one big knot when Manny stopped right in front of her.

"Damn. It must be my lucky day. I almost didn't recognize you with your clothes on." Bailey's face turned crimson. Suddenly, a deep growl came from behind her. When she turned around, Irish stood there with his arms crossed in front of his chest, glaring at the guy. With his eyes narrowed and standing there with his chest puffed out, Irish looked fierce, and Manny took his stance as a warning and stepped back.

Irish took a step forward and placed his hands on her shoulders. He squeezed, and she knew he was pissed. This was so not good. The entire table went silent and waited to see what would happen next.

"What did you just say to my girlfriend, asshole?" Bailey put her hands over Irish's.

Manny held his hands up. "Whoa there, man. I didn't know. She may want to be a little more careful. If she were my woman, I wouldn't let her out of my sight, let alone let her venture into a place like my friends and I run."

"What in the hell are you rambling about?" Irish exclaimed. Irish wasn't aware of the *situation* that had occurred at Deep Waters.

"The day spa, my friends and I run," Manny smiled all cocky. Bailey thought the man seriously had a death wish. "It's a very hands-on experience for women only if you get my drift."

Bailey covered her face with her hands as the situation turned worse.

"No, I'm not getting your drift." She tried to intervene, but Irish hushed her, which kind of pissed her off. "Maybe you need to be a little more descriptive."

What the hell? Are they seriously speaking to one another about me like I'm not even standing here?

Before the conversation could go any further, she decided it was time that she spoke up. She cleared her throat, shook Irish's hands from her shoulders and stood between the two men.

"Excuse me, Manny, but in my defense, I wasn't seeing anyone at the time. And second, I was oblivious to what services your establishment offers. Now before this situation gets out of control, I think it's best if you just turn yourself around and go back to your table."

The jackass had the audacity to grin and then wink at her. She heard Irish mumble something under his breath, but then the guy did what she had insisted. He turned around and went back to his table of friends who looked on with interest.

"Asshole," she heard Irish say before she felt his hands on her shoulders again. He turned her around and boy did he look angry.

"Irish, I'm sorry—" He cut her off.

"We'll talk about it later," he said, then motioned for her to take her seat and he took the one beside her. For the next forty-five minutes, he barely said anything, and she couldn't help but wonder what he was thinking. Shit...she didn't know what to do.

Right after lunch, Irish excused him and Bailey. They were walking to his vehicle. His long strides make it difficult for her short legs to keep up. Finally, she pulled on his hand, making him stop. "Irish, you're scaring me. Please say something."

He shook his head and continued walking. "I can't right now."

"Why not?" She pressed.

He turned toward her with his hands on his hips. "Because I'm pissed off right now, and I don't want to say something I may regret."

140

"I can see that, but not talking about it is making it worse," she countered. She wasn't going to let this go on.

He raised his hands in the air. "What do you want me to say, Bailey? A man…. a man who, by the way, is not me, saw you naked, and then had the nerve to throw it in my face. So, excuse me if I'm not dancing around, acting happy and shit."

Her temper met his. It wasn't fair that he was taking it out on her. "Just so we're straight, he didn't see me naked. Yes, I was naked, but I was under a sheet. And remember, when this happened, we weren't dating."

"Like that makes me feel any better," he retorted.

"Irish, look at me." He was staring at something over her shoulder, but she was determined to make him talk to her and realize that the situation was all a misunderstanding. She shook him, and he finally looked down into her eyes. She could see the anger and hurt. "I swear to you nothing happened with that guy. As I said, when I realized what was going on, I made him leave the room, then I got dressed as fast as I could and got the hell out of there." She placed her hands on his chest, and he covered them. He was breathing heavily, and his nostrils flared. "You believe me, right? Because if you don't, then we have a serious problem."

He backed her up until her back was against his vehicle. He took her face between his hands and bent, so he could really look into her eyes. "There was never a moment that I didn't believe you. I'm a man, Bailey. A man who is very possessive and protective of people I care about, including my girlfriend. It upset me to stand there and hear another man talk the way he was about you."

She smiled and wrapped her arms around his waist. "Well, if it helps, I'm sorry for placing myself in the situation to begin with. Believe me, that won't ever happen again."

He gripped her chin and tilted her face upward and stared into her eyes. "Damn straight, it won't. Maybe I'm just insecure, but damn if I am going to knowingly let another man put his hands on what is mine."

She giggled. "Deal. Now kiss me."

141

"You don't have to ask me twice." He lowered his head and tenderly made love to her mouth. Things started to get a little hot and heavy when his large hand slid under her skirt and caressed the back of her thigh. The warmth of his palm on her skin had her moaning. When his hand slid further up toward her ass, she reluctantly pulled away and took a couple of deep breaths. The man was sexually lethal. She rested her head against his chest as he buried his face against her neck, and he placed tiny kisses to her skin as she listened to his heartbeat rapidly in his chest.

"You are going to be the death of me, woman," he whispered.

She pulled back enough to look at him, and she could see the emotion in his face, mainly his eyes. The anger before was gone and replaced by arousal and desire. And it wasn't just feeling aroused that had her wanting to demand him to take her home and make love to her. No, it was something else much powerful, more meaningful. She swallowed hard...*It was love.*

He touched her cheek. "You okay?"

She smiled softly. "Yeah, everything is perfect."

"Do you have plans for the rest of the day?" He asked, and she shook her head no. "I need to blow off some steam, and you gave me an idea."

"I did?" She asked, wondering how she managed that.

"Are you still interested in learning to shoot?"

She smiled wide. "Yes!"

He grinned and opened the door for her to get in. When she stepped up, he gave her ass a slap, making her jump. She turned to reprimand him, and he cocked his eyebrow, daring her to say something. Instead, she kept quiet and buckled her seatbelt. Today had been a turning point in their relationship. She felt it, and she had a feeling that Irish had too.

CHAPTER NINETEEN

"Hey, sweetie, why are you sitting in here all by yourself?" Bailey asked Sienna as she walked into Sienna's bedroom. Sienna looked saddened as she sat at her little pink and green Disney table.

Sienna let out a deep sigh. "Uncle Ky promised me he would come to my tea party. But his friends are here now." That was when Bailey noticed that Sienna had her table set with her Disney tea set, complete with teacups, saucers, and teapot. She had even placed her favorite stuffed animals around the table and she wore her yellow Belle from Beauty and the Beast dress, with a matching tiara. She looked adorable.

She crouched down in front of Sienna. "Oh, honey, I don't think he forgot. He just got a little sidetracked. I'm sure he'll be here as soon as he finishes up with his meeting."

"Do you know when they will be done?"

"No, but whatever they're meeting about must be really important because I know for a fact that your uncle wouldn't have forgotten your tea party. He loves to spend time with you, and I'm sure he is just as upset as you are right now that he can't be here. How about you come and sit with me on the couch, and we can watch a movie until he's finished."

Sienna shook her head. "No, I'll stay here and wait. Maybe the rest of my friends can have their tea, and then when Uncle Ky finishes, he can have some," she said, motioning towards her stuffed animals.

Bailey smiled. "I think that is a perfect idea. If you need me, I'll be in the living room."

"Okay…"

Bailey waited patiently on the couch. She could see the guys through the glass door. It was getting later, and Sienna was still in her room. She had ventured out for a few minutes and fixed herself a snack and fill her teapot with water.

When Bailey had checked on her a few minutes ago, Sienna still sat at the table looking defeated. Her sad expression broke Bailey's heart. She knew Irish hadn't intentionally forgotten about the tea party. He had been surprised when Ace called this morning and asked if they could all meet at his house. Irish had called her right after he had hung up with Ace and asked if she could come over to keep an eye on Sienna since he wasn't sure how long their meeting would last. She hadn't minded one bit. She loved spending time with Sienna, especially outside of the classroom. Bailey was still adjusting to the balance of the relationship inside and outside of the classroom. There was a certain professionalism she had to maintain to be sure she wasn't showing favoritism.

Bailey knew something was going on with Irish. He had been quieter than usual and a little moody the last few days. The way he had blown up yesterday at the situation with the guy from the day spa had been a good example. She was pretty sure something at work was the driving force behind his mood. He'd also been working late, and he mentioned he could be called out any day. Even though she wanted to question him on it, she knew to just let it go.

She lifted her head when she heard the sliding glass door open, and Irish poked his head in.

"Hey, are you okay?" Irish asked.

"Yeah," she replied.

He walked in, closing the door behind him. He sat down next to her, and she laid her head on his shoulder.

"You look like you're pondering something."

She pulled her bare feet up and tucked them under her. "No. I'm good. How much longer do you think you guys will be?"

"Not too much longer. Why? Do you have somewhere you need to be?" He leaned in and started suckling her neck, making her laugh. That brought back a memory from yesterday when they went to the shooting range. She not only had surprised Irish, but she'd also surprised herself with how well she could handle a gun. Her favorite, for now, is a Glock 17,

144

9mm compact handgun. However, she really wanted to get her hands on the weapon that Irish used. When she asked him about it, he just smiled and said it was his baby. But when he had her laying on her belly, trying to hit the target with the Glock, he kept distracting her by kissing her neck just like he was now.

She sat back and looked at him. "I don't, but you do. Your niece is heartbroken because she thinks her uncle forgot her tea party."

His eyes widened, and he stood up. "Oh, shit! Where is she?"

"In her room. Sitting at the table waiting."

"How long has she been there?"

Bailey looked at her watch. "About three hours. She did come out to the kitchen to get something to eat but went back to her room."

He ran his hand down his face and sighed. "Shit. I can't believe I forgot that. Why didn't you come and get me?"

She pulled back and looked at him like he was crazy. "I wasn't going to waltz out there and interrupt your meeting. You all looked so serious and deep in conversation. Potter, at one point, looked like he was ready to kill someone. Plus, I told her that you hadn't forgotten and that you were just delayed."

Bailey was right about one thing. Potter was pissed. They had been discussing an upcoming mission, one that involved women and children being slaughtered. But right now, he needed to make things right with Sienna. He had made her a promise, and by God, he would honor that promise.

He took Bailey's hand and rubbed his thumb over her knuckles. "What do I do? How do I make it right?"

"I'd suggest you finish up that meeting of yours and get to that tea party."

He grinned and leaned in and gave her a big wet kiss. "What would I do without you?"

"Don't know. And hopefully, we won't have to find out."

A few minutes later, Irish explained to the guys his dilemma, and they all put their heads together. With some last-minute help from Bailey and

Alex, who showed up, they were now all stuffed into Sienna's bedroom, sitting around her table having a tea party fit for a queen.

Irish was going to owe the guys big time. Not only had they all agreed to take part in the tea party, but they went above and beyond the Call of Duty by dressing the part. Ace and Dino had hot pink feathered boas wrapped around their necks and wore silver clip-on earrings. Stitch wore an oversized white garden party hat with some bright ass yellow flower on it. Frost, God help him, let Sienna put lipstick on him, and he too had some weird contraption clipped to his head. He thought he heard Alex call it a fascinator or something like that. Whatever it was, he looked funny as shit. It looked like a bird coming out of his head. Potter had a silver tiara with pink hearts sitting on top of his head and chunky costume necklaces made of pearls. Diego wore earrings, bracelets, and a tiara similar to Potter's. Irish, on the other hand, was thankful Sienna chose him to be a Prince, and he got to wear a big gold crown. Bailey and Alex promised not to take pictures, but he knew they had anyway. He would pay them back if they ever decided to use them.

Irish noticed a plate sitting on the table that was covered in foil. Curiosity, of course, got to him. "Sienna, what's on the plate?" He pointed to the plate, and she smiled.

"I made tea sandwiches."

"Tea sandwiches?"

"Yes, silly. You can't have a tea party without tea sandwiches." She took the cover off, and his stomach growled at the sight of the food. He was hungry. She handed him one, and he looked it over. It smelled fishy. Then it dawned on him she had made tuna fish, remembering there were a couple of cans in the pantry.

He waited until she passed them all out before eating his. Tea sandwiches were supposed to be finger sandwiches. These, on the other hand, were full sandwiches cut in half. Everyone politely thanked her before eating. When the meaty chunks of the sandwich hit his taste buds, he knew instantly something was off. Whatever was between the slices of bread was not tuna fish, and before he could warn the others, it was too

146

late. Skittles swore and make a face as if he'd just eaten a piece of shit. But if Skittles' sandwich tasted like the one he had just bit into, he couldn't blame him. Seconds later, Stitch started gagging before spitting the remnants of his sandwich into a napkin. Ace was doing everything he could to swallow his, but it wasn't working too well. His face was all scrunched up, and he looked a little green. Frost and Diego were coughing, trying not to make a huge scene. Dino couldn't take it, as he spit his into the wastebasket, then grabbed the tall pitcher of iced tea and downed what was left in it. That left Potter. Fucking Potter did what Potter normally did. He took it in stride and ate the fucking nasty ass sandwich as if it was the sweetest and tastiest, damn cupcake. Ace made a mad dash for the door and ran down the hall. A few seconds later, Irish heard him throwing up.

Bailey and Alex came into the room, looking concerned and asked what was wrong. Irish got up from the table because he didn't want Sienna to feel bad for likely poisoning the entire team. He had no clue what she had given them. He explained, and Bailey said she would check the kitchen and see what she could find.

Irish turned his eyes on the sweet, innocent-looking angel who stole the hearts of the entire team with her jubilant personality. She sat there with her too-big purple tea party hat, her jewelry on, and in her yellow princess dress. She looked like a hot mess, but all that mattered was her happiness, and right now, she was far from happy. Her eyes were wide as saucers, and Irish thought she looked about ready to cry. *Fuck me....*

He walked over and knelt in front of her. He could still smell whatever was in the sandwiches. He shuddered and felt his stomach protest at the pungent scent. "Honey, what did you put in the sandwiches?"

"I made them with the tuna fish in the can," she whispered.

Ace had come back and stood in the doorway, holding the small wastebasket from the bathroom. He still looked a little sickly. Bailey and Alex walked back into the room and judging from the amusement in both of their eyes and the smirks on their faces, Irish had a feeling this was a story they all would be talking about for years to come. Alex looked as if she was ready to burst as she rubbed Ace's back, making sure he was okay.

147

Bailey lifted her hand and showed Sienna a can. Irish couldn't quite see it but could tell it was the size of a tuna fish can.

"Sweetie...is this what you used to make the sandwiches with?" Alex snorted a laugh when Sienna shook her head yes, then looked around at all the sets of eyes on her. The poor thing looked frightened and intimidated. She probably thought she had done something wrong and Irish could see the tears in her eyes.

"I used the tuna fish that you give Mr. Whiskers. You know, the one that has the picture of the fish on it."

Irish closed his eyes and swallowed the bile back down. Jesus fucking Christ...she had fed them all canned cat food. That stinky ass shit he hated feeding to that cat. That thought alone had him wanting to grab the trashcan out of Ace's hands and toss his cookies. He looked back at Sienna and slowly spoke, so she understood him clearly.

"Are you saying that you made the sandwiches with Mr. Whiskers dinner food?"

She grinned and shook her head, yes, and the guys couldn't hold back their laughs. Shit, he was never going to hear the end of this.

"Well, one of the cans was the other type of can. The white one that you use sometimes. I couldn't reach the other cans, so I took one of those."

That was when it sunk in, and he looked over at Potter, who was grinning. No wonder he ate his as if he enjoyed it. He got the sandwich with the "real" tuna fish. *Fucker.* Potter got up and lifted Sienna in his arms and gave her a big hug. She looked tiny in the giant man's arms. He kissed her on the cheek.

"Thank you so much for inviting me to your tea party. Your sandwich was so delicious. I can't wait to come to your next party."

She smiled wide, and her eyes lit up. He would owe Potter for turning an embarrassing situation for Sienna into a happy memory. Ever since Potter became a father to Alejandra, he had become much more friendly and approachable, especially when it came to kids.

"Of course, Uncle Potter. You can come to all of my parties."

148

He grinned and set her back down. Then as if on cue, Mr. Whiskers sauntered into the bedroom, jumped up onto the table, and began to lick the plate clean. Irish cringed while the others made comments. There was no way he could ever open another can of wet cat food again without gagging. The cat was getting dry food from here on out.

Bailey finished cleaning up the kitchen as Irish walked Skittles out. When Irish returned, he shut the front door and locked it.

She was putting the left-over pizza in the refrigerator when strong arms came around her waist. She jumped, and Irish chuckled. He pulled her against him. With the front of his body pressed against her back, his strong, hard body felt warm and inviting. Apparently, he was aroused if going by the long thick appendage she felt pressing against her backside. She took a deep breath when he rocked his hips forward. Instincts had her pushing back against him. She heard his breath hitch, then felt his lips against her neck as he placed tiny kisses along her skin. Shivers racked her body, but it brought a smile to her face. She loved it when Irish put his hands on her. She was getting warmer on the idea of wanting to have sex with him.

She turned in his arms and hugged him around the waist. Her cheek rested against his chest, and she felt content, safe, at home.

"You really didn't know what Sienna was making in the kitchen when she made those sandwiches?" He asked, making her chuckle. Irish wouldn't let it go.

"When I asked if she needed help, she said she was fine. I swear I didn't know what it was."

Irish shook his head and then laughed himself. "Fucking cat food!" Bailey couldn't hold it in any longer and started giggling uncontrollably. By the time she got herself under control, she was wiping tears from her eyes.

"You know the guys are going to have fun with this, right?" Oh, she had already heard some of them talking during dinner on what they were planning to do.

"You're probably right, but the one that I would be extra worried about is Alex." She grinned at him, and he snorted.

"That doesn't surprise me one bit. That woman loves to play jokes on people, and she's good at it. She strikes when you least expect it. Ask Stitch. During one of our deployments, she went into his apartment and emptied his shampoo bottle and filled it with lube."

Bailey gasped. "No!"

Irish chuckled. "Oh yeah. It was funny as shit."

"That is wrong on so many levels, but totally funny, especially since it happened to Stitch. He seems so organized and a total neat freak."

"I know, it was awesome, but now I have to keep a close eye on her."

Irish got quiet, like he was in a deep thought. "Are you staying the night?" He asked.

She looked up at him, and her eyebrows scrunched together. "I don't know." They'd spent most of their free time together in the last couple of weeks, but each evening always ended with him giving her a good-night kiss before she went back home to her condo, alone. Tonight would be the first time she'd stayed the night, since the hurricane.

She looked at him. "Do you want me to?" *Please say yes, please say yes.* She repeated to herself. Not that she was expecting to have sex with him. At least not tonight because Sienna was here, but she wanted to sleep in those strong, muscular arms of his.

He smiled. "I do. I've already locked the house up and set the alarm."

"Hmmm...I guess I'm a prisoner for the night then."

"Prisoner.... I like the sound of that. I know a lot of torture techniques." He lightly bit down on her neck, and made her squirm and laugh.

"Ky..." She pulled back and saw the hungry look in his eyes. "Sienna's sleeping just down the hall."

His arms moved around her waist, and his hands rested on her ass. "I know. I'm sorry. You are just so tempting. It's hard to control myself when I'm around you." He gave her a quick kiss. She couldn't wait to curl up with him. Then she remembered she didn't have any clothes. She usually kept a spare set in her car for whatever reason. She looked down at what she was wearing and cringed. Jeans were not going to be comfortable to sleep in. She only had a tank top that she wore under her hoodie, and she definitely wasn't wearing just a tank top and panties to bed.

"You okay?" She heard Irish ask and looked up him.

"Umm..." He cocked his head to the side and looked at her with a serious expression. It was funny to watch the guys and how protective they all were when they assumed one of the ladies was in a pickle. "I don't have any clothes with me. What you see is what I've got," she told him, gesturing to her jeans.

His face took on a devilish grin, one, like the Grinch does when he is up to no good. "I don't see that as being a problem. I see it as a win for me. I guess you'll just have to go to bed naked." She blushed, then put her hands on her hips, preparing to scold him when he started laughing. "I'm just kidding. You can borrow one of my t-shirts and a pair of my boxers."

She smiled to herself. *Oh goody, I can steal more of his clothes.*

"That works; let me finish putting the dishes away, and I'll join you on the couch. We can watch a movie. I'll even let you select the movie." She cringed when she saw Irish grin. Yeah, she was going to regret that decision. Irish liked scary movies. She, on the other hand, despised them. She also wanted to talk to him about Sienna's birthday that was coming up in a couple of weeks.

A little while later, she found herself snuggled with Irish on the couch as they watched Halloween, the original. She hated the Halloween movies. The boogeyman in that movie freaked her out. If she walked into a store and saw that white mask sitting on a shelf, she would turn around and walk out.

At one point in the movie, she had tried to crawl behind Irish, but he just held her in front of him and chuckled. She felt his warm breath on the back of her neck. She was getting more comfortable with Irish on an intimacy front. She still got shy when he would make comments about her body, but deep down, she loved hearing the compliments.

151

Deciding she would use conversation to distract herself from the movie, she flipped over, so she was face-to-face with him. He was a sight to take in with his disheveled hair and the light scruff on his cheeks and jaw. She used her thumb and rubbed his scar on his chin, and he grinned. For some odd reason, she loved that scar. It was a unique part of him.

"Sienna's birthday is coming up in a couple of weeks."

His eye's widened. "Shit, that's right. I totally lost track of the days. Do you have any ideas on what I can do?"

Bailey had an idea, but she wasn't sure if she would be overstepping, but she wanted to do something special for Sienna, especially since the last two months had been a major adjustment for her with moving and starting school.

"Well, I have an idea, but…" She nibbled her lip, and Irish looked at her.

"I'm open to all suggestions. This is new for me. I don't know the first thing about throwing a birthday party for a little girl."

"Well, it's sort of over the top, and you can say no if you want to because—"

He squeezed her hip. "Bailey, just spit it out." She forgot she was dealing with a master of impatience. He was grinning, so she knew he wasn't scolding her.

"I was thinking since the last few months for her has been whirlwind of change that we could do something really special for her."

He cocked an eyebrow. Ok, he was really getting impatient. It was kinda, sorta funny.

"Well, as much as she loves Disney, what if we planned a weekend trip and took her to Disney World. That is if you and the guys are not off saving the world. Maybe we could even invite a few of the others if they want to come. Sienna would love it." She waited nervously as he pondered the idea.

"I love the idea, but right now, I don't know if I can afford something that extravagant for all of us. I mean, I have some money saved, but I had plans for using it."

152

Without thinking, she blurted out, "I'll pay for it."

He looked at her like she was crazy. Yeah, teachers don't have the highest paying salaries, but she had enough money to probably buy one of the "lands" inside the Magic Kingdom. Only he didn't know that.

"Bailey, you're a teacher. I know damn well teachers don't get paid what they should. I appreciate the gesture, but I just don't see it happening. I mean, you're talking airfare, hotel, rental cars, not to mention the cost of the park tickets. Tickets alone are highway robbery. Then you have food, plus all the shit they get you to buy at the parks because you can't say no to a little girl who wants something."

If he weren't being serious, Bailey would have laughed. He was way overthinking it, so it was time for her to step in and diffuse the situation. She sat up and used the remote to turn the TV off. Thank God because the movie was getting to another scary part. It was a good thing she was staying over because after watching that, she didn't want to go back home alone.

Irish sat up along-side her. She gave herself a quick pep-talk. *Okay, you can do this. He deserves to know. Plus, you trust Irish; you know he won't share with anyone what you are about to tell him if you ask him not to; you know he won't be upset with you for withholding this information until now, and most importantly, you know in the end he will still like you for you and not your bank account.*

She took a deep breath. *You got this girl.*

She scooted over until she couldn't get any closer without sitting in his lap and grabbed his hand. "What I am about to tell you is something that nobody, except for my cousin, knows. I don't want any secrets between us, but I also don't want you to think differently about me."

She was so nervous. It's not like it was a subject that someone just brought up out of the blue with their boyfriend. *"Hey babe, by the way, I'm worth millions."* Seriously, how do you tell someone you're sitting on a nest egg worth twenty-million dollars, give or take?

153

She must have zoned about because he squeezed her. His eyebrows were drawn in, and he looked concerned. "Bailey, whatever it is, you can tell me. I'm a pretty open-minded person."

"You know my family is wealthy." He nodded, and she took a deep breath. "When I turned twenty-one, I inherited a trust fund that my grandfather left me. Nobody, not even my parents, I think, know about it. It's something I keep quiet about."

She watched him carefully as he digested that. She couldn't tell if he was upset, worried, or whatever. His face was just blank. "Why are you telling me this now? Did you think that by you having money, it would turn me off? Because I'll tell you right now, rich, poor, middle-class, I don't give a fuck how much or how little your bank account has. What I care about is what is inside here," he told her firmly, pointing to her chest where her heart was.

She stared up at him. She wasn't exactly sure the reaction she was expecting, but she couldn't help but feel all warm and fuzzy from his heartfelt words. She wasn't used to that type of compassion. That someone actually cared for who she was rather than what she stood for. The tears pooled in her eyes. "That has to be the nicest thing anyone has ever said to me. Not that you haven't been nice, it's just...."

He smiled and ran his finger down her cheek. "I know what you mean, sweetness."

"I'm sorry for not telling you sooner. It isn't something that I want to advertise." She was getting herself worked up. She took a breath and exhaled. "I don't want to keep anything from you, ever. You have to understand, with the amount of money I have, I don't have to work, but I do because I love doing what I do. I love being a part of something. But what I want more than anything right now is to give you and Sienna something back. I was on my own until I met you. You both have welcomed me into your lives and your home. I want Sienna to have a childhood that she'll remember and smile about when she's older. Not that you and your parents haven't given her that already. And please believe me, this isn't about me throwing my money around or trying to impress you. This is about me saying thank you and wanting to share in the memories that you both will have for the rest of your lives. I've had that trust fund for almost six years, and I've never touched a penny of it. I never wanted to until now. I always said that I would use that money when I had a family of my own. I want to help friends and even strangers in a time of need. Please, Ky, you and Sienna are the closest thing I have to a family."

He sat and was silent for a few minutes as he stared at the blank screen on the TV. As the seconds ticked by, she felt as if she was sitting on pins and needles. Christ, she wished he would say something. Then as if he heard her mind, he looked at her. A blank expression encompassed his face. Her body was rigid, and she held her breath as he started to speak. "I appreciate you are being forthcoming, but Bailey," he released her hands, then hauled her on top of his lap and took her face between his hands. "I meant what I said before; I want you because of the person you are inside. And what you just told me confirmed that you are that person I've always believed you were. I want you to experience everything with Sienna and me."

He leaned forward and kissed her. "I'll make you a deal, sweetness. I like the idea, and I agree that Sienna will love it, but how about it comes as a gift from both of us?"

Bailey's smile was so big she knew she had to have looked goofy, but she couldn't help it. Her dreams of finding love and happiness were becoming a reality. She leaned down and kissed him. His hands held her head firmly while he ravished her mouth. She moaned as his hands moved under her tank top, making their way over her ribs to her breasts. He pushed the cup of her bra down, finding her budded nipple and pinched it, awakening every cell in her body. He thrust his hips upwards, and she felt his hard cock under her ass. She pulled from his lips and panted. She felt flush and hot. She was turned on and wanted so much more, to give him so much more, but Sienna was just down the hall asleep.

"Sienna's here," she stated as she ran her fingers through his hair.

Irish's eyes had taken on a wild and lust-filled look. "I know, but that doesn't mean we can't fool around a little bit." He nipped her lip, and she gasped, feeling a sensation hit her belly that was new to her.

"God, you're so damn adorable." He carefully maneuvered her onto her back and ran his large hand up her jean-clad thigh. He didn't stop until he reached her belly then pushed her shirt up, exposing her breasts. He bent his head and licked her aroused nipple. The moment his warm tongue made contact with the sensitive little bud, she about shot off the couch, and he chuckled. "Easy, baby. I won't go too far." He continued to lick and suck, making her body feel good.

He settled between her thighs, and thrust his hips, making his cock hit her pussy, and she couldn't stop the moan from coming out. "Oh god, Ky. That feels so good." She began to rock her hips to his rhythm. Her body's sensors were on overload. Between his mouth on her breast, teasing her nipples, and his cock rubbing against her clit through the barrier of their jeans, she felt the sensation build within her body until she couldn't hold back any longer. She lost all train of thought and exploded.

Irish pulled back just slightly, still massaging her breast. "Holy shit, you are so responsive."

"Oh, my God. That felt so good," she stated, coming down from her high, and he smiled. "Just wait, it gets better," he said and winked. But their little lust fest was cut short when the floor behind the couch creaked.

Irish sat up first, but not before making sure that Bailey was covered. He looked to the right, and there stood Sienna a couple of feet away from the couch with her nose scrunched up and teddy bear in hand looking at them. Then she turned her head sideways. "Uncle Ky, are you and Ms. Bailey playing or exercising?" Throwing his exact words back at him.

Bailey sat up along-side him, and he wanted to chuckle because her face was so red. She looked well-loved, and he could only imagine how beautiful she'd look when he made love to her. His dick got harder, but then he remembered Sienna had asked him a question.

"What?" He asked, but Bailey started laughing, and then he understood. Jesus, she must have seen him humping Bailey, just like the cat had done to his pants. He looked at Bailey for help once again, because honestly, he didn't have a fucking clue what to say.

"Sienna, you know that tickle monster game Uncle Ky plays with you where he runs after you, and if you don't get to the safe base, he tickles you, and then you become the tickle monster, and then you get a chance to go after him?" Sienna nodded. "Well, I didn't make it to the base, and your uncle held me down and tickled me until I cried." Bailey made a pouty face, and Irish cocked his eyebrow. *How in the hell does she come up with this shit on a whim?*

"Uncle Ky, that wasn't nice. You need to say you're sorry for making Ms. Bailey cry," Sienna scolded him. How the fuck did this get turned around, making him the bad guy? From his view, he should be made the hero considering he'd just made Bailey cum while fully clothed. Not that he could tell a five-year-old that.

He turned toward Bailey. "I'm sorry." She was biting her lip, trying not to laugh, which made him want to bend her over his knee and spank her ass for being a little minx.

"You need to hug her too. Sorrys should come with hugs. That is what grandma always says."

*Fuck me...*He hugged Bailey and whispered in her ear. "Paybacks are a bitch, sweetness."

After getting Sienna a glass of water, which was why she wandered out of her room in the first place and tucking her back in bed, Irish joined Bailey back on the couch. She was curled up in the corner with her legs tucked under her. He picked her up easily and sat down with her on his lap, and she snuggled against his chest. The moment was long gone now.

"That was too close," she said, and he agreed and kissed the top of her head.

"I need a shower." She said, sliding off him, and he wanted to protest. He liked having her in his arms and holding her.

157

"Can I join you?" He asked without thinking, and she put her hands on her hips. He laughed and held up his hands. "I'm only joking."

"I'm locking the door."

He looked at her like she had grown a pair of horns. "Like a five-dollar lock would stop me. I'd have that door opened in five seconds."

"Five? You might want to brush up on your skills, SEAL boy! I'd thought you'd be faster than that," she retorted.

"You are going to pay for that, sweetness."

"Can't wait," she replied with sarcasm and winked at him. She turned and walked out of the room with her hips swaying as she went, and all he could do was smile. She was awesome, and more importantly, she was all his.

CHAPTER TWENTY

"Well, do you have any update? Time is ticking, and Ralph is starting to make threats if I don't have his money by the end of the month." Bentley asked Randy as they sat at the bar at the Country Club.

Randy was getting irritated with Bentley. If it weren't for him, Bentley wouldn't even know where Bailey was. Randy had found out that Bailey was indeed seeing the guy who had shown up at that run-down bar in the town she lived in. The guy's name was Ky Daniels, and he was in the Navy. He owned a house and had his niece living with him. What had him puzzled was when they tried accessing his military record, his investigator was shut down. According to the investigator, that usually meant the records were classified. There were several reasons for a person's military to be non-accessible, but one seemed the most logical because of his location. If he were a betting man, which he was, he'd be willing to bet this Ky Daniels was Special Forces, a Navy SEAL.

Without knowing for sure, Randy had to tread the water very carefully. He didn't know much about the elite unit, but he knew enough to know they were trained killers and not to be taken lightly.

Randy took a drink of his scotch then turned to look at Bentley. The man looked like shit. He could tell he was getting worried, and he should be. He never should've gone to a loan shark unless he knew he'd be able to repay his debt plus the interest. The Ralph guy that Bentley borrowed money from had been charging him twenty percent per week.

"I've been working on a plan, but I need to be sure I have everything in place before I put it into action."

"I don't see why you don't just drive up there and throw her ass in the car. Why do you need a fucking plan?"

"There are things I've been told by the guy who has been keeping tabs on her."

Bentley raised his eyebrows and scowled. "I know my daughter enough to know she doesn't deserve what my father left her. She doesn't even care about the money she has. She's had fifteen million sitting in an account for over five years and hasn't touched a dime of it. Shit, with interest, it has to be close to twenty million now."

"Actually, she wrote her first check the other day."

"She did?" Bentley asked, surprised. Randy was surprised as well when the manager of the bank called him to inform him of the transaction. Bailey thought she was hiding the money, but once he found the banking institution she was using, all it took was greasing a few palms with some cash, and people talked.

"She wired five million dollars to some organization called the Jacob Hardesty Foundation."

Bentley gasped and nearly choked on his drink. Randy knew that information would piss him off. Bentley was a scrooge; he never donated money to charities.

"She gave five million to a charity?"

Randy nodded. "She did. It's an organization that helps veterans and their families. The founder is a friend of Bailey's."

"What else does your contact up there say"

"She has a group of girlfriends she hangs out with, along with a group of guys. The guys are all in the Navy."

Bentley squinted his eyes and set his glass down onto the bar. "Is she dating one of them?"

"It seems that way."

Bentley slammed his hand down onto the bar top. His face was red, and he pointed at Randy.

"That can't happen. I don't care what it takes; you get her ass back here within the next three weeks."

"Actually, with my plan, I don't even have to leave. We are going to make her come to us."

"Explain."

Randy proceeded to explain in detail how Bailey would come willingly, and once he had her here, she'd never leave, even if it meant ending her life. Of course, after he got what was owed to him.

CHAPTER TWENTY-ONE

Bailey pulled into Irish's driveway and smiled when she saw his vehicle parked there. He had called her earlier and invited her over for dinner but called again about an hour ago to let her know that something had come up at work, and he might be a little late. He told her that if he wasn't home when she got there, to use the key he had given her to let herself in.

She was excited to see him. The past four days, he'd been at some sort of sniper training in Coronado, California. Every night he had called her, and they'd talk until she couldn't keep her eyes open. It wasn't the same as seeing him in person. She missed his arms wrapped around her while he kissed her goodnight.

She pulled her overnight bag from the backseat and lifted it onto her shoulder and made her way into the house. Irish had given her specific instructions to bring a bathing suit and pack an overnight bag. She had been giddy all day since he had called. She had spent the last two hours pampering herself. Sienna was having a sleepover at Tenley and Potter's house with Alejandra, so that meant she and Irish had the house to themselves for the night, meaning tonight could be the night she finally lost her virginity.

She let herself into the house and paused when the aroma of spices filled her nose. She inhaled; it smelled divine.

She dropped her bags by the door and walked into the kitchen and took in the sight. The table was set for two and even had candles lit. Light jazz music filled the air, and then there was Irish. She took in the sight of all six feet plus of him. The pair of loose-fitting jeans with a light blue, long-sleeve button-up shirt, and the sleeves rolled up to his elbows, exposing his muscular forearms, made him look as if he had just stepped out of a GQ magazine. He turned and gave her a lopsided smile, and she nearly fainted. He took her breath away, looking all sexy, standing in front of the stove.

"Hey, sweetness," he said, walking over and placing his hands on her hips as he looked her over. She was glad she had taken Alex's advice and opted for the new grey sweater dress she'd bought the other day. She paired it with her black suede, high heeled boots. If his smile was any indication, he was obviously happy with her choice. He licked his lower lip, then lowered his mouth to hers. "You look gorgeous."

She smiled against his lips. "Thanks. You don't look too shabby yourself." She closed her eyes as he kissed her. It was a quick kiss, then he wrapped his arms around her and pulled her against his chest and just held her. She'd missed him so much, and he'd only been gone for four days. How was she going to cope when he would be gone for an even longer time on deployment and had no clue where he would be?

"You got quiet. Is everything okay?" He asked softly.

She looked up at him and gazed into his blue eyes. They held a gleam to them. He looked happy. She smiled, hugging him and snuggled closer. "Everything is perfect. I just missed you, that's all."

He squeezed her tighter and rubbed her back. "I missed you too."

They stayed that way for a few minutes until she stepped back and lifted her nose in the air.

"What smells so good?" She walked toward the stove, and he followed her.

He turned off the stove and lifted the lid to one of the pans. She closed her eyes and inhaled the delicious aroma.

"I hope you like chicken parmesan."

"It's one of my top five dishes. What type of sauce do you use?" She asked, dipping her finger in the pot and taking a taste of the thick, red sauce. She closed her eyes and savored the taste as the fresh tomato and spices hit her taste buds. "Oh, my stars in heaven! This is fantastic."

He gave her a boyish smile, and Bailey swore he looked a little embarrassed. She thought it was cute.

"It's my mom's recipe," he said as he plated the food and walked it over to the table.

She stared at him in amazement. Damn, she couldn't have asked for anyone better. He was kind, compassionate, loving, sexy, could cook, and he was a freaking SEAL.

"You made this from scratch."

"Yep."

"Wow!"

"What? I told you I like to cook."

"No, I didn't mean it in a bad way. I love to cook too, but I couldn't make this. My spaghetti sauce comes straight from a jar."

He leaned down and kissed her then held her chin. "Well, I'll just have to teach you."

"I'd like that."

He smiled and motioned for her to take a seat in the chair he pulled out. He took the seat across from her, and they both dug in, making conversation as they ate.

Later, after they both cleaned up the kitchen, Bailey stepped out onto the patio and looked around. Irish had done a lot of planning to make this evening as perfect as possible. The arbor over the hot tub was strung with white twinkle lights; the same light jazz music that was played in the house could be heard through the Bluetooth speaker outside. He had even placed white candles around the patio, creating an ambiance of romance. As her eyes moved, she locked gazes with his as he sat on the edge of the hot tub with the bottom half of his legs submerged in the water. She absorbed his trim, muscular physique. His muscular chest along with the dips and ridges of his abs teased her. She had the urge to run her hands all over his body. The man was carved like a sculpture.

She gripped the towel around her tighter. She had chosen to wear her black halter top bikini. She felt a little self-conscious. It was the most her body had been exposed to his eyes. Well, except for their little romp on the couch a few days ago. She had her faults with her body, just like most women did. There was always something they disliked about themselves. Hers just happened to be her boobs. She had big boobs, and in her opinion, they were too large for her body, although Irish would beg to differ. He seemed to like her boobs very much. He curled his finger, motioning for her to join him. She swallowed hard, knowing once he put his hands on her, she would be done for.

Irish slowly pulled the towel from her body. His eyes started at her feet and went up from there, very slowly. His eyes zeroed in on her breasts that poured from the top, with her nipples standing at attention. Now, whether that was from the chilly air or just her arousal, she wasn't entirely sure. Either way, he must have liked what he saw because when his eyes met hers, he grinned.

"Just when I think you couldn't get any more beautiful, you surprise me. Come here, sweetness." He held his hand out, and she accepted as he helped her over the edge and into the steamy water.

The water felt good as she sunk into the swirling water. Irish followed her, bringing two bottles of beer with him. He placed them on the ledge behind them before he lowered himself next to her. She tried to settle her nerves, but it felt impossible. She was both anxious and nervous. She leaned her head back and looked up at the sky. The moon was shining, and the stars were twinkling against the black velvet sky. The mixture of the hot tub jets swirling and the jazz music playing added to the romance of it all. She couldn't have asked for anything more beautiful and calming.

She flinched ever so slightly when Irish placed his hand on her thigh. Her heart started to beat faster, and she took a deep breath. He must have sensed her nervousness. He spoke in a low, calm, but deep voice as he caressed her thigh from knee to hip. "Bailey, I want you to know that nothing will happen tonight that you don't want to. I want us both to just enjoy each other tonight."

God, when she didn't think he could be any more compassionate and understanding, he goes and says something like that.

She reached out and placed her hand against his cheek, loving the feel of his light scruff. "Your words mean so much to me. It's hard for me to

165

relax when I'm feeling so much right now. I honestly don't know what to say or do right now."

"What is your mind telling you to do?"

"It's not my mind that's driving me. It's my heart. It is telling me to trust you and let you lead me."

Irish smiled, then picked her up and placed her on his lap. The water bubbled around them. He kept one arm around her as she straddled his waist. He put his other hand on the nape of her neck and pulled her face toward his.

Irish felt quite proud of himself for pulling off tonight. He'd admit he did seek out a little bit of advice from Alex. He owed her a pedicure. He knew Bailey was nervous, and he didn't want to screw this up. He could feel her body tremble, even as she sat in hot water. He wanted this evening to be meaningful and memorable. He was trying to be patient and let her get comfortable, but damn, seeing her sexy, voluptuous body, she rocked in that little black bikini was seriously testing his patience. His dick was so hard that she had to feel what she was doing to him. The way she looked at him right now had his hardened and empty heart feeling light and filled with love.

"I want you to trust me. I want to make you feel special and cared for. I want you, and only you."

"I do trust you, Ky. I had long forgotten what it felt like to be cared for until I met you. You have no idea how just being around you and your friends have made me feel. Like I told you the other night, I feel like I'm finally part of a family of some sort."

"I understand, honey."

When he licked his lower lip, her arctic blue eyes darkened. She leaned forward and took a deep breath as her soft, delicate hands stroked his chest. Tonight was at her pace, and he waited for her next move. What she said next shocked him to his core.

"I want you to love me, Ky."

166

His heart began to beat faster, and he gripped her hips, maybe a little too hard, and she gasped. But he felt like a caged animal. He was ready to rip her bathing suit off and devour her. "What are you saying, Ba?" He spoke the words slowly.

The little minx gave him a sexy, shy smile, then kissed his forehead, his cheeks, his nose, then right before she kissed his lips, she said in a sweet sexy, angelic voice, "I want you. I want to feel you inside me."

Irish took everything Bailey was willing to give him. He stroked his tongue into her mouth while his hands explored her body. From her ass to her breasts, he touched every inch of skin he could. When his hand slid up her back, he felt the ties to her bathing suit top. He pulled on the material then pulled the string by her neck, holding the rest of it. One tug and the top fell into the water. Her breasts were pressed against his chest. He started to reach down and remove the bottoms when he heard the giggles followed by Sienna's voice. *What the fuck?*

"See, Aunt Tenley. This was what I was trying to tell you and Uncle Potter. Mr. Whiskers does the same thing to Uncle Ky's jammies."

Bailey froze at the sound of Sienna's voice, and Irish thought he heard her whisper, "Oh shit." He pressed Bailey closer to him and looked over her shoulder, only to see Tenley, Potter, Alejandra, and Sienna standing just outside the sliding glass door. Tenley was biting the inside of her cheek, and Potter stood there with his hand over his mouth. *What the fuck were they doing here?*

"Uncle Ky, are you and Ms. Bailey playing again?" Sienna asked, and Irish had to shake his head to make sure this was really happening. He had Bailey, who was practically naked on his lap in his hot tub and his friends and niece standing in front of him. Bailey hadn't moved a muscle, but he could hear how hard she was breathing.

He looked at Potter, who looked to be holding on by a thread not to burst out laughing. Tenley was trying to usher the girls back into the house when suddenly Ace and Alex walked out the door. *Oh, for the love of God!*

"What in the hell are you all doing here?" Irish asked as he tried to reach for one of the towels for Bailey to cover up with.

Potter spoke up. But Irish could hear the humor in his voice. "Well, Sienna forgot her teddy bear and insisted she couldn't sleep without it. I tried calling and then tried calling Bailey's phone but didn't get any answer. You always answer no matter *what* you're doing, so I got concerned and called Ace, and he agreed he meet us here to make sure things were okay." Irish wanted to kick himself in the ass for not bringing his phone outside with him. *Motherfucker!*

"Did you ever think that maybe I was a little busy?" He gave Potter and Ace a look, and Ace just grinned.

"Irish, give me the towel so I can go and get changed," Bailey whispered to him, and thank God Alex came over and helped, so Bailey wouldn't be exposed. But just because Alex was helping didn't mean she hadn't found the situation amusing.

Irish climbed out and grabbed his towel when he heard Dino's loud, boisterous voice from inside the house.

"Are they okay?"

Irish turned and faced the door as Dino walked out onto the patio. He looked at Potter and Ace with his hands on his hips. "Did you call the entire team?"

Ace chuckled. "No, just Dino. But we can get the rest of them here if you'd like."

"Fuck you!"

Potter laughed. Dino looked at Ace and asked what he had missed.

"Just Irish playing games with Bailey in the hot tub," Potter said, wiping tears from his eyes. "Holy shit, wait until the rest of the guys hear about this."

Irish pointed at the three men whom he trusted with life. "Don't you fucking dare, Bailey's probably embarrassed enough as it is. I don't need you assholes making it worse."

"Maybe next time you'll answer your phone," Ace said, shrugging his shoulders but still laughing.

A little while later, Irish sat in the kitchen at the table with Ace, Potter, and Dino. The women were with the kids in the living room, watching something on TV. What started out as an unbelievable romantic night with his girlfriend had now turned into a get together with his buddies.

"So, this turned out a bit awkward for ya, don't ya think?" Dino asked but didn't wait for Irish to respond. "I got to admit Bailey is a fox. She's got curves in all of the right places."

"Oh, don't you even go there, asshole. I know exactly what you're doing," Irish warned him.

"Really? And what are you suggesting that I'm doing?"

"You're trying to get me riled up. But you know what? I'm not taking the bait." Irish relaxed back in the chair and lifted his beer to his lips, still shaking his head.

"Well, I'm not the one who almost got caught with my pants down while I got my jollies off with my girlfriend in the hot tub. Oh, wait a minute; that was Bailey, who was caught with her pants down." Potter and Ace burst out laughing.

Potter looked at Irish and shook his head. "Playing or exercising?"

Irish lifted his hands into the air. "What the fuck was I supposed to say? The damn cat was fucking my pajama pants. I told her the first thing that popped into my head. How would you explain that to a five-year-old?"

"I would have told her the truth."

"Are you out of your fucking mind? Like I'm going to have a conversation like, well honey, you see normal humans and animals find a mate to hump, but your bastard of a cat instead likes to roll up my pj's and have his way with them."

"I hope you washed those pants," Potter said laughingly.

He shot a glare at Potter. "You're an asshole."

Potter went to respond when Ace's phone rang. "Shit...It's the commander," he said as he answered and walked out of the room.

Irish knew what that call meant. In a matter of five seconds, the friendly banter between friends ceased, and things got serious. There was a situation brewing in Algeria that they had been briefed on a few weeks ago, and they were put on notice that if the situation escalated any further, they could be shipped out to assist the Algerian security forces in eliminating the problem.

What a way to end the night. He needed to find something over the top to do for Bailey after the circus that occurred tonight.

CHAPTER TWENTY-TWO

Irish wiped the sweat from his brow. Somebody needed to call Satan and tell him he could have his weather back. Where they were was hotter than the hinges in hell. He sat atop an abandon building, looking through the scope of his sniper rifle. He scanned the area all around him. Incoming Intel led the team to the outskirts of the town of Tizi Ouzou. They were on the hunt for a man by the name of Asad Madani. According to the Algerian security forces, Madani had emerged as the leader of a new militant group that pledged its allegiance to ISIS. With ISIS out to take over land and destroy anything or anyone who got in their way, the US government, along with the Algerian government, wanted to shut down the group as quickly as possible before it gained a bigger following.

Madani's regime was cruel and ruthless. Their sole focus was power and control. Madani wanted to grow his empire, and to do that, he would send soldiers into small towns and villages to recruit. All male heads of households were forced to join the regime. If they refused, their families were executed. In instances where there were no males in the household, the women and children were brought to the compound and forced into labor camps or in some cases sold.

Madani was hard to track down. The regime was good in keeping his whereabouts a secret. He was rumored to only travel the region at night and under disguise. The joint team had received word through intel that Madani had been smuggled into the compound when a truckload of hostages had been brought in.

The large compound sat in the middle of an abandon small town and consisted of five buildings that had been built around a courtyard. Based on the intelligence gathered, three buildings were residences and offices. The two remaining buildings were solid construction with no windows and only one entry point. The one-story structure was a weapons armory. The building next to the armory was an L-shaped structure and was believed to be holding an unknown number of women and children from nearby towns and villages. The hostages went through a thorough inspection process as soon as they arrived at the compound. Depending on their gender, age, and physical abilities, they were then assigned to roles within the regime. Boys were always separated from their family and taught the history of the regime. Women and young girls were used as cooks, cleaners, and sexual entertainment. In some cases, both genders were used as human sacrifices—forced to walk through mine fields and suicide bombers. If someone disobeyed or couldn't carry out their role, they were executed on the spot. They were a ruthless group.

The images Irish had, made him sick. His thoughts went to Bailey and Sienna. He never wanted Bailey or Sienna to be exposed to the shit he'd seen. It was hard at times for himself to stomach some of the sights and situations he'd had to take part in, but he did it because that's what he'd signed up for. When he enlisted in the Navy at eighteen, he knew he wanted to be a SEAL. However, wanting to be one and actually becoming one were two entirely different things. With grit, determination, and even a few tears, he succeeded in earning his Trident pin and becoming a Naval Surface Warfare Operator.

"Heads up…we got movement on the eastside. Irish, our target should be in your sights in three, two, one."

Irish focused. "Got him." Skittles was crouched beside him, keeping an eye on the other side of the compound. Ace and Stitch were on the top of another nearby building.

Ace swore. "This mission has been FUBAR since we were boots on the ground." Irish agreed silently. When they had first arrived, they were told that the local intel could have been incorrect, and their presence had not been needed. But shortly thereafter additional intel had come in that the mission was a go.

Irish studied the Madani, and by the way he kept looking around suspiciously had Irish's gut telling him something wasn't kosher. Suddenly, a young boy was led out of one of the buildings by a man and handed off to Madani. Irish focused in on the boy who Madani held by the back of his neck. He only looked to be maybe thirteen, and judging from the pained expression on his face, he wasn't there willingly. He was probably one of the hostages that had just been brought in. Too young to be put in a situation like this.

"Shit…" Skittles swore at seeing the kid as well, and Irish couldn't agree more.

"Ace…what's Frost and Dino's location?" Irish asked, his eyes still focused on Madani and the boy.

Frost chimed in. "We're on the north side. Finally found the entry point on building five; however, the whole structure is wired to explode if breached." It was where the women and children were held.

"Fuck! Frost, you, and Dino pull back and meet Potter and Diego a block over. I have a feeling our informant double-crossed us. Madani appears a little overconfident. Stand-by."

Irish knew the situation wasn't going to end well. It was becoming clear that Madani had been tipped off, and he knew troops were in the area. Irish's overwatch was five buildings down from the compound. He had a perfect spot, high enough to get a good view of the entire area. Soon, the sun would fully set, bringing the area into total darkness.

Seconds later, Ace's voice came through his earpiece. "Frost…sit-rep?"

"Thirty seconds."

"Irish, orders are to eliminate the target. Take the shot when you got it. Frost, you and Dino move your asses!"

"Copy that." Irish peered through the scope and lined up the shot. He blocked everything from his mind but the man sitting in the crosshairs of his rifle scope. The only sound he could hear was the thumping of his heart. He drew in a deep breath with his finger steady on the trigger. Suddenly, the boy made an abrupt move and attacked Madani.

"Shit!" Irish exclaimed, as he watched Madani double over with his hands over his stomach. When he righted himself, his hands were stained with blood. The kid must have stabbed him. Madini shouted and a group of

173

men nearby went after the boy, who ran toward the building rigged to explode. One of Madani's men aimed his gun at the boy, and Irish didn't hesitate; he took the guy out with one bullet. Seconds later, the entire compound erupted in a firefight as more men rushed out of the other buildings, armed and ready to fight. Ace and Stitch fired from the opposite side. The only plus side of the situation was it gave Frost and Potter additional time to get to their meet up point.

Irish searched for the boy and saw Madani had him in his grasp. Irish lined up his shot, took another deep breath and pulled the trigger. Madani's body jerked before it crumpled to the ground.

Irish was sweating, and his stomach was twisted in knots, but he wouldn't let those actions faze him. His focus was to eliminate the target, protect his team, and protect the innocents. He fired off a few more rounds before his mind went back to the boy. Irish sought him out in the middle of the fiasco. He was crouched down behind one of the vehicles parked near the building. Movement nearby caught Irish's attention. It was one of Madani's men. He bent down next to Madani's body on the ground and pulled a black box from Madani's pocket. When Irish realized it was a detonator, he shouted.

"Fuck!"

Irish wanted to yell to the kid to run, but there was no way he would hear him. Just as the kid emerged from behind the vehicle, the guy holding the detonator saw the kid and grinned evilly as he pressed the orange button. The next two or three seconds felt as if time had stood still. No sound, no movements, no nothing. Then as if the depths of hell erupted from below, a huge fireball shot upward into the air. The massive blast rocked the surrounding area, including where Irish was. He dove for cover as the raging inferno tore through the compound and other nearby buildings. Irish felt the heat the shockwave carried. When he lifted his head and the smoke cleared, the entire compound had been leveled. But what will haunt Irish for a long time was the look on the boy's face just before he was murdered.

❧

Right after it was confirmed from the Algerian government that Madani was indeed dead, the team hauled ass out of town. The plane ride home was done in mostly silence. Even though the government would consider the mission a victory, Irish knew the victory came with a cost.

They would never know, nor did they want to know how many women and children's lives were taken in the blast. The team had no idea that Madani had a detonator on his person. Irish could care less about the terrorist because he got what he had coming to him. What Irish was having trouble coming to grips with was the young boy. He'd been going over and over the entire scenario numerous times in his head, thinking if there could have been a better alternative, but each one kept coming back to the same conclusion. There was nothing he could have done differently. It was apparent that Madani wasn't going to let anyone live, including himself. Thankfully, none of the guys tried to talk to him about it. He knew they were giving him some time to process the situation, but it was only a matter of time before they would finally make their move.

Thirty-two hours later and back stateside, Irish cracked his knuckles as he walked into the ballroom at the hotel where Alex's grand opening gala was being held. He and the team had arrived back at base a little over four hours ago. They weren't sure if they were even going to make it back in time, which not only would have pissed Alex off, but it also would've have pissed the guys off as well. This was a huge night for Alex and her accomplishments. It had been a year in the making, and Alex had busted her ass night and day to get to this day. She deserved to have her family and friends in attendance showing their support. However, the world could be an evil place at times, and unfortunately, its timing sucked.

He took a step and felt himself sway. Damn, maybe those three shots along with the beer he had in the hotel bar had been a bad decision. But he needed something to take the edge off. At least, to get through the next couple of hours. He felt uneasy and off-kilter. He sarcastically chuckled to himself. Of course, he was feeling off-kilter. He was borderline drunk. Jesus, he should've told Ace he was going to stay home instead of coming here and acting like everything was hunky-dory. He was in a piss poor mood and had no desire to mingle. But he told himself he had to suck it up, make an appearance, then call it an early night before going home to decompress. Sienna, Alejandra, and Cody were all with a babysitter for the night at Tenley and Potter's house, so he had the house to himself. He knew Bailey would want to stay with him, and as much he would like to bundle her up and take her home with him, right now, he just needed to be alone.

He had done some thinking at the bar while the alcohol took its course. He thought about how he should be happy to be alive and back home with a beautiful woman waiting for him. But then the demons took over his thoughts. As this was his first deployment since they had been dating, before the unfortunate turn of events in Algeria, he was smitten and excited to finally get to come home to a set of waiting arms, like some of his other buddies. As much as he wanted to see her face light up when she saw him, he didn't want to face her scrutiny. She was smart and excelled at picking up on others' emotions. She didn't need or deserve to see him at his lowest. He'd had breakdowns before after missions, especially when they were intense, but they came nowhere close to what he was feeling right now.

He was pulled from his thoughts when he felt the hand on his arm, then steadied himself. "Dude...Are you fucking drunk?" *Ace. Just fucking fantastic.*

He ran his hand down his face, feeling the beard he had grown over the last couple of days. He looked at Ace. "I don't know what I am right now." Numb, depressed, tired, there were several adjectives he could give. He stumbled again. *Shit.* This time, Potter and Stitch were there to settle him.

"Alex will kill you if she sees you like this, not to mention the grilling you would get from her."

He looked at Stitch. "I'm not worried about Alex. I don't want Bailey to see me like this. You guys have to get me out of here."

"And when she asks where you are?"

"Tell her the truth. I had to go home and that I will call her later."

Christ, all he needed was Bailey to see him in this state. He closed his eyes and used the wall behind him to support his weight. He knew the guys would get him home. He could sense movement; then he heard that voice. That voice he'd longed to hear for the last week. *Goddammit!*

"Ky?"

He cracked open his eyes, and there she stood looking every bit as beautiful as the last time he'd seen her. But then he really looked in her eyes, and he saw the concern. Her eyebrows were drawn in.

She stepped forward and hugged him. He didn't move. Not that he didn't want to, he was afraid that if he moved an inch, he would end up face down on the floor. He buried his face in the crook of her neck and shoulder and tried to let her presence and comfort help take some of the tension away. But it didn't.

He pulled back and looked down at her. "Are you okay? You don't look so well," she said to him.

He put on a fake smile—the one he was accustomed to when he wanted to bullshit his way through something. Being in Special Forces, you become a pro at that type of shit. Hell, every one of them could win an Oscar. "Yeah, just a rough trip, and I'm pretty tired." Just then, he saw a boy walk by the dessert table across the room, followed by the sound of a glass breaking, and just like that, he was thrust back into Algeria. He shook his head and stumbled again. Someone grabbed his arm.

"Ky, are you sure everything's okay? Your face looks a little pale," Bailey asked, reaching for him, just as he got a sickening feeling in his stomach. The vision of the boy being overtaken by the blast played back in his head. It was like watching b-roll footage. It just kept playing over and over. His head started spinning, and he became nauseous. He bent over with his hands on his knees and tried sucking in a couple of deep breaths. He knew what was coming. He was crashing, and it was coming full speed like a freight train with no brakes. Suddenly, the walls started to close in on him, and he heard the mumbled voices of concern around him. He felt the hand on his back, and something within him snapped, sending himself

177

instantly back into the mist of the battlefield. *Protect his team from the enemy.*

He turned so fast he made his own head spin. Like the trained man he was, he took hold of the enemy. Once he had the individual secured, so no harm would come to his teammates, he took a breath. Then he heard the voice of an angel. His angel.

"Ky…"

"Bailey, don't move."

"He's not going to hurt me, Ace. Are you Ky?" Why was Ace talking to his angel? And why would he be worried about him hurting her? He shook his head. No, his angel was home and safe where she belonged. This was a ploy to get him to let his guard down.

"Irish…come on buddy. Come back to us. Take a deep breath and look around; all of your friends are here. We are at the hotel, celebrating Alex's opening." Irish stared at the white wall above the head of the individual he had restrained. He was processing Ace's words. He was safe. His team was safe. He was home. That one word had him focusing on the person he held in his grasp. The person was small in comparison to him. His brain finally engaged, and all he saw was a set of glassy blue eyes staring back at him. Those eyes were his home. He felt the blood drain from his face as his hold loosened, and he pulled his angel into the safety of his arms. He buried his face in her hair. It was all coming back to him. Her scent, the feel of her body, but most of all, her kindness as he felt her arms go around his waist. He stood there, absorbing the comfort she brought him.

Bailey wasn't sure what was happening or going through Irish's mind when he grabbed her by the shoulders and pushed her against the wall. His eyes were focused but not on her. It was as if he was reliving something in his mind. Then, when Ace told her not to move and started talking to Irish in a way like he was coaching him, she realized what the issue was. Irish was apparently having a flashback of some sort. She'd read up on signs and symptoms of PTSD, but just recently, since she started dating Irish, she'd been reading more on it.

She felt Irish pull back, but all she wanted to do was hold him and comfort him. When he looked down in her eyes, she wanted to cry. She was doing all she could to hold back the tears that wanted to fall. This beautiful man she loved with all her heart was obviously hurting, and she didn't know what to do. She wanted to hold him and chase his demons away. She reached out to take his hand, but he pulled it back as if her hand would bite him. Then he shook his head.

"You need to let me be alone for a while." And here it was. It was almost textbook in what she had read. He was going to push her away. *Well, guess what, buddy...it ain't going to happen. At least not if I can help it.*

"I don't want you to be alone. Please…. let me at least take you home. Please don't shut me out."

He stared at her with a look she'd never seen before, and she was frightened. Not that she was scared of him physically, but she was scared of what his next words might be.

He dropped his hands to his side. "I can't do this."

She didn't understand. "You can't do what?" She asked as her voice cracked.

He stared at her again as if he was having trouble forming the words he wanted to say. She watched him swallow hard as if he was trying to swallow a boulder that had lodged in his throat.

"Us. This. I can't be what you need." And there it was. Those words are what she had dreaded since she and Irish had started dating. He was walking away, and she felt the first crack in her heart.

"So that's it? You're just going to throw away everything we have between us. Just give it all up and walk away?"

He made an odd sound with his mouth as he stood there with his hands on his hips, looking at her. "It's not like we were married. Hell, we've only been dating for what…a month. I'd consider that an accomplishment in my book."

She almost didn't hear the gasp that came from Alex, because she was focused on the hurtful words. His words hurt more than anything her parents had ever said to her. And that was saying a lot. As much as she wanted to fight for them, she knew it would be a lost cause. He was dead set on pushing her away, and if that is what he truly wanted, then she would walk away, even though it would be difficult to give her heart to another man because Irish would always own a piece of hers.

She knew her eyes were filled to the max, and with one blink, the tears would come raining down. But she vowed to hold herself together until she was out of the public eye. She stared up at Irish for probably the last time.

"I'm sorry it had to end this way. I wish you'd take the time you need, and then we could talk, but it looks like you've made your decision, and I will be the grown adult and walk away gracefully. Hurt, but gracefully. In the end, I hope you find peace and happiness someday."

She turned to Alex and everyone else that had gathered around. They all looked angry, but she refused to show defeat, even though she was humiliated and dying on the inside. Her heart was ripped to shreds, and there wasn't a damn thing she could do about it. He'd made his decision, and she would honor it.

"Alex, congratulations again on your success. If you will all excuse me, I'm going to see myself out." Her voice cracked so slightly on the last word. Her meltdown was coming in three, two, one. Just as she stepped around the group of people and her face was out of their line of sight, the first tear rolled down her cheek. She heard others calling out to her, but she never wavered.

As she made it outside, she saw a taxi down by the main lobby entrance. She ran down the sidewalk but stumbled when the heel of her baby blue Jimmy Choos caught in a crack. She went tumbling to the ground and hit the concrete hard. She cried out, feeling the sting to her legs as they scraped against the rough surface. What else could go wrong tonight? She was already at her lowest and wasn't that the literal truth as she laid on the sidewalk outside of the hotel. She buried her face in her hands and cried.

Suddenly, a set of hands lifted her to her feet. When she finally looked up, she was shocked to see Diego. Sweet Diego. That man had a heart

180

made of gold. He looked angry, but then he surprised her when he hugged her and consoled her while she held on and began to sob. He whispered soothing words to her as he rubbed her back. When she didn't have any tears left, she pulled back and wiped her face. She had to look like a train wreck. The little make-up she was wearing was probably all over her face; she felt some strands of her hair against her neck, so she knew her hair had come loose. She just wanted to get into a cab and go home and lock herself inside. She was embarrassed, angry, but most of all, hurt. Hurt by the words from the man she had fallen in love with.

Diego touched her chin and tilted her face towards his.

"Are you okay?"

She shook her head. "No, Diego, I'm not, okay. I feel like someone stuck a knife through my heart, and if that wasn't bad enough, they decided to twist it."

"What can I do for you?"

"Just get me in that cab. I'll get myself home." He looked like he wanted to argue, and that was the last thing she wanted to do right now, so she gave him a pleading look. "Please. I just need to go home." He nodded and opened the door.

Before she got in, he turned her towards him. "You promise to call me if you need anything, you got that?" Knowing he would be one of the last people she would call but not wanting to upset him, she nodded. Taking her nod as acceptance, he leaned forward and kissed her forehead before he stepped back and shut the door. Something in the back of her mind told her to look back, and when she did, she saw Irish running towards her, but then Diego stopped him. He looked so distraught. Part of her wanted to stop the driver and go to Irish. But then her brain stopped that thought. He pushed her away. It was his choice. Let him deal with the consequences.

Irish watched Bailey walk away. The way her eyes glistened as the tears started to form almost had him dropping to his knees and begging her for forgiveness. He didn't want to push her away, but he had to. He wasn't the man for her. She was innocent and pure. He, on the other hand, was far

181

from that; he killed people for a living. The inside of his head was spinning. He started pacing until Ace grabbed his arm and spun him around.

"What the fuck is your problem?" Ace growled, looking ready to beat the shit out of him. Hell, he wanted to beat the shit out of himself.

Irish ran his hand down his face. "I don't know what came over me. I've been on edge since that goddamn mission, and when I saw a kid over by that table, I had a flashback. Jesus, Ace, did you see what I did to her? I thought she was the fucking enemy. I lost my fucking mind and pinned her against the wall. She doesn't deserve that shit."

"Yeah, well, you are lucky that I don't beat the fuck out of you. One, for the way you treated Bailey. And two, for not talking to one of us. We were there too."

He shook himself from Ace's grip. "Where did she go? I need to find her. I have to find her and make this right."

"She ran, man."

"She ran where? It's a fucking hotel, and I know she didn't drive."

"Out the door. I think Diego went after her." Skittles stated looking angry, disgusted, and pissed off. Irish couldn't blame him. He'd be feeling the same if he saw one of his teammates treat their woman how he'd just treated Bailey. *Fuck!*

Irish took off in the direction Bailey had gone. He ran outside through the automatic doors and looked to the right, and saw Diego helping Bailey into a cab. "No!" He sprinted after them, but by the time he made it down the sidewalk, the cab was pulling away with half of his heart in the back seat.

Diego turned around just as Irish approached. No words were spoken between the two SEALs as they both just glared at each other. Before Irish could say a word, Diego pulled his arm back and punched him in the face. He stumbled backward and rubbed his jaw. *Okay, he deserved that.*

Diego pointed his finger at him. "I hope you fucking realize what you just threw away. You hurt that woman in ways you'll never forgive yourself for." He walked away, leaving Irish standing there staring where the cab once sat.

He closed his eyes and willed away the tears he felt forming. He sensed someone standing nearby, then felt the small hand touch his arm. When he opened his eyes, he looked down to find Alex standing there, and damn, was she pissed. He waited for the steam to start coming out of her ears and the horns to grow out of her head.

"Alex – "

She cut him off quickly. "No, you are going to shut up and listen to me. I would call you an asshole, but I don't think that is a strong enough word. Your actions reminded me of a bully. Bullies are far worse than assholes in my book." She had tears in her eyes. Great, now Ace was really going to kick his ass. One for ruining a special night for Alex and two, for making her cry.

Her facial features softened as she stared at him. She was the only woman who could intimidate him. And she was doing a damn good job at it right now. "Look, Irish. From my understanding, things didn't really go according to plan wherever you guys were. But how dare you take those emotions out on Bailey when all she was doing was trying to be helpful. Granted, I understand you guys sometimes need some downtime when coming home but did you ever consider just telling her the truth instead of getting drunk, then coming in here and acting like the woman who loves you means nothing to you?"

Alex's last sentence had him sobering up instantly. Bailey loved him. He looked at her, and as if she could read his mind, she smiled softly and said, "Yeah, you horse's ass, Bailey is in love with you."

"Irish, I was in your shoes when I got home from Afghanistan. I almost threw everything away when I turned into a hermit instead of dealing with my issues. I've never experienced anything like that before. Nor did I have any training or concept in handling PTSD. Sure, I've seen and been around people, but I had never had it happen to me. But you don't have an excuse; you've been trained and should know when to seek out help. Hell, you have people waiting to talk to you as soon as you get home."

Irish remembered how depressed Alex was and wouldn't speak to anyone for a couple of weeks after returning from the Middle East. He thought back to how hurt the team felt. Is that how Bailey felt right now? Damn, she was right. He was trained to handle what normal citizens couldn't. He'd seen before the damage a monster like Madani could do, so why was this so much harder to deal with?

His shoulders slumped. "You're right, and I'm sorry, Alex."

"It's not me you need to apologize to."

"I don't know what to do, Alex. I don't think a simple apology is going to be enough."

"My advice is to let her be for the night. I highly doubt she would want to talk to you even if you tried. I know I wouldn't. You hurt her."

"I lost my cool. That's never happened to me before."

"That's not the only thing you lost," Ace said in a stern voice as he joined Alex.

And wasn't that the truth. He most likely had lost the one woman he found love in. God, what happened if she didn't accept his apology?

He heard Alex say something else to him, but it was drowned out from the noise in his head. All of a sudden, he felt clammy, Jesus what was happening to him. His vision became blurry. Someone grabbed his arm and spun him around, making him dizzier. It was Ace and Potter. They were talking, but his ears weren't working. His chest tightened, and he couldn't breathe, then his knees buckled. Right before he blacked out, all he saw was an image of Bailey's smiling face. His sweet, caring, and loving Bailey.

Bailey rested her head against the cool window of the cab. Her eyes were still leaking tears. Even the older cab driver had asked her if she was okay. She felt her phone vibrate again and knew it was probably Alex. As much as she needed a friend right now, she didn't want to talk to anybody. She was afraid of what she might say, so she thought it was best just to ignore all of their calls until she could think rationally.

As the driver pulled up to the entrance to her building, her phone pinged with a text. After paying the driver, she pulled her phone out. When she saw the name flashing on the screen, she wanted to scream. Her fucking mother. Like tonight hadn't been bad enough. She read the message.

Bailey, it is important you call me right away.

Bailey snorted. Yeah, the only thing important right now was drinking herself to sleep. Then she got an idea. Maybe a few days away at her cousin's place would do her mind some good.

CHAPTER TWENTY-THREE

A few days had passed since the night Irish had made a total ass of himself. He still hadn't spoken with Bailey, and to say he was concerned was an understatement. When he picked Sienna up from school this afternoon, he noticed Bailey wasn't working bus duty like normal. When Sienna informed him, that Bailey hadn't been at work for the last three days, his internal alerts started going off. She hadn't answered any of his calls or texts, which he just chalked up to her still being pissed at him. But after he spoke with Ace earlier, it seemed she hadn't returned anyone's calls or texts as Alex, Tenley and Autumn had tried to contact her as well.

Irish picked up his bottle of beer and took a swig. He hadn't had a drop of alcohol since the night of Alex's gala. Tonight, he was hoping to relax at Bayside, have one drink along with his dinner, then go home and strategize what his next move was to win back Bailey. That plan went to shit when he spotted Derek walking toward him. *Shit!*

Derek took the seat next to him at the bar and ordered a beer. He didn't say anything for a minute or two, and Irish knew right away Derek wasn't there to just hang out. After taking a drink of his beer, the bartender had set down, Derek spoke. "I thought you would be over at Ace and Alex's with the rest of the crew having dinner."

He thought so himself but decided at the last minute he wasn't up for socializing, mostly since the women were still pissed at him. He looked over at his commander and shrugged his shoulders, then took a slug of beer. "I'm not very good company to be around."

Derek's lips twitched up. "Girls still giving you the silent treatment?"

"Yeah. Can't say I blame them either."

Derek nodded his head and took another drink. "You see the shrink, yet?" Well, that hadn't taken long. Irish nodded his head, knowing if he hadn't already seen the head doctor, Derek would have his ass. It had taken less than an hour before Derek caught wind of went down. He was there at the gala but had been on the other side of the room.

"You know, Irish, what happened over in Algeria is a hard situation to overcome. We see a lot of bad shit in our careers and spend a good majority of our time trying to protect women and children. You need to know and understand you did nothing wrong on that mission; you followed a direct order. None of us knew what Madani had planned. And unfortunately, the kid was caught in a really bad situation. You acted accordingly and did what was needed. You did your job by covering your teammates' asses so they could live to see another day. So, don't sit here wallowing in your pity and thinking about the 'what ifs.' Because I will tell you, son, it will do more harm than good."

He knew Derek was right. He was a soldier; he followed orders. Yes, there had been times where he disagreed with the order given, but he still followed through with said order. He went to say something, but Derek held his hand up.

"I'm not going to sugar coat it. You fucked up. And in some minds, it was unforgivable." Irish could only nod his head because Derek was one hundred percent correct. "Look, Irish. I'm not here to lecture you on the fundamentals of a relationship because some time or another, we all fuck up at one point. So, you're down a point right now. You need to figure your next move and get back in the game."

"Well, it's sort of hard when the other team won't take my calls or answer my texts. Not hearing from her is actually concerning. I don't even know if she's okay. The others haven't heard from her either."

Derek stared at him for a couple of seconds.

"Let's just say that she has been in touch with someone."

Irish wracked his brain. Who else was there that Bailey would have been in touch with? None of his teammates or their women have heard a peep from her since that night. How would Derek know? Unless.... motherfucker!

Irish turned to face Derek. "You!" If Irish had been watching Derek so closely, he would have missed the slight twitch in lips.

"Alex was concerned and asked me to try reaching out. So, I texted her."

"And she answered you?"

"Like I said, she's a smart girl," Derek said, chuckling.

Irish had a million questions, and Derek knew it because he held up his hand. "I don't know where she is or what she is up to. All that I know is that she assured me she was safe."

With those words, Derek laid down a twenty on the bar and got up, leaving Irish alone to think. His commander was right. He needed to put the incident behind him and focus on what was in front of him, starting with what he wanted out of life. And that was easy to figure out. There were three things he cared about the most in his life, Sienna, Bailey and his career.

"Hey cuz, whatcha doing out here all by yourself?" Bailey turned in her chair and looked at her cousin, Jonathan. He closed the sliding glass door and walked across the wooden deck and sat down in the lounge chair next to hers. She had arrived in Alabama the morning after the shit show with Irish at the gala. After talking to Jonathan that night and some convincing by him, she decided it was best to get away for a few days and to think. In the four days she'd been there, she had done quite of bit of thinking. The problem was, whatever she was thinking about always came back to Irish.

There were more civil ways he could have handled the situation, but he didn't, and that was something that he would have to live with. Even though there are no excuses for his behavior, she couldn't help but wonder what had happened on that mission that triggered his outburst. She would never forget that blank lost look in his eyes. It broke her heart, seeing him hurting like that and not being able to do a damn thing about it.

She looked up at her cousin. He was watching her intently. He had been worried about her when she had arrived in town. But she assured him she just needed a little TLC and time to reflect on several things in her life.

Jonathan was a very handsome man and a very successful lawyer.

188

"I just wanted some fresh fall air and to try to clear my mind a little."

He walked over and took the seat in the chair across from her. "I got all of the papers you wanted drafted today. I can go over them with you later. If you're good with it, then all they'll need is your signature. Then I will get them filed." He gave her a serious look. "Are you sure this is what you want? You know this is going to cause you more headaches with your parents. I don't trust them and wouldn't put it past them to try and get back at you."

She half-smiled at him. "It is. And let them. I will have them arrested so fast they won't know what hit them. They are lucky I haven't already pressed charges since finding out that they paid employees at the bank off."

One of the reasons Bailey had been so uptight was because of her parents. She had a funny feeling in her gut that her parents were after something. On the second night, Jonathan and his friends were having drinks and invited her to join them. When she found out the guy was one of the most sought-after private investigators in the area, she explained the situation about her parents to both of them, and without any hesitation, the guy said he would check into it. It hadn't taken him long because the next night, it had become clear her parents had known for a couple of years about her trust fund. They had found out the attorney's name that her grandfather had used to handle the fund. The guy wasn't very ethical because he had given her parents copies of everything he had on her. Of course, he had been paid a very nice sum of money for the information. Needless to say, the man would soon be out of a job and facing charges as soon as she delivered the evidence to the police.

As for her parents, they would be served papers of their own. She was legally divorcing them. She wanted nothing to do with them and wanted no association with them whatsoever. She would keep the Anderson name but only because of her grandfather and the respect she had for him. By breaking the ties with her parents, should anything ever happen to her, they couldn't get their hands on anything of hers unless it was specified in her Will, which would be a cold day in hell. And speaking of her Will, she had

Jonathan draw up a new one, making sure there were no loopholes her parents could use.

"Have you decided yet on when you're heading back home?" Jonathan asked her. She knew he was worried about her going back home by herself, especially in the coming days, once her parents got wind of her surprise for them.

"Probably in another day or two. If that's okay with you since I kinda just showed up here out of the blue and disrupted your life. Plus, I miss my students." She was mostly missing Sienna. She started to wonder what Irish and her were up to. As it was just shy of 8:00 pm, they were probably curled up on the couch, watching Disney Jr. God; it had only been a couple of days, and she was already missing them both badly. How was she going to handle going back there and possibly running into them? *Of course, you're going to run into them. You're Sienna's teacher.*

"Sweetie, you know you are welcome here anytime. You don't need an invitation to visit. The same goes for my parents. They love you as if you were their own daughter," Jonathan said, bringing her attention back to him and not the man who still held her heart.

She smiled. God, she wished she had parents like her aunt and uncle. They were wonderful people who knew the meaning of family.

"Thanks, that means a lot."

"Anything for my favorite cousin."

CHAPTER TWENTY-FOUR

Bailey was going over some paperwork at school. She had returned to Virginia Beach two days ago. She was happy to be back working and spending time with her students. It kept her mind from wandering. Well, at least while she was at school. At home, it was a little different. As much as she was still hurting, she still missed Irish, and being away from Sienna was very hard. She had grown attached to her in the month and a half she'd known her. She found out from Sienna that Irish told Sienna that Bailey had to take a trip. But it was sort of funny because nobody knew where she was, and she didn't want them to know, even though she felt guilty about not telling anybody and knowing they would be worried about her. At least Derek knew she was safe. Damn, that man drove a hard bargain. And talk about intimidating. When his name showed up on her phone, she knew better than to send him to voicemail. He wasn't particularly happy about her little disappearing act. But after she explained that she hadn't meant to make everyone worry, he seemed okay with the explanation and assured her that if she needed anything to call him.

"Uncle Potter!" Sienna called out, catching Bailey's attention and bringing her back into the present. She looked up, and yep, there stood Potter. All six-foot-five of him, standing there staring at her with a pissed off look. *Well, damn. Time to pull up those big girl panties and face the music.*

She stood up and holy shit on sticks, her legs felt like Jell-O because they shook so bad. This was going to be a bit awkward, she thought. "Uncle Potter, look, Ms. Bailey is back."

Potter continued to stare at her, showing no emotion. "I see." Bailey swallowed hard. Oh yeah, he was pissed, alright.

"Are you picking up Sienna today?" Bailey decided to ask to break the ice. Maybe sticking just to the basics was best.

191

He walked farther in the classroom, closer to where she stood by her desk. He towered over her, and suddenly the room felt even smaller.

"Yeah, Irish had a meeting on base and is running late."

She held her hand up. "Potter, you don't have to explain. Whatever Irish does in his time isn't any of my business. I'm just glad I'll get to see some of you around here at the school once in a while."

"Where have you been? We've all been worried," he asked. She felt a little bad for not returning any calls or messages, but she didn't feel like hearing excuses made on Irish's behalf since they were all his friends. Plus, technically, Derek knew she was safe. So obviously, Derek didn't pass the message on.

"I had some personal stuff I needed to deal with." Potter raised his eyebrows. Did the man think she was just going to spill all the details just because he asked? "Some private matters that I don't want to discuss."

He looked shocked and taken back by her response. Then he nodded his head. "Okay. Well, I'm sure I'll see you around. I mean, now that you're back, I'm sure you'll be catching up with Alex, Tenley, and Autumn."

She nibbled her lip. "Yeah, I'm not so sure about that."

"Why not?"

"They're Irish's friends. Wouldn't that be making them choose sides? That isn't fair to them."

Potter's expression softened. "Honey, if you think you can get rid of those three women, you've got another thing coming. They all adore you. You are part of their gang with or without Irish. And I, along with the rest of the guys, still expect to see you at our get-togethers still. Like I said, we've all missed you and have been worried about you. We were almost to the point we were going to have Skittles try and track you down."

"Really?" She asked, surprised they would have done something that extreme.

"Really," he told her.

"Well, if it means anything, I've missed you all as well, but don't you think that would be a little awkward? You know, me and Irish being in the same place at the same time."

"Fuck him!" Potter winced as he said that, realizing he was in a school, and she had to laugh. But then he said something that made her feel uplifted and as if she did belong in their circle of friendship. "Irish fu-...fudged up. He's paying for it. Trust me when I say that he is hurting probably more than you. But if he has an issue of you being around, he'll need to get over it because you're our friend too."

She wasn't sure she wanted to come between friends and teammates, but she appreciated his words. "Thanks, Potter. You don't understand how much your words mean to me."

He winked. "I've been in your shoes before, so I do understand." She tilted her head to look at him. "The part of being and feeling alone. I'll tell you all about it one day, but right now, I have to get these two young ladies home before we come back tonight."

"Oh, you and Tenley are coming to watch Sienna in the play?"

"Yep, *all* of us will be here." She didn't miss how he emphasized the word all. Of course, Irish would be here. His niece had one of the biggest roles. She was playing the part of a ladybug. "I take it I'll see you tonight."

Even though she didn't have to be, there was no way she was going to miss the play. She smiled. "Yeah, I'll be around for a little while."

"I mean it, Bailey. I'll expect to see you around."

She smiled. "We'll see, Potter. No promises." He frowned at her, but then stepped forward and hugged her. And God, did it feel good to be cared about.

As she watched Potter leave with Sienna and Alejandra, she spotted Mr. Pega, the principal, and he walked in. He was usually one of those people who had a permanent smile on their faces, so seeing a frown and look of concern, she knew something was wrong.

And boy, was she right. With the news that Mr. Pega delivered, her life had been knocked off its axis, and she was pissed seven ways to Sunday.

She was determined to seek and destroy those responsible for ruining her life.

❦

"Bailey, you don't have to be here tonight," Jonathan told her as they stood in her classroom.

She shook her head. "Nope, I have to be. I promised Sienna that I would be here. Mr. Pega was nice enough to let me come tonight."

"He's still an asshole. So is the entire school board for that matter," Jonathan said with an attitude, and Bailey appreciated his backing.

Though Bailey was trying to forget the awkward conversation with Mr. Pega this afternoon, it was hard not to. Considering the conversation ended with her losing her job. As of this afternoon, she had been relieved from her teaching position. The reason, because someone sent some inappropriate pictures of her to some of the members of the school board. Pictures of her in just her panties and bra. Of course, the images were photoshopped because she would never pose in something like that and have pictures taken. Someone was out to destroy her reputation, and she had a good idea of who that someone was. Randy had the resources and connections to do something of that nature. In his mind, he probably figured that if she lost her job, lost her friends, and lost her boyfriend, she would run home with her tail between her legs.

"What are you going to do?" Jonathan asked her.

She looked up at her cousin and shook her head as she packed a few more of her belongings into one of the boxes. "I don't know. The reality of it hasn't even sunk in yet. Maybe I'll do some charity work or something."

"Shit, Bailey. You don't even have to work."

"I know that. But I need to do something. There is no way I'm just going to sit around and be a trust fund baby. Then I'd be acting like my parents."

"Don't even compare yourself with those worthless pieces of shit. Why not take a little bit of time for yourself and go on a long trip? Go explore the world."

"I don't know. We'll see."

Before she made any plans, she first needed to figure out how she would make it through tonight without running into Irish or any of the others. She looked down at the bouquet of pink roses lying on her desk. Pink was Sienna's favorite color, and ever since she was given the lead role in the play, she'd been talking about how it would be cool to have someone give her flowers after the show like they do on Broadway.

Alex entered the multi-purpose room of the elementary school. She and the rest of the gang were excited to watch Sienna perform in her first school play.

Her and Ace had arrived a little early, hoping to get a chance to see and talk to Bailey. When Potter called Ace earlier and told him that Bailey was back, it made everyone relax some. Everyone, including Irish, had been worried. After he finally got his head out of his ass, thanks to a talk with Derek, he tried going to her condo. After letting himself in, he realized she hadn't been home in a couple of days. Alex took a deep breath and looked around the room.

"Are you sure she's even here?" Ace asked her.

"Potter said she told him she'd be here. Plus, I know how much she cares for Sienna. She wouldn't miss her performance." Alex walked out into the hallway with Ace right on her heels. "Let's check her classroom. Maybe she's there."

As they made their way down the hall, they saw the light coming from Bailey's classroom. As they walked closer, they heard voices. One was Bailey's, and the other was a man. Ace put his finger to his lips, signaling for Alex to be quiet. As much as Alex hated eavesdropping, she was curious as to who the male voice was.

"What are you going to do?"

"I don't know. The reality of it hasn't even sunk in yet. Maybe I'll do some charity work or something."

"Shit, Bailey. You don't even have to work."

"I know that, Jonathan. But I need to do something. There is no way I'm just going to sit around and be a trust fund baby. Then I'd just be acting like my parents."

"Don't even compare yourself with those pieces of shit. Why not take a little bit of time for yourself and go on a long trip? Go explore the world."

"I don't know. We'll see."

Alex didn't like what she was hearing, and apparently, Ace didn't either by the frown on his face. It appeared that Bailey might be leaving. He motioned for Alex to go into the room.

She knocked and popped her head around. "Hey, stranger!"

Bailey turned around and gasped. "Alex!" Then saw Ace walk in behind her. She prayed that rest of the gang wouldn't follow. She wasn't ready for that.

She met Alex halfway and hugged her. "Oh girl…do you know how worried we've been about you?" Alex said to her.

Bailey pulled back, and Alex noticed she wiped her eyes. "So, I've heard, but why?"

"What do you mean, why? You're our friend, and we couldn't get a hold of you. When Sienna told us you hadn't been at school, we all became concerned."

"Yeah, sorry about that. I had some things I had to take care of."

"So, we heard. But too important to even return a call or text and let your friends know you were at least okay and not lying in a ditch somewhere?"

Bailey heard the sadness and hurt in Alex's voice, and she felt bad. It wasn't her intention to hurt anyone.

"I'm sorry, Alex. I had a lot on my mind this past week and was up to my neck dealing with some personal stuff. I never meant to hurt or insult anyone. I just needed some time."

"What's with the boxes?" Alex asked, moving the conversation along and looking around the room. The only items she had packed up were the ones that were hers that she'd personally bought. Though some of the items she was going to let the school keep just because she knew the students would be disappointed if she took those with her. That included the library corner she created with the bean bags and a ton of books that she had bought with her own money.

Not wanting to hash out all over again about losing her job over some fake internet pictures, Bailey just shrugged her shoulders. "Just making some changes." As the words left her mouth, she happened to glance over at Ace, and when she saw him squinting his eyes at her, she knew right away she wasn't pulling the wool over that man's eyes. But thankfully, she was saved any further interrogation when Jonathan cleared his throat.

"Oh, I'm sorry…Ace, Alex, I'd like you to meet my cousin, Jonathan Perner. He's from Alabama and staying a few days with me."

Jonathan smiled and shook Ace and Alex's hands. "It's nice to finally meet some of the folks Bailey's been gushing about for the last few weeks. She talks very highly of all of you. You and your friends are in the Navy, right?" Jonathan asked, and Ace raised an eyebrow at that comment, and Bailey had to hide her smile. Ace was so protective of his team. Jonathan only knew Irish was in the Navy. He didn't know he was a SEAL.

Ace looked at Bailey with that intense stare down thing the guys sometimes do. "What? Why are you looking at me like I committed a crime? You are in the Navy, right? Or have you all been lying to me? Because if so, that means I lied to my cousin." She gave him a wink and raised one of her eyebrows back at him. She heard Alex mumbled the word "smooth" under her breath.

She relaxed a little when Ace's face finally showed that he got what she was saying. Yes, she told her cousin that they worked for the Navy, but she never actually told him what they did. She'd never betray them like that.

"And that is why we all have great respect for her. She has a trait that we all respect. Loyalty," Ace replied to Jonathan as he gave Bailey a nod with his head.

"Well, I'm just glad she was able to meet great people like yourselves and that she has friends watching her back."

Ace chuckled. "You don't have to worry about that. She's got more eyes on her than she probably realizes. Though it would help if she'd let people know if she decides to pick up and leave town in the middle of the night."

Bailey felt a little embarrassed as Ace and Jonathan spoke about her like she wasn't even in the room. She cleared her throat and gave her dear cousin a look that said, knock it off. He chuckled then pulled her into his side. "Sorry, cuz. I just like knowing that you're safe." She rolled her eyes, and Alex laughed.

"Get used to Bailey. You're stuck with us." Alex said, and Bailey smiled. But she wasn't so sure she agreed with Alex's comment. She glanced at her empty desk and started wondering what her future in Virginia Beach really held for her now that she was unemployed and boyfriend-less.

Alex looked at Ace. "Hey, honey, why don't you and Jonathan go save us some seats. There is something I want to talk to Bailey about, and I'm sure you guys don't want to sit here and listen to girl talk. Plus, maybe you can give Jonathan some insights on what you really do for the Navy." Bailey had to hide her smile when Ace just quirked his eyebrow up at his fiancé.

Ace nodded his head and gave Alex a quick kiss on the lips. Bailey loved watching the two of them interact. They were so in-tune with one another and obviously so madly in love with each other. That was what was hurting her so much because she was in love with Irish.

The two guys left the room, and Bailey was left standing there with Alex. And from her posture and the blank expression on her face, Bailey knew she had some explaining to do. And she would explain everything to Alex; after all, Alex, along with Tenley and Autumn, had been good to her.

"So, we only have a few minutes before that caveman of mine will come back looking for us. So, what's the deal, chica. Where the hell were

198

you for a week that you couldn't have even sent a text to let us know you were okay, and why in the hell is your desk empty? Are you leaving?"

Well, so much for keeping things under wraps for a little while longer. Leave it to Alex to notice every detail. She thought about asking her what she was talking about, but that would just be insulting the woman's intelligence, and Alex was too good of a friend for her to treat her in that way. Nope, the best scenario was to come right out and be honest with her.

Bailey cleared her throat and leaned against her desk, half standing, half sitting on it. "I was in Alabama." Alex went to say something, but Bailey held her hand up. "Let me finish because I know what you're going to ask, and that answer is no. I was not at my parent's. I stayed with Jonathan. He and his parents live about an hour from Birmingham. He's been helping me with some personal things relating to my parents and Randy. With Jonathan's recommendation, I hired a private investigator to look into my parents. It seems my parents have known about my trust fund for a while. They paid off the attorney to give them information."

Alex shook her head and stepped closer. "Bailey, I'm so sorry."

"It's nothing for you to be sorry about, Alex."

Alex glanced at the boxes stacked on the desk again. "So, what's the real deal with the boxes?"

"I got fired today," Bailey said on a sigh. Damn it to donuts. She really didn't want to hash all this out tonight.

"What? Why?" Alex exclaimed.

Again, it only took one word to answer. "Randy."

"What did that fucker do now?" Leave it to Alex to not hold back.

"He had someone photoshop some risqué pictures of me and sent them to every member of the school board."

"Oh, shit!"

"Yeah. So, needless to say, I'm out of a job as of about four hours ago. Since I was coming up for the play, Mr. Pega, the principal, let me clear out my stuff tonight."

"God, Bailey. I'm so sorry. I don't even know what to say right now."

Bailey waved off Alex. "Nothing to say. I explained those were not real pictures, but without any proof, I can't really argue my case."

"Well, hopefully, Sienna's birthday trip to Orlando next week will cheer you up some. She's so excited."

Bailey nibbled on her bottom lip. "I don't know, Alex. That will be a little awkward, don't you think?"

"Bailey, I'm not going to lie. Irish fucked up, big time. The man has been miserable, believe me. He misses you and wants to talk to you. Don't get upset, but he even went to your condo a few nights ago and let himself in so he could make sure you weren't hurt or something."

Bailey's eyes widened. "He broke into my condo?"

Alex smiled. "Well, technically he didn't break in, considering he had a key. And well, we were all worried about you, and when you wouldn't respond to our calls or texts, we thought something might have happened to you."

Bailey was shocked, but at the same time, her heart grew a little, knowing they had truly missed her.

She looked at Alex. "Fine, but don't expect me to stay in the same room as him."

"Good luck with that," Alex chuckled.

"Oh, here, before I forget. These are for Sienna for after the performance." Bailey handed Alex the bouquet of pink roses. "Give them to Irish. I'm sure he forgot about them."

"Wow, Bailey. That is really sweet. Sienna is going to love them, but why don't you give them to Irish?"

Bailey shook her head. "Nice try. I'm not ready to talk to him yet. Please, Alex. With everything that's happened in the last week and now with me losing my job, I'm hanging on by a thread right now."

"Deal."

CHAPTER TWENTY-FIVE

Irish looked around the auditorium in search of Bailey. After groveling for what had to be close to ten minutes, Potter finally broke down and told him that she would be here tonight. He was just about to take his seat when he caught sight of the blonde-haired goddess. She was walking into the room with Alex, but what stopped him in his tracks was the tall, dark-haired man Bailey had her arm around. He watched her closely as she introduced the guy to who he assumed were some of the other teachers she worked with. He saw her smile at something the guy said, but he knew that wasn't her "real" smile. No, her real smile would light up the room.

"Here, asshole!" Alex said, shoving a bouquet of pink roses in his face. Asshole had become his new name amongst the women. But he took it in stride because he deserved it.

He took the roses from her. "What are these for?" He asked as their large group started to take their seats. He would have to wait until after the performance to talk with Bailey.

"Well, they're definitely not for you."

"Alex!" Ace growled her name in warning, and she turned and gave Ace the Ice Queen glare.

She glanced back at Irish. "They are for Sienna."

His jaw dropped. "Shit! I completely forgot. Listen, Alex, I know you are still pissed off at me, but thank you. I want this night to be perfect for Sienna."

"Oh, they didn't come from me."

"Who?" He asked.

She looked at him like he had asked a ridiculous question. Alex let out a deep sigh. "Bailey gave them to me to give to you to give to Sienna."

He knew he looked surprised, and when he took a glance in the direction where he knew Bailey was sitting, their eyes locked. He saw the sadness she still held in her eyes, and his gut twisted, knowing he did that to her. He held up the roses and mouthed the words "thank you," and she smiled at him. A real smile, and he couldn't help but think he still had a chance to redeem himself.

Right after the final curtain call, Bailey and Jonathan headed out to the car. She planned on taking him to Bayside for dinner tonight. As they made their way to her car, she spotted Derek and Juliette walking to theirs.

Juliette waved. "Hi, Bailey!"

"Hi, Juliette. How are you?" Juliette was Tenley's mom and Derek's girlfriend, though rumor had it, wedding bells could be in the future for the couple.

"I'm doing great. That was some play tonight. Sienna looked so adorable."

"She sure did." Derek took that moment to walk over, and Bailey saw the way he eyed Jonathan and then looked at how her arm was looped with his. Did Derek think Jonathan was with her? As in she was on a date? *Ewww....*

Quickly, she introduced Jonathan to both Derek and Juliette. As they spoke for a few minutes, Bailey saw some of the guys from the team start to exit the building, and they were headed in their direction. Now she wished she would've gotten in the car instead of talking with Derek and Juliette. She quickly said her good-byes and said they might catch up with them at Bayside since it appeared the gang was heading there to celebrate Sienna's performance.

Irish watched in shock as the guy with Bailey had his hand pressed against her lower back as he guided her to the car. His temper started to rise. Could she have seriously moved on in just a matter of days?

He glanced over at Alex, hoping she may know who the guy was, but she just shrugged her shoulders. Fuck!

As Irish approached Derek and Juliette, he wasn't going to beat around the bush. "Who was the guy with Bailey?" He asked but didn't miss the glance Juliette gave Derek. Derek kept a straight face, of course, and just shrugged his shoulders. "A friend, I assume." Irish knew for a fact they were hiding something, and he was going to find out, even if he had to play dirty. His friends couldn't lie to Sienna.

Bailey guzzled the last of her drink, then set the empty glass on the bar. She was debating staying and having another, but honestly, she wasn't in the mood to socialize. She had spoken briefly to most of the guys on the team and, of course, Alex, Tenley, and Autumn. Now she was ready just to go home and curl up in her bed. She touched Jonathan's arm. "Hey, I'm going to head home." Jonathan was drinking a beer and eating buffalo wings. They were the best wings in town.

Her eyes darted to the other side of the room and to the table where her friends were. They were all smiling and laughing, having a grand old time. Well, except for Irish, who was in a dead stare with her. And damn if she didn't feel the intensity from his eyes alone. When she talked with everyone earlier, they had told her how much they'd missed her, and she would be lying if she said she didn't miss them too, especially Sienna. That little girl had carved a niche in her heart just for her. At least at the school, she was able to see her, but now that she'd lost her job, she wouldn't see her anymore.

Her cousin's voice brought her out of her trance. "Why don't you just talk to him? It's obvious he wants to speak with you, and I know you want to talk with him."

She looked at Jonathan. "I don't think I'm ready yet."

"Okay. If you say so, let me finish my beer, and I will get my food wrapped up, then we'll go?"

"Stay," she said, and fished her keys from her purse, then handed them to him. "Take your time. I'll walk the beach home. The brisk night air will be good for me. I need it after today. Maybe it will help clear my head a little."

"Are you sure? I mean, do you think it's safe?"

"Positive." She laid some cash on the bar to cover her drink and enough for Jonathan to have a couple more if he wanted. He gave her a hug and told her to be careful; then she slipped out the side door. God, she loved that side door.

Irish couldn't take it any longer. That should be him with his arms around her and hugging her. He wanted to know who the pretty boy was she was with. Everyone played dumb, but he had a feeling they knew exactly who the guy was but weren't sharing the information. Again, he thought of sending Sienna to ask, but that was a pussy move.

He needed another beer anyway, so instead of asking the waitress, he got up and headed to the bar. He'd wait there until Bailey came back. She was avoiding him on purpose, and he was done with it. He was going to talk, and she was going to listen.

He stepped up to the bar right next to the guy and ordered another beer from the bartender. He waited a minute or two and looked down at his watch. What in the hell was taking her so long?

"If you're waiting to talk with Bailey, it's not going to happen," the voice beside him said.

"Excuse me?" He clearly stated with an attitude. Who was this guy to tell him he wasn't going to talk to Bailey?

"She left," Jonathan said, nodding at the side door.

Goddammit! He hated that fucking door. He should've known. He thought about going after her, but she had a good start. At least he could find out who this guy was. God, he hoped he was just a friend because he wasn't sure what he'd do if she were already dating this guy.

"I'm Irish, by the way." he said, introducing himself and putting his hand out there.

"I know who you are, and I'd say it's nice to meet you, but I'd be lying," Jonathan said, but he shook Irish's hand.

"This is going to be a bit abrupt, but I need to know. Are you dating Bailey?"

Jonathan laughed and then wiped his mouth with a napkin. "No. The last time I checked, relationships with family members was illegal. I'm her cousin. Jonathan Perner.

Irish couldn't help the smile that spread across his face. He glanced over to his friends and saw Alex watching him. Her lips twitched just before she turned her back and continued her conversation with Tenley. The damn woman knew exactly who Jonathan was. She just wanted to see him suffer a little while longer.

Irish felt a little awkward. "So, I'm guessing she's told you about me?"

"She told me enough. Can't say I blame her for not wanting to talk to you."

"No, me either." Irish stood there, silently playing with the label on his bottle. "Look, I need to talk to her. I need to apologize and explain some things. I had a lot of shit on my mind that night, and things just spiraled out of control. Not that I'm using that as an excuse, because it's not. I let my job get the better of me, and I took it out on her. I said some pretty shitty things to her. Things that I wish could take back."

"Do you love her?" Jonathan asked out of the blue, shocking Irish.

"Excuse me?"

"I asked, do you love her?" He said slowly.

"Yeah, I do. I think I fell in love with her the moment I met her."

"She has that way about her. She's an absolute sweetheart."

"Where has she been the past week?"

"With me. She came to visit my parents and me for a few days. I would never refer to her parents as family. They are conniving, deceitful, and mean. They will stop at nothing to get what they want. And that includes hurting their own daughter for their own personal gain."

"Yeah, I kinda got that impression from what she's told me."

"I don't think you do because if you did, you wouldn't have said to her what you did. There is so much you know and don't know."

"I know. I fucked up. Big time."

"Yeah, you did."

"So, how do I make her see she is the one for me?"

"I honestly don't know. She was broken. Complete and utterly broken on the inside when she got to my place. I've seen her down in the dumps before, normally over something her parents did. But this time, I'll admit, I was worried about her. And now, with the news, she was dealt today, well, let's just say it didn't help matters." He picked up his beer and took a big chug of it.

Irish stood up straighter. "What happened today?"

Jonathan debated saying anything, but then he thought that Ace or Alex might tell him anyway since they knew. "She lost her job."

"What?"

Jonathan explained what happened, and Irish felt his temper rise. This guy Randy was seriously looking for a death wish. It made Irish want to be with her now even more. They were leaving next week for Florida, and he still wasn't a hundred percent sure if Bailey was still planning on going.

"Look, she's supposed to go to Orlando with a group of us next week for Sienna's birthday. We all want her to go. I want her to go. There will be some downtime where she and I can talk."

Jonathan turned to face him. "Look, Irish, she needs someone who is going to be there for her. Someone who will fight for her and, most of all, someone who will love her. And love her for the woman she is and not the other materialistic things that come with her."

"I get it, man. I want to be that someone."

Jonathan looked out the window before turning back. "She loves you, Irish. She's hasn't actually told me that, but I can tell."

"I love her too."

Jonathan eyed him for a few moments. "Listen, I will make sure she gets on the plane as long as you swear to me you will never again treat her the way you did."

Irish shook Jonathan's hand. He knew for a fact he would never again behave the way he had with Bailey. He knew he was being given a second chance, and he wasn't about to fuck it up.

CHAPTER TWENTY-SIX

Irish looked at his watch as his leg bounced up and down nervously. They only had about ten more minutes before the flight crew closed the doors to the plane, and Bailey hadn't shown yet. Everyone else in their group, Alex, Ace, Frost, Autumn, Cody, and Alejandra, were seated and buckled in. They all were in First Class. Next time, he knew not to let Bailey pay for the airfare. She not only bought their three tickets, but she bought everyone else's too.

"Irish, will you settle down. She'll be here," Alex said.

"How do you know? Did she call you?"

"Because she told me she would, and I believe her. She wouldn't bail on Sienna."

He looked at his watch again, eight minutes. Sienna was sitting in the window seat next to him. Bailey's chair across the aisle from his was still empty. He pulled his phone out and was getting ready to send her a message when he heard the flight attendant greet someone, and he perked up. It had to be her. His hopes were dashed when a man, probably a few years younger than him, came into view. He was a Marine, dressed in uniform.

The blonde flirty flight attendant with fake boobs pointed to the empty seat across the aisle from him. Was she insinuating that the seat was empty? Oh, hell, no. That was Bailey's seat. But then he heard Bailey's voice, and his heart began to beat a little faster. She appeared right behind the Marine, and he turned and spoke to her.

"I can't thank you enough, Ms. Anderson. What you've done means the world to my family and me."

Irish watched as Bailey gave the Marine her gorgeous smile. He'd missed that smile.

"Please, call me Bailey, and it wasn't a problem in the least. Just make sure as soon as you get off this plane, you run like heck and get to your wife and daughter." She leaned over and said something to Alex. He saw Alex smile and nod her head, then pull out one of her business cards and hand it to Bailey. Bailey turned back to the Marine, handed him the card and told him to call when he had some information.

"Bailey?" He questioned, and she gave him a half-smile and nodded to the Marine, who was taking the seat Bailey should be sitting in.

"We'll talk later," she told him. "He needs that seat more than I do." And with that, she walked toward the back of the plane. He watched her put her bag in the overhead compartment, then took a window seat about two rows from the rear, and he wondered what the fuck was going on? Why would this guy need the seat more than her? He sat back down, and the Marine was staring at him.

"Is Bailey your girlfriend?" the guy asked him, and without any hesitation, he said yes.

"Well, she is definitely a keeper. There needs to be more people in the world with a heart like hers. If it weren't for her, I wouldn't make it home in time to see my little girl before she goes in for heart surgery."

Irish swallowed hard. Jesus, not that age mattered, but he wondered how old his little girl was because the guy only looked to be in his mid to late twenties.

"If you don't mind me asking, how old is your daughter?"

"Seventeen months. She was born with a heart defect. ASD or Atrial Septal Defect. There are three types of ASD. Charlotte, my daughter, has Secundum. The defect is in the middle of the atrial septum. It's the most common form of ASD. They say at least half of all babies born with Secundum ASDs close on their own. But Charlotte's heart hasn't shown any signs of the hole closing. I was shipped out three months ago to Pakistan. About two weeks ago, the doctor told my wife they would have to do the surgery. I thought there would be some time before it would be scheduled. I was pretty surprised when I got the call six days ago, saying they were going to operate tomorrow at Shand's Medical Center in

Gainesville, FL. Luckily for us, it actually works out because my wife's parents live just about an hour from there."

Irish's thoughts immediately went to Sienna. He couldn't imagine going through something that terrifying with a child. Then having to deploy to another country and leave your spouse behind to handle everything. He always thought that spouses of military personnel were the true heroes.

"Well, I hope everything works out for your family. I'll make sure I send up a little prayer for Charlotte."

"Thanks, man. I appreciate that. And please tell your girlfriend I said thank you again. I don't know how it happened, but my flight into Gainesville got scheduled for tomorrow instead of today. I tried to get on one of the later flights, but they were all sold out, so Orlando was the closest I could get a seat on."

"How does Bailey actually play into all of this?" Irish asked.

"She happened to be standing next to the ticket counter when I was explaining the situation to the gate attendant. Unfortunately for me, to get on the Orlando flight, I had to go with another airline, which meant purchasing another ticket. Not that it mattered. I'd pay my life savings to get back to my little girl. However, when I'm deployed, I don't take my credit cards, and I must have stuck my damn check card in my checked bag because it wasn't in my wallet, and I only had three hundred and fifty dollars in cash on me. The cost of the ticket was $765. Anyway, Bailey stepped in after hearing everything and paid for my flight, no questions asked. Then, as we were boarding, she told me to take her seat in first class. She said I deserved it more than she did. I tried to argue with her, but she kept insisting. I told her I wanted her address, so I could pay her back, but she said if I wanted to pay her back for me to make a donation to this organization." He held up Alex's business card, and Irish couldn't help but smile. Not only did Bailey step in and help a complete stranger in need, but she also aided a friend who was doing amazing work to assist our veterans that were in need of medical assistance.

The Marine shook his head, and Irish swore he saw the man's eyes glaze over with tears. "I owe your girlfriend my life. If she hadn't been standing there, I don't think I would've made it in time."

Irish nodded his head. "She is definitely an angel, and the first woman I've ever loved."

The guy smiled. "Well, you be sure to treat her right. There aren't many like her and my Nicolette."

Irish and Bryan, the Marine, ended up talking almost half the flight. The more they chatted, the more Irish liked the guy. He even invited him and his family to Virginia Beach once Charlotte was better. Once Bryan knew he was in the Navy, they exchanged some military stories. Nothing classified, just funny stories of mishaps, mainly during boot camp. Then he introduced him to the rest of the gang on the flight. Bryan and Alex spoke for a while about her Foundation and what all it involved. The guy was pretty impressed and said he would spread the word when he got back to base to help drum up donations.

Now Irish sat there, his mind on the woman who was sitting all alone in the back in the plane. He debated going back there to talk to her, but he didn't want to piss her off. She told him she would speak to him later, so he just needed to be patient. He tried reading a book, but that lasted about three minutes. Then he tried to close his eyes. Falling asleep was easy. They were trained to take naps when they could. But even that simple task seemed impossible. He kept turning around, looking back toward her seat. He couldn't see the top of her head anymore.

Autumn leaned forward in her seat from behind him. "Irish, do you want me to go and check on her?"

He grinned. "Is it that obvious?"

"Well, considering you keep fidgeting and looking back there every five seconds." She smiled at him.

"I want to go back there, but I don't want to upset her."

She patted his shoulder. "I'll be right back."

Autumn wasn't even gone for two minutes when she was walking back to first class. He raised his eyebrows.

"She's sound asleep."

"Thanks," he said and turned to face forward. He closed his eyes; maybe he could try getting a couple of minutes of shut eye now that he knew she was okay.

The group was headed to the restaurant inside the hotel, and Irish had yet to see Bailey. After they got off the plane and collected their bags, a limo took them to the hotel. Another surprise from Bailey, however, Bailey hadn't ridden with them. According to Alex, Bailey told her she had some business she needed to tend to and said she would meet them for dinner. So, here they were but still, no sign of Bailey. He asked Alex, and she said she hadn't heard from her. In the back of his mind, he couldn't help but be worried about her.

They had just sat down when Frost spotted Bailey. Irish turned around, and his chest tightened at the sight of her. She looked cute in a pair of dark grey Capri sweatpants and a white tank top. With her hair pulled back in a ponytail, she looked youthful as she walked through the hotel lobby, pulling her bag behind her. But when he caught a glimpse of her face, he frowned. She looked tired and upset. When she got in line at the lobby desk, he looked at Alex.

"What is she doing?" Alex's cheeks turned a little pink, and she tried looking away as if she was trying to avoid his question. "Alex?" He asked again.

She sighed. "Fine. Bailey told me she would come on the trip but that she was getting her own room."

Irish looked back in the direction where Bailey stood. Enough was enough; she wasn't going to avoid him any longer. "Like hell she is," he said, standing and storming off in the direction of the lobby.

Bailey stood in line to check-in at the hotel. She was tired. Between not sleeping the past few nights, traveling, then having to spend the last two hours dealing with the bank that used to hold her trust fund, she was

211

literally spent and ready to pass out. At least she managed to get about forty-five minutes of sleep on the plane.

As she went to step up to the desk, she felt a hand squeeze her shoulder. She jerked and looked over her shoulder and met Irish's intense eyes. She swallowed.

"What are you doing?" He asked.

She licked her dry lips. "Checking in."

He held her gaze. "Why? I already checked *us* in."

"Yeah, about that. I don't – "

He cut her off, then looked at the desk clerk who was watching them intently. "She's with me, and I already checked us in, so she won't be needing a room." Before she could argue, he was pulling her through the lobby, down a hallway before stopping in a hidden alcove far away from prying eyes. Her back hit the wall, and he placed a hand on her hip and the other against the wall above her head.

"Look, I know I was an asshole and hurt you. But I've been patient. I've given you time and space like everyone has told me to do. But dammit, enough is enough. I've missed you so much. I know an apology doesn't even begin to make up for what I did. Just know that I intend to make it up to you. We both have a lot to talk about but know this; I won't give up on us. I made a commitment to you that first night you slept in my arms, and I intend to stand by it. I won't let you go. At least not without a fight. And sweetness, know that I have never lost a battle, and I don't intend to now."

Bailey knew her eyes were wide as saucers, and as much as she should be feeling angry and fearful at Irish's barbaric behavior, that so wasn't the case. Her body felt on fire; she was aroused by his determination, and holy shit, she wanted him. She missed the domineering and bossy Irish.

Before she could even consider rebutting his comments, he swooped down and kissed her. There was no holding back either. He kissed her fiercely and thoroughly. Their tongues tangled as if they were meant to be one. He pulled away but suckled her neck right in a spot that made her squirm. She was so turned on.

212

"Jesus, I've missed you," He huffed out.

She held on to his waist and took a couple of deep breaths. "I've missed you too."

She noticed he was looking at her shirt, and she looked down and saw her breasts were pouring from the top of it. He reached down and fixed it for her. When his eyes met hers again, and she saw the love they held, she knew deep down everything would work itself out. It may take some time, but things would be okay. Fifteen minutes later, after taking her stuff to *their* room and having another impromptu make-out session, they finally joined the rest of their friends for dinner.

As soon as they sat down, all eyes were on them, and then a smile appeared on Alex's face.

"Well, I guess we can all assume you two have kissed and made up." Ace and Frost both chuckled. Autumn was covering her mouth, trying not to laugh, and the kids, well, they were just being kids and not paying any attention to the adults.

"Why would you think that?" Bailey asked, then looked at Irish. He held a straight face.

"Well, judging by that large hickey on your neck, I just assumed," Alex said, giggling.

"Sonofabitch!" She whispered, and she could hear Irish snickering next to her along with the others. She looked over at him and gave him the evil eye. "That is so not cool." She touched the spot on her neck, where Irish was sucking just minutes ago. "You marked me?"

All Irish did was smirk. Then he leaned over and kissed her cheek. "Next time, it won't be your neck that I mark."

She shut her mouth and felt how warm her cheeks got. Hell, it just wasn't her cheeks that felt warm. Her body felt needy. How in the hell was she going to get through this weekend?

CHAPTER TWENTY-SEVEN

The following evening, everyone entered the hotel dragging their feet. Alejandra fell asleep on the boat ride, so Frost carried her, and Sienna was out cold in Irish's arms. Spending over twelve hours in the "Happiest Place on Earth" would do that to an adult, let alone a child. It was a magical day, especially for Sienna, and that was what the trip was all about. Sienna got to meet all her favorite princesses, along with some other characters, and Bailey couldn't help but splurge on the Bippity, Bobbity, Boutique for Sienna and Alejandra. They both got to be pampered and turned into princesses. Cody had fun, too, as his favorite was the Pirates of the Caribbean ride.

As for the guys, their favorite part was when the ladies told them they were ready to go back to the hotel. Although they said they enjoyed themselves, the women knew they were uncomfortable in large crowds. Alex explained to Bailey how large crowds raise the guy's level of anxiety. They can't get a read on everyone around them, and when the crowd is too large, that interferes with getting to a safe exit, should something go wrong. Bailey completely understood.

They all set plans to meet for breakfast tomorrow morning, and then everyone went to their rooms. Bailey was hoping to catch the fireworks. As she had never been to Disney World herself, the fireworks were the one attraction she'd wanted to witness.

She and Irish got to their room, and Irish carried Sienna into the one bedroom. The other bedroom, Irish had given Bailey last night, and he slept on the couch. Bailey pulled the covers back, and Irish laid Sienna down. Her little eyes started to flutter open.

"Ms. Bailey, I am so happy that you came back to us," Sienna's tired voice said.

Bailey was stunned by her comment, and she looked to Irish, and he smiled. "That makes two of us," he said, giving her hip a little squeeze.

She looked back down at Sienna and smiled, then kissed her cheek. "Me too, sweetie."

Irish kissed Sienna next and pulled the covers up over her, and she was lights out in seconds. Bailey and Irish closed the door and walked out into the living room.

"You know, you are going to have to fight her to get that princess dress off her tomorrow morning, right?" Bailey told him as she walked toward the bedroom to drop her shoes.

"Well, it was your idea, so you can deal with it," he said sarcastically, and Bailey just smirked.

"We'll see."

He held out his hand to her. He looked so good standing there, looking all casual in his cargo shorts, fitted V-neck t-shirt, and his bare feet. "Come on, the fireworks will start soon, and we have a perfect view from the balcony."

She took his hand, and he led her to the balcony. She scanned the view. It was so beautiful. They could see the park lit up, and all of the other hotels across the lake looked absolutely stunning at night. Suddenly, the first sparkler went up into the air, over the castle, and exploded into various colors. Her breathing stopped at the magical sight, and she felt a tear roll down her cheek. It was then that she realized she was grateful to have gotten to experience this for the first time with the people she loved.

She felt Irish's arm go around her waist as he pressed his warm body against her side. She looked up, and he looked so serious but loving at the same time. He reached out and wiped the tear from her cheek. His breathing shuddered before he spoke. "You're so beautiful." He turned her fully, so she was facing him.

"I know I promised we would talk, and we really haven't had the chance to. I can sit here and make excuse after excuse for how I treated you, but it won't do any good. I fucked up, Bailey. I let something that happened on that mission eat at me until I couldn't take it. Instead of just taking you aside and talking to you, I exploded and took all of my frustrations out on you. I am so sorry, sweetness. I've been miserable without you. I want you with me. I want us to live together; I want you, me, and Sienna to be a family." He took a deep breath. "I love you, Bailey. You and Sienna complete me.

"The night we met, not only were we in the right place at the right time, but we were both at a point in our lives where we were ready to test the waters. There may be a thousand loves out there that never happen, simply because two people who were meant to connect miss each other by just a couple of minutes. But we didn't. We did meet, and damn if we didn't connect. It was fate, Bailey. Please, baby. Please tell me that you forgive me, and I haven't lost you."

She needed to make him understand that he was her life, and without him, she would never be happy. "I hadn't experienced true happiness until I met you, Ky. I got that from you, Sienna, and all of the wonderful friends I've made since moving to the beach. When you said those awful things to me, I felt like all of that happiness was ripped from me." She heard her own voice crack, and she felt the tears well in her eyes. "You, coming into my life has meant so much to me."

Bailey knew she had to look like a wreck with the tears streaming down her face. She had been expecting an apology of some sort, but never in a million years did she think Irish would be confessing his love for her. She loved him too and couldn't see her life existing without him.

Irish waited for what seemed like minutes as Bailey stared into his eyes. Those arctic blue eyes had caught his attention from the start. A tear fell and rolled down her cheek. Then another one fell, before long, the dam had burst, and she was sobbing and sniffling. She reached up and placed her delicate small hands against his cheeks.

"I don't want to lose you either. You, Sienna, and your friends have been more of a family to me in the few weeks we've known each other than my parents have been my entire life. But dammit, Ky, you hurt me. Those hateful words you threw at me were not only hurtful but humiliating." She paused, and his grip tightened around her waist. "The days we spent apart made me think a lot. Mainly about what I missed. I missed how happy you made me feel when we were together. I missed the warmth of your face and sparkle in your eyes when you would look at me. I missed how safe I felt being with you."

He pulled her closer and studied her closely. "What are you saying, Bailey?"

She shook her head and looked away for a second before turning her stunning, sparkling eyes on him. "I must be crazy, but I have to go with what my heart is telling me. I love you, Ky. I love Sienna too, and I want us to be a family as well."

That was all he needed to hear. He lifted her and kissed her as the fireworks continued to explode all around them. Who knew coming to Disney World would turn into their own fairy tale with a "happily ever after."

Irish set her back down onto her feet and pulled her close. "You know, you are pretty cute when you get all fired up."

She looked up at him and gave him an incredulous look, and he grinned. "What? You do."

"Well, just don't go pissing me off too much because this cuteness can turn real ugly fast," she stated, and he barked out a laugh and kissed her again and again and again. Nothing mattered at the moment because he was with the woman he loved.

CHAPTER TWENTY-EIGHT

Bailey ended the call with her mother and was so confused by the conversation they just had. She walked into the living room where Irish and Sienna were watching a cartoon together. They were getting ready to head downstairs for breakfast. Today, they had planned to go to Universal Studios. She had been looking forward to it, but then she got a call from her mother. At first, she was hesitant to answer because she was most likely calling to ream her a new ass because they got served with the papers. On the other hand, she wanted to know if they had been served.

She sat down next to Irish, and he put his arm around her, and she leaned into him. They had kissed and made up last night, and she was still feeling the high from all of the snuggling and pampering Irish had given her.

"Who were you talking to?" He asked.

"My mother," she said and felt his arm around her tense. She looked up at him and saw just how fast his happy expression morphed into a frown. Irish hated her parents, and he made it known any chance he got. "She called to tell me that my dad had a heart attack yesterday while he was at the office."

"Shit." Then he asked, "What does she want from you?"

"She said that my dad wanted to speak with me. In-person."

"What are you going to do?"

She thought about the papers that she'd filed with the court. Her mom hadn't mentioned them, so she didn't think they had been served them yet. If she went to see him now before they were served, there shouldn't be any problem.

"I'm torn. One part of me wants to say fuck you to him because of how he has treated me my entire life, but the other part is telling me to be the better person." She hadn't told Irish yet about the paperwork. This wasn't the time to get into it either. She would explain once they got home and were alone. "But I won't really know unless I go."

"When do you need to leave?"

"I would have to leave this morning and drive."

She could tell he wasn't happy she was considering going. But she knew he wouldn't stop her either.

Irish kissed Bailey. "Be safe, and call me when you get there, okay?"

"I will." She hugged him again, and he squeezed her tight. "I love you."

"I love you too, sweetness." He kissed her temple. She said bye to the others, then got into the car. Before she drove off, she looked at him and smiled and waved.

As she drove out of the parking lot, Irish watched until he couldn't see the car anymore. Ace and Frost were standing there with him.

"Don't worry; you'll see her in a few days, Romeo," Frost said, slapping his back, and Ace chuckled.

Irish tried to laugh at his buddy, but something deep down told him that he'd made a huge mistake in letting her go see her parents alone.

Bailey pulled the car into her parents' driveway. It had taken her an extra two hours to get there because of an accident on the highway.

It was going on six o'clock. Her parents were probably upset that she hadn't made it in time for dinner. They ate dinner at five o'clock sharp every night. It was like clockwork, and they never deviated from it. Even if they had dinner at the country club, it was always a five o'clock reservation. She only hoped they had saved her a plate of food because she was starving.

She took a deep breath and got out of the car. She decided to leave her bag until she saw how things would pan out. There was no use lugging it inside if things went south, and she left. As she walked up the front pathway to the front door, she noticed a white BMW sedan parked by the garage. She wondered who's it was because her parents would never leave one of their cars parked in the driveway. She blew it off, assuming it was one of her dad's associates checking on him.

When she got to the front door, she rang the doorbell. Yep, pretty sad, she had to ring the doorbell to gain admittance into her childhood home. She looked at the designer doorbell and snorted. Only her mother would have had something that obnoxious installed.

She heard footsteps on the other side of the door. The oversized door opened, and she expected to see her mother but was shocked to see her favorite housekeeper Ms. Kay. Ms. Kay had worked for her parents since Bailey was a little girl. She had to be in her late sixties now and a person Bailey would call a friend for life.

Ms. Kay smiled wide and pulled Bailey into a crushing hug. "Oh, sweet child! It is such a blessing to see you!" She exclaimed in that deep southern accent she'd carried all her life.

Bailey smiled and hugged her back. Well, as far as her arms would reach around the heavy-set woman. Ms. Kay had somewhat of a sweet tooth, you could say. "Hi, Ms. Kay."

The older lady pulled back. "Let me get a good look at you." She looked Bailey over and cupped her cheek. "You look good, child. You look relaxed and happy. Kind of glowing. Have you met a man?" Bailey felt her cheeks heat up, and Ms. Kay smiled wide. "Oh, you and I are going to talk later, little lady. Considering the pink in your cheeks, I want to hear all about this man of yours," Ms. Kay said, as she smiled and gave Bailey a wink.

Bailey laughed but then got serious. "I am happy, but I'm here because of my dad. How is he doing?"

Ms. Kay scrunched her eyebrows together and gave Bailey an odd look. She went to say something, but the sound of her mother's shrill voice interrupted the conversation.

"I thought I heard the doorbell." Bailey turned toward the doorway as her mother waltzed into the room. Dressed in a red pantsuit paired with a pair of heels, you would think she was on her way to one of her country club meetings. This was everyday wear for her. God forbid she didn't look less than a million bucks at any time of the day.

"Hello, mother."

Her mother looked her over like she was under a microscope. Then she turned and looked at Ms. Kay. "You can get back to your duties. I'll escort Bailey to her father's office as he is waiting to see her."

Bailey noticed the odd look that Ms. Kay gave her as she exited the room. It almost seemed like a warning.

Once Ms. Kay was gone, her mother turned back to her, and it didn't take long for the insults to start flying. "You look like shit. You're gone for a matter of a few months, and you let yourself go. Randy won't be happy with your appearance."

Bailey looked down at herself. She was wearing a pair of jeans and a long-sleeved black t-shirt. Her hair was pulled up into a ponytail, and she wore no make-up. She hated wearing makeup, and if she did feel like wearing it, she didn't put too much on other than a little eyeliner and mascara. But it wasn't the insult that had her stomach clenching. It was the comment her mother made about Randy.

They started walking down a long hallway toward her father's study. It was located on the main floor of the house in the left-wing. The house was a mansion. Actually, more like a museum. Growing up, she wasn't even allowed in certain areas of it. But that wasn't to say she never broke the rules and explored when her parents weren't home.

When they got to the end of the hall, she pushed the large wooden door open that led to her father's office. She hated this room and was always fearful when entering it. Mostly because she was only summoned here when she was in trouble for something, and it usually ended with her getting a beating from her father. A slight tremor shook her body as she stepped over the threshold.

She looked around, seeing nothing had changed. It was still the very cold room that she remembered. It was painted dark forest green, accented with dark wood furniture and trim to match. His huge desk sat to the right in front of a large window that was covered with dark green curtains to match the walls. To the right was a fireplace with a seating area.

There were family pictures around the room, but not a single one of them included her. She stared up at the large portrait of her mom and dad that hung above the fireplace. She remembered when the artist met with them to do the painting. The artist had been a little taken back when her parents had informed that they didn't want her in the portrait.

When she looked back toward the other side, there stood her father standing in front of his desk. The drink in his hand had her doing a double take. *Was he drinking brandy?*

The door behind her slammed, and she jumped. That's when she saw Randy, standing about a foot behind her. She had been set-up and was royally screwed.

She reached for her back pocket to pull out her phone, but it wasn't there. Dammit, she must have left it in the car. She took a step back when Randy came closer. She turned her body, so she had both her father and Randy in her line of sight.

"What is going on? Mother said that you had a heart attack and wanted to see me, but considering you're standing here drinking a brandy and look like total shit, I'm going out on a limb to say that she lied." She could hear the shakiness in her voice, and she knew her father would feed off that. He was a pit bull who fed off of people's weaknesses.

Her father smirked and set his drink down on the edge of his desk. He reached for a packet of papers behind him. "Your mother and I were served these on Friday."

Bailey's eyes widen. Oh shit, it was the emancipation papers.

He picked up another set of papers and took a few steps toward her. These are papers of my own that you are going to sign.

She gave him a ridiculous look. "I'm not signing anything that comes from you. At least not until I have my attorney look it over."

He took another step toward her, and he looked angry. "Oh, you're going to sign these before you leave here."

"Oh, yeah. And how are you planning on making me."

"I'll let Randy tell you. After all, you belong to him."

Her eyes widened, and she shouted back. "The hell I do. I don't belong to anyone."

"She's all yours, Randy. Do what you want with her. Just make sure she signs the fucking papers." With that, her father walked out of the room, leaving her alone with Randy.

Bailey tried to make a run toward the other side of the room, where she knew there was a secret door that led to the outside. She only got a few steps before she was yanked back. She broke free from Randy's grasp but lost her footing, and Randy used that to his advantage. He pushed her backward, sending her into the sofa table. Her back slammed into the wood table, and she cried out.

"This is just the beginning," Randy stated as he licked his lips and then covered her mouth with his. He held her around the waist with her arms pinned to her side. Without the use of her arms, it was difficult for her to make him stop. She bit his lip, and he released her mouth.

"Now that is no way to treat your husband?"

"Husband? Are you delusional?"

"Not at all. You see, once you sign those papers, you will become my wife, my property."

"What happens if I don't? Because I'm telling you right now, I will never sign them. I will never be anything to you."

"Oh, you'll sign them. Even if I have to beat you until you do."

"Then you might as well kill me because I never will," she yelled, then spit in his face. When he went to wipe his face, she raised her knee and hit him in the groin. He shouted and grabbed himself. She managed to get her feet moving. Her back and hip were very sore, making her movements a little slower. No sooner had she made it down the long hallway and into the entry foyer, Randy came at her again. His face was red with rage. She was going to have to fight her way out. As he got closer, she turned and counterattacked just like Murphy at the dojo had taught her to do if she ever found herself in this situation. Although now she wished she would've taken up Irish on his offer to teach her some more evasive defense moves.

223

Before she could get her body set, Randy charged her, taking them down to the marble floor. The side of her head made contact with the floor, and her vision blurred momentarily. Randy straddled her body, pinning her to the floor. He gripped her throat and squeezed. Using his other hand, he slapped her across the face.

"You stupid, stupid, bitch." He looked at her with wild and crazy eyes and hit her again. "You really think I'll let you leave here. Leave me!" He shouted at her. She was terrified and cried out from the pain she was in. "You don't have your big bad Navy friends to back you up this time."

Bailey was shocked that he knew Irish was in the Navy. Her surprise must have shown in her expression.

"That's right; I know all about your boyfriend and his friends. They can't help you now."

"He's my boyfriend, and I love him!" She shouted.

Just when Bailey didn't think Randy could look any crazier, he suddenly spiraled into a fit of rage. He grabbed hold of her shirt and ripped it. She screamed, hoping Ms. Kay or one of the other staff on-site would hear and help her. She looked around for anything nearby to help her. Her eyes landed on an umbrella leaning against the wall by the door. She reached for it just as Randy stuck his hand in her shirt and squeezed her breast. She felt his other hand trying to undo the button on her jeans. He was going to rape her right here in the open. Using all the power she had, she stretched her arm enough to get her fingers around the base of the umbrella. Once she had a good grip, she swung it down and hit him in the back of the head. He fell sideways, holding his head. When he pulled his hand away, there was blood. He roared and lunged at her again. This time, she was prepared and swung the umbrella like a baseball bat, striking him in the forehead, and he dropped to the ground moaning. She heard footsteps racing down the hall. She felt dazed herself. Before she could muster another thought, Ms. Kay was there pulling her into a hug.

"Oh, my lord, child. Did he do that to you?"

All she could do was cry while Ms. Kay held her.

"Come child; we need to get you out of here. Can you drive, honey?" Bailey would make sure she was good enough to drive. At least far enough away from this place.

"I have to get out of here," she mumbled and looked down and saw blood coming from the gash in Randy's forehead. She was surprised her parents hadn't come around, considering all the ruckus they were making.

Ms. Kay took her hand and walked her out through the side kitchen door to avoid being seen. Once she got Bailey into the car, Bailey thanked her.

"Oh, honey, you don't have to thank me. I can't believe that man did this to you." She touched Bailey's cheek. "I've always known that man was evil. You did the best thing by getting away from here. I'm done after tonight. Not after this. They need to be stopped."

Bailey felt bad. She knew Ms. Kay worked her ass off to support her family. She needed to work, considering her parents probably didn't pay her ditty squat.

"Ms. Kay, please don't quit your job because of me. I'll be fine once I get out of here."

Ms. Kay pulled her into a hug. "Oh, honey, I think I only stuck around because of you."

Bailey pulled back. "Me?"

"Sugar, I knew I couldn't leave your upbringing to your parents. Besides your grandparents, who do you think convinced them every year to have you home for the summer while they galivanted around the world."

"You did that for me?"

"Of course, I did. I would do anything for you, honey."

Bailey hugged her. "I love you."

Ms. Kay closed her eyes and hugged Bailey tight. "I love you, too, baby girl. Now, listen, you get on outta here before ya parents come looking for ya. Are ya sure you're okay to drive?"

Bailey nodded her head, although she wasn't so sure. Her head was throbbing, and her entire backside hurt. Driving for eleven hours wasn't going to help or probably the smartest thing to do. But what choice did she

225

have? She thought about driving to Jonathan's, but he was out of town at some seminar, and his parents were on vacation, so going to their house was out. In all honesty, all she wanted was Irish right now. She wanted his comfort and security, but she couldn't have that either, so she would just settle for getting home.

Bailey pulled the rental car into her parking spot in front of her condo. She was exhausted and running on adrenalin and caffeine. It was almost four in the morning, and she had driven straight through. She wasn't sure how she managed it, but she did. A few times, she thought about stopping at a hotel to rest, but she was afraid Randy or her parents would be hot on her tail. The drive had taken longer than it should have. With her injuries, she had to make more stops to stretch. At least now, it was still dark outside, and people were sleeping. Nobody would see her battered face as she made her way up to her condo.

She got out of the car slowly. Her body was stiff and sore. She opened the back door and grabbed her bags. She looked at her cell phone. There were multiple texts from Irish he had sent last night. One telling her how much he missed her, another telling her how much he loved her, and a third one telling her good night. She started to cry again. She needed to call him, but if she called now, he would know something was wrong, and he would worry. He didn't need that since they would be getting up soon to catch their flight home. Instead, she sent off a text letting him know she was home and that she loved him.

There was one phone call that couldn't wait. She needed to call Jonathan and ask how she could get a restraining order against her parents and Randy. She should've called the police, but knowing her parents, they probably had the local police chief in their back pocket.

She got into her condo and dialed her cousin. On the third ring, his groggy voice answered. "This better be good, Bailey."

She felt bad for waking him, but God knew what her parents and Randy were already planning. She hated them. It brought tears to her eyes, thinking how devious there were.

"Bailey, are you there?" She heard Jonathan say.

"Yeah." She managed to croak out.

"You don't sound okay; what's wrong? Aren't you in Florida with Irish?"

"No. I was there, but then my mother called and fed me a line of bullshit about my father having a heart attack, so I left and drove to their house yesterday."

"Oh, shit. Bailey, what happened? I was going to call you today. I heard from the county processor, and he informed me that your parents were served on Friday."

"Yeah, I know." She could hear the shakiness in her voice, so she knew that he could hear it as well. "It didn't go well. Randy was there."

"Fuck. Did that bastard hurt you?" Jonathan asked, sounding wide awake now.

She started to get emotional again and proceeded to explain in detail how her own flesh and blood left her helpless with a man who was going to rape her. After what seemed like an eternity, she finished. "I didn't know who else to call." She sniffled as more tears fell.

When Jonathan didn't say anything, she knew he was angry and most likely processing everything she told him. She could hear him over the phone moving around and taking a couple of deep breaths. After about a minute of silence, he finally spoke.

"Bailey, how bad are you hurt." He asked, and she was shocked at the calmness in his voice.

She walked into her bathroom and looked at her injuries in the mirror. She had a nasty bruise on her cheek and a busted lip. When she lifted her shirt and turned, she gasped at the discoloration on her back. Her right hip had a bruise, but it was her head that concerned her the most. The throbbing was getting worse, and she felt a little nauseous. Both were signs of a concussion.

"I don't really know. I have bruises all over," she whispered and then started to cry again.

"Bailey, you need to get yourself to a hospital. What did Irish say when you called him? I don't like you being alone for two reasons. One, you're injured, and two, I don't trust your parents or Randy not to show up."

"Irish doesn't know. I haven't called him yet. We talked the night before last for a long time, and things are good with us."

"Goddammit, Bailey! Why didn't you call him first? And another thing, why did you wait? You should've called either Irish or me right away. Between the two of us, we could've gotten to you somehow."

"I'm sorry. I was just so focused on getting away. I didn't want to call Irish because I didn't want to put a dampener on Sienna's birthday weekend. I was going to call him this morning."

"He needs to know Bailey. He knows people and can probably get someone to come over and take you to the hospital." He paused, and Bailey knew he was upset. "God, Bailey, I want to be there for you, but I'm stuck here in Minnesota at this seminar. Give me a couple of minutes to make some calls to some friends of mine in Birmingham. Your parents aren't getting away with what they did."

She didn't know what else to say, but okay and thanks.

"You're family Bailey, and this is what a real family does for one another. They are there for each other in good times and bad. I know you don't have much experience with that, but you'd better start understanding that."

She teared up again. "I love you, Jonathan."

He exhaled, "I love you, too. I'm going to call Irish, honey, and tell him what happened."

"He's going to be so mad."

"And he should be. You've taken enough shit from your parents. They need to be stopped, along with Randy."

"Okay. I know I shouldn't sleep, but I'm so tired." She'd been up since yesterday morning, and the last real food she consumed was breakfast.

"Bailey, don't you dare go to sleep. Not until you get looked at." After assuring him, she would try to stay awake, she hung up the phone and exhaled as she walked into the kitchen. She hadn't been to the store, so food was scarce. She found a cucumber and a tomato in the refrigerator and decided to slice them up to make a salad with some Italian dressing. When she pressed the butcher knife into the tomato and almost sliced her finger, she decided to abandon the salad even though her stomach protested the decision. Instead, she grabbed a bottle of water and went to her bedroom to take a shower.

Irish had just gotten out of the shower. Sienna was still asleep, but he would have to wake her soon, so they could pack and leave for the airport. He thought about calling Bailey but figured she was likely still asleep, considering she didn't get to her parents' house until after six last night. He wanted to hear how things went. He'd been a nervous wreck all day worrying about her.

He stepped into his boxer briefs, then shorts, and pulled on a t-shirt. On his way to Sienna's room, he heard his phone vibrating on the table. This early, it had to be one of the guys. He picked it up, but when he saw Jonathan's name flashing on the screen, the hairs on the back of his neck stood up. The only reason he would be calling this early was if something happened to Bailey.

Quickly he swiped the screen. "Hello?"

"Hey, Ky. It's Jonathan. Sorry for the early call, but Bailey ran into some trouble at her parents last night, and I'm worried about her. I didn't know who else to call."

Irish's gut clenched. "What happened. Is she okay? Is she with you now?"

"No, she's already home. I don't have all of the specifics because she wasn't making sense over the phone, but apparently, the whole story about her father having a heart attack was a ruse to get her home and to keep her there."

Irish listened as Jonathan explained what he knew. The more he heard, the angrier he got, and the more he worried about Bailey and how bad her injuries were. When Jonathan mentioned Randy's involvement, Irish's body went rigid.

"Randy is the asshole who she's been trying to get away from? The one who sent the pictures and ruined her career?"

"Yeah, that Randy. Like I said, it was all a setup. When Randy showed his face, things got a lot worse." Irish sat down on the couch and ran his hand through his hair. He was very worried and wondered how bad things had gotten.

"How bad?"

He heard Jonathan's sigh and braced himself. "He attacked her, Ky. She's injured. I don't know to what extent, but she didn't sound good over the phone."

He slammed his fist down on the table. "Why the fuck didn't she call me?"

"Because she didn't want to ruin Sienna's birthday. She was planning on calling you this morning before your flight, but I didn't like how she sounded on the phone. That is why I'm calling you now. Do you have anyone who you can call and have them check on her?"

"Yeah, I'll make some calls." They spoke for a few more minutes, and Irish thanked him again for calling and promised he would keep him informed. After he hung up, he dialed Bailey's number as he walked next door to Ace's room and knocked on the door. He needed to talk to Ace and call the guys back home and have them check on Bailey. When Bailey's phone went to voicemail, he hung up and became really concerned. What if she was unconscious?

The door opened, and Ace stood there. "Dude, it's six-fifteen in the morning, and you look like shit. Who the fuck pissed you off already?"

Irish had a blank expression on his face. "Bailey's in trouble."

Those three words brought Ace to full attention. Alex was at the door now, standing next to Ace, looking concerned. Both of them were already up and dressed. Irish conveyed to them what he knew. Now the two of them were pissed off and concerned as well.

230

"Irish, I'll call Tenley and Stitch and have them go over to her place. Between the two of them, they can assess her injuries and determine if she needs to go to the hospital," Alex told them.

Thank God Alex was thinking rationally. All Irish was thinking about was driving to Alabama and dealing with her parents and Randy. Tenley was a nurse, and Stitch had a good amount of medical training, so Bailey would be in good hands.

"Have you tried calling her yet?" Ace asked, pulling Irish into the room and closing the door. He couldn't stay long because Sienna was still sleeping next door.

"I tried, but it went to voicemail." He started to pace. "I had a bad feeling when she left. I knew I shouldn't have let her go. At least not alone. Fuck!" He looked at his watch, "I need to get Sienna up and ready. Plus, I need to pack still."

Alex walked back over, holding her phone and touched Irish's arm. "Okay, Tenley is heading over now. Potter is going with her, and Stitch is meeting them there. Why don't we go and let Frost and Autumn know what is going on?" She turned to Ace. "Ace, you, Frost, and Irish wait for Stitch and Tenley's call. Autumn and I will handle getting the kids up and everything packed and ready to go. I'm also going to call my Uncle Tink. When I spoke with my dad yesterday, he mentioned that a couple of Tink's guys were working a case over in Tampa, and they have one of the company planes. They are supposed to be heading back home this morning. Maybe they could swing over here and pick us up. That would get us back a little earlier."

Irish didn't know what he and the guys would do without Alex sometimes. Although she wasn't an actual team member, she played a very vital role. She kept everyone grounded. He walked over and hugged her.

"Thank you," he whispered. She squeezed him back. "She'll be okay, Irish. She's strong."

And didn't he know that.

Bailey blinked her eyes open and groaned. Her head felt as if the "The Little Drummer Boy" was inside her head beating on his drum. Make that several drums. She felt a little queasy. She tried to move closer to the edge of the bed, where she had put a trashcan in case she had to vomit. When she moved, her body protested. Her entire body was sore.

She looked at the clock; she needed to call Irish, but in all honesty, she just didn't have the energy. She wanted to close her eyes and hope that when she woke up, all of this had been a bad dream. She felt so numb and foolish. How could parents do this to their own child?

She heard her front door open, and her heart stopped. Fear consumed her at the thought that Randy had come back for her. She knew he had to be pissed, and he wasn't the type to just sit back and let something like that go. It was just a matter of time before he sought revenge.

Her breathing grew rapid, but then a familiar voice called out, and damn if she didn't feel like a balloon being deflated.

Tenley walked down the hall of Bailey's condo leading to the master bedroom. Potter and Stitch were both with her. She pushed open the bedroom door and had to hold back her gasp as she spotted Bailey curled up in the middle of her bed. Her face was buried in the pillows, and her shirt was bunched up, but the three of them couldn't miss the ugly bruises that painted Bailey's back.

She looked at Potter and Stich, and she could see how upset and angry they were. They both nodded for her to go first. She took a few steps closer to the bed. The last thing she wanted to do was scare Bailey. She could hear the muffled sobs coming from Bailey. "Bailey," she whispered. "It's me, Tenley. I have Potter and Stitch with me. We came to check on you, sweetie."

She heard the sniffle again and knew Bailey was awake and crying. She probably was not only in pain but was also embarrassed by all of this. Tenley felt like crying with her. She couldn't understand how a parent could treat their child, even grown, how Bailey's mother and father had treated her.

She gently sat on the edge of the bed and touched Bailey's shoulder. "Hey, sweetie. Can you turn over for me so we can check and make sure you don't need to go to the hospital."

She waited a few seconds and was relieved when Bailey lifted her head. That was until her eyes zeroed in on the busted lip and bruise on her cheek. "Oh, honey." Tears formed, and she tried hiding them. She was a nurse and saw these types of injuries all the time. However, her patients were usually not her friends. This one hit home.

Bailey wiped her eyes and looked at her and then over toward the doorway where Potter and Stitch stood with their arms crossed in front of their chests, looking four ways of pissed off.

"What are you guys doing here?"

"Irish called us. Your cousin called him and told him what happened. He's been trying to call you."

"I was going to call him in a little while. I left my phone out in the kitchen. He is going to be mad at me. I was just so tired, and everything hurts." She started to cry again, and Tenley's heart broke even more.

Stitch knelt next to the bed and brushed Bailey's hair from her face. "Sweetheart, he's not mad at you. He's just very worried. That's why he called us. Tenley and I are going to take a look at your injuries."

Tenley was grateful when Bailey relented and nodded her head.

Irish pulled into the parking spot at Bailey's condo. When Stitch called him right before they boarded the plane, he felt a little better, knowing her injuries didn't require a hospital visit. Thanks to Tink, they were able to catch a ride on his company plane, getting them home almost four hours earlier than when their commercial flight would've arrived. Dino and Skittles had his vehicle moved from the airport up to Hampton Roads Executive, where they had landed. Frost and Autumn graciously offered to take Sienna back to their house until Irish could get her.

He pressed the code to get into the building, then entered the elevator. Once the elevator made it to the sixth floor and the doors opened, he found himself jogging to the end of the hallway where Bailey's unit was. When he got there, the door opened, and Potter stood there with a frown on his face. Not that it was a surprise because Potter rarely ever smiled unless it was for his wife. But his face was cold. It was how he expressed himself during a mission.

"Where is she?" He didn't mean to be rude, but he needed to see her.

Potter nodded toward the bedroom. "She's asleep. She's bruised up pretty good. She's scared but apparently put up a hell of fight. She told us that she broke the asshole's nose before hitting him in the head with an umbrella. Stitch had some painkillers, so he gave her some until she could see her doctor. She falls asleep, but then she wakes up in a panic."

Irish could tell that Potter was just as upset as he was.

"You know this isn't over, right? It's only a matter of time before he comes after her."

"And I hope he does because I'll be waiting. And believe me. He will be walking away with more than a broken nose and bump on the head. That's if he can even walk."

Potter nodded his head, and Irish knew the team would have his back.

Irish quietly pushed open the bedroom door, and his eyes landed on his little pixie curled up in a ball under the covers. He toed off his shoes and climbed into the bed. He moved some strands of hair from her face, and his eyes landed on the bruise on her cheek and her busted lip. He closed his eyes and clenched his jaw.

Willing his body to relax, he molded his against hers. She stirred and moved closer to him, and he breathed a sigh of relief.

Bailey felt the big warm body press up against her backside. She knew it was Irish. She had heard him out in the living room talking with Potter and Tenley.

"Hey, sweetness."

Carefully, she rolled over and met his eyes. They were intense, and she knew he was looking at the bruises on her face.

He cupped her cheek. "Jesus, baby." He leaned and pressed his lips tenderly against hers. She closed her eyes.

"What can I do for you?" He asked, moving her hair out of her face and caressing her jaw with his thumb.

"Just lay here with me. That's all I want right now."

He gave her a serious look. "I won't let them get away with what they did." He wrapped her up in his arms, where she was safe, and kissed her temple. "And you did good, baby. You fought back and got away."

"I'm sorry for not calling you. I was so focused on getting away, and I wasn't thinking straight. The whole drive was a blur. I only stopped for gas and some ibuprofen. Landing on a table and a marble floor isn't great for the body."

After a few moments of silence, she continued. "I don't want to keep anything from you, Ky. I mentioned back in Florida that there were some things I need to fill you in on concerning my parents."

"I'm all ears whenever you're ready. But you seem tired, so why don't you get some rest, and then when you wake a little later, I'll heat us up some food that Juliette sent over, and then we can talk."

"Juliette sent food over?" He nodded.

"That was sweet of her. All of your friends are so nice."

"They are your friends too, and yes, you can't ask for any better friends."

"Where's Sienna? She doesn't know about any of this, does she?"

"No, I just told her you had some business to take care of. She is over at Frost and Autumn's house."

"I had so much fun with her."

"I did too. Once we get through all of this, I want to take you and Sienna somewhere. Just the three of us."

"I'd like that. And I will even let you pay for it." By the end of the trip, Irish had realized that Bailey had somehow managed to pay for the entire trip for everyone.

He barked out a laugh, and he heard her snicker. "I'm going to hold you to that. Now rest."

"Will you stay with me?"

"I wouldn't want to be anywhere else right now."

235

She nodded her head. "Good, I feel safer with you here with me." He kissed the side of her head, and she snuggled closer to him.

"I love you, Ky."

"I love you too." Once she fell asleep, he'd go out and call the guys and start making a plan to take down Randy and her parents. By God if he was going to just stand by and let them get away with hurting his woman.

CHAPTER TWENTY-NINE

A couple of hectic days had passed since the fiasco at her parent's house. To start, with the help of their friends, Bailey had moved in with Irish and Sienna. She and Irish had a lot of long talks. She explained about the emancipation papers and about her parents knowing about her trust fund.

During those conversations, she got her ass handed to her for not calling him when the incident with Randy first took place. She apologized and told him that it would never happen again. He, of course, forgave her, especially when she initiated a little make-out session that almost got out of control until they both realized that Sienna could walk through the door at any moment.

Bailey turned off the shower, stepped out and caught sight of herself in the big mirror in Irish's bathroom. With the bright lighting the bruises along her skin really stood out, and she frowned, knowing Randy was out there somewhere. He wouldn't give up until he got his hands on her. The police were looking for him too. Her parents, on the other hand, claimed they knew nothing and tried to make it seem like Bailey had made everything up.

She was still feeling a little sore. She hadn't been able to sleep well because of the nightmares that plagued her. Just this morning, she awoke screaming and trying to fight off Randy; however, when she finally came to, she realized she was hitting Irish. She cried and told him how sorry she was. Irish assured her she had nothing to apologize for and just held her.

She didn't feel like getting dressed yet, so she just threw on her bra and panty set. It was Halloween, and she and Irish were meeting everyone in town for the Annual Fire Department's Haunted House fundraiser. For the little kids, they were hosting a trunk or treat. Sienna was over at Potter and Tenley's house, and they would be bringing her to the fundraiser. She couldn't wait to see her all dressed up in her lion costume. She smiled, knowing how cute Sienna was going to look. She grabbed her baby blue silk robe that hit just above her knees and threw it on.

She walked into the bedroom and was surprised to see Irish sitting on the edge of the bed. He was bent over with his hands cradling his face. As she started walking toward him, he looked up and grinned. She got a funny sensation in her belly as she took in the sight of him in just a pair of jeans and nothing else. He looked so damn sexy, and then it hit her. She wanted him. She was ready to let him all the way in.

She stood in front of him, and he pulled her gently between his legs. Not feeling shy anymore when it came to touching him, she put her hands on his bare shoulders. His muscles felt tense, but they slowly relaxed as she caressed his skin. The black-out curtains were pulled shut, and the only light was from the lamp on Irish's side of the bed that gave the room a soft glow.

"What's the matter, sweetness? And don't tell me nothing because your eyes give you away. Are you in pain?"

"No, I'm feeling good right now."

He gave her hips a little squeeze. "Well, something is bothering you."

"I don't want you to think I'm a scaredy-cat. But I have a really bad feeling that something terrible is going to happen. Randy isn't going to stay hidden forever. He is going to want revenge."

He pulled her in for a hug. "Listen to me. I don't want you feeling scared. I know it's probably hard not to."

"You weren't there. You didn't see the evil in his eyes when he attacked me."

"Don't remind me."

She could tell he was starting to get upset again. He had been blaming himself for not being there with her and that if he had been, she wouldn't have been injured.

"Stop…I didn't bring this up to upset you. I brought it up because I am concerned about Randy coming and finishing what he started."

238

Irish pressed a finger to her lips and gave her a serious look. "That man will never lay another hand on you." He pulled her closer. "I love you, baby."

"I love you too." She looked him over and then ran her hands up and down his chest. He took a big breath and closed his eyes. When he opened them, her heart felt full because of the love and compassion his eyes alone held.

Irish always said that she would need to take the lead when it came to their first time being intimate. And by golly, she was ready to. Without further ado, she gently held his face between her hands and locked gazes with him. "I need you, Ky."

At first, Irish looked frozen, then she saw the blue hue of his eyes darken with desire. He pulled her tighter in his embrace and spoke in that deep low whisper that turned her on. "What are you saying, Bailey."

She smiled. "I want you to make love to me."

"Bailey, I would love to, but I don't want to hurt you, baby. You still have bruises," he told her as he ran his hands from her thighs up to her ribs.

"I promise you; I'm okay. I need you. Please, I want to feel you inside of me."

Irish took in everything about the woman who stood before him. She was so beautiful and sexy, standing in just her robe. His chest tightened, and he felt a sensation he couldn't quite explain. But then a conversation he had with his mom a few days ago came to the forefront, and he understood what his mind and heart were telling him. He smiled because it was just as his mom had told him, how he would know when he met the woman who he was meant to marry.

He stood up, and walked over to his nightstand, and opened the top drawer and pulled out the purple velvet pouch. He opened it and emptied its contents into his hand. He closed his fist around it tightly and closed his eyes.

He walked back over to Bailey and placed his hand against her cheek and gazed into her blue eyes. After several seconds of complete silence, she asked, "What's wrong?"

Still staring at her, he asked, "Do you know how much I love you?"

"Probably as much I love you. You're my soul mate. You're the one my grandma told me that I would find one day."

He smiled and wished he could have met her grandparents. "As you know, I'm not a mushy, romantic kind of guy. I try at times, but I know I suck at it." She snickered but then took his hand that was on her cheek and held it in her hand.

"I don't care about any of that. All I care about is that you love me and that I make you happy."

He took a deep breath and squeezed her hand. "I am happy. But you would make me an even happier man if you said that you would marry me and be part of mine and Sienna's family forever."

Irish couldn't hold back his smile at the way her eyes widened, and her lips parted. Though it was only like five seconds before she spoke, it felt like five minutes. A tear fell from her eye, and she didn't even try to wipe it away.

"Ky…" She whispered.

He loved that he had just shocked the shit out of her. He lowered down to one knee, still holding her left hand. He brought it up to his lips and kissed her ring finger before looking up into her tear-filled eyes.

"You are everything I ever dreamed of, and the one I thought only existed in my imagination, but then you walked into my life and showed me that love could happen to anyone. I love you and want to spend the rest of my life with you." He brought up his other hand and opened it, revealing a white gold antique diamond ring.

She gasped and covered her mouth. "Oh my God, it's beautiful."

"It was my grandmother's. She was a great woman and a wonderful wife to my grandfather. I want to carry on the tradition, and I hope you accept it and become my wife and mother to Sienna."

♔

Bailey was in utter shock. Here she was, wanting to give Irish something she'd waited all her life to give to the man she loved, and he just completely pulled the rug out from under her.

She looked at the ring again. Not that it mattered what it looked like. What mattered was that Irish had chosen her to give it to. It was a special token that was important to him and his family. She felt honored and loved and would cherish the gift for the rest of her life. She wiped some of the tears from her face and then looked at Irish, who had the most adorable grin.

"So, what do you say, sweetness…Will you marry me?"

She smiled from ear-to-ear, even though tears continued to cascade down her cheeks.

"Yes, Ky. I would love to marry you and spend the rest of my life with you and Sienna."

Bailey didn't think she'd ever seen a smile that big on Irish's face before. He jumped up and scooped her up and twirled her around while she laughed. She clung to his shoulders as he held her close. He set her down, then took her face between his hands and kissed her. He placed the gorgeous and most meaningful piece of jewelry on her ring finger. "Thank you, Bailey."

She smiled at him as she wrapped her arms around his waist. "You're welcome. Now, will you make love to me?"

He chuckled as he picked her up and laid her down onto the bed they shared. "I think that is the perfect way to celebrate our engagement." He licked his lips and stared at her. She had a feeling that things were about to get a little wild.

Irish was on an adrenaline rush, just like when he was on a mission. Except this mission was one that he wouldn't mind executing time and time again. Not only was he finally getting to make love for the first time to the woman he loves, but she had also accepted his hand in marriage.

With her silk robe open to his view, he couldn't take his eyes off her. She was naturally curvy, despite the weight she had lost over the week and a half they'd been apart. She was his fantasy come true, as she laid there spread out on their bed like a goddess, waiting for him to take her.

"You are absolutely gorgeous," he told her as he unbuttoned his jeans and pushed them down. He grinned when he saw her eyes go wide. He wasn't wearing any underwear. Then she snorted out a laugh, and he gave her a stern look. "Did you just laugh at my dick?" He felt a little insecure at the moment, but then she sat up and pulled him down on top of her, and she smiled.

"So that's your lucky charm?" She asked with a huge smile on her face, and he couldn't help but laugh now. And he felt better, knowing she was laughing at his tattoo. Yes, he had lost a bet on St. Patrick's Day a couple of years ago, and the deal was that if he lost, he had to get a tattoo on his dick. So, as it was St. Patrick's Day, and he was a lady's man, he got a four-leaf clover with the words Lucky Charm tattooed just above his cock. It hurt like hell, but a bet was a bet.

He leaned down and licked her nipple. "No, it's your lucky charm."

He wasn't a small man, and knowing she'd never had sex before, he would be sure to take his time, so he wouldn't hurt her. He gave her a stern look. "You promise me that if you feel any pain at all, you tell me, and I'll stop. I'm not small, and you also are still recovering from your injuries." He started to get angry again, and it must have shown because she took his face between her hands.

"Get them out of your mind, Ky. It's just you and me right now." She kissed him; then she looked his body over. She licked her lips, and he groaned.

"Honey, I'm really trying to take my time, but with the way you are staring at me and licking those plump, beautiful lips, you are wearing on my patience."

Her face turned red, and she went to look away, but he wouldn't let her. He took her chin with his fingers and tilted her face towards his.

"Look at me."

"I'm sorry. I'm just nervous. You are so much more experienced, and I'm making a mess of this."

242

He smiled. "No, you're not. I may be more experienced, but that is a bonus for you. Just relax, okay?"

"Okay," she whispered.

"Good. Now, you seemed to be a little overdressed." Her cheeks turned pink again, and he wanted to laugh at how adorable she was when she got embarrassed. But as he pulled the robe from her body and saw her fully naked for the first time, the woman had no reason to be embarrassed at all.

He nestled his body between her thighs and pressed his body against hers. He didn't want to rush this. He wanted it to be perfect for her, but he wasn't lying when he told her it was hard to hold back. Especially now, feeling her soft skin against his and how wet and warm her pussy felt against his cock. She grabbed onto his shoulders and looked at him. He could see different emotions swirling in her eyes, but what made his heart beat faster was the love he saw.

He took her face between his hands. Their gazes were locked onto each other. He could feel her heartbeat. He lined up his cock at her entrance and slowly started to push in. He looked down at her, making sure she was okay before he went any further. He pulled out a smidge and entered her again, letting her adjust to his size. She held his gaze and squeezed his shoulders.

"Make me yours, Ky."

With those words, he shoved in until he couldn't go any further. He heard her gasp, but before he could ask her if she was okay, she thrust her hips upward. He was close to losing all control. She felt so good, but this wasn't about him. This was all for Bailey. She showed him what love was. Slowly, he made love to her. Being deep within her and connected overwhelmed him. His emotion felt like they were on steroids. Never had sex felt so intimate—so right. Her tight vaginal walls squeezed his cock, sending him quickly over the edge. Beads of sweat formed along his brows as he fought to get himself under control. Seconds later, he felt Bailey's body tense before a soft moan escaped her lips. She was absolutely beautiful as she came. He stroked into her a few more times and followed, filling her with his seed.

He lowered his body, putting some of his weight onto her, and she wrapped her arms around him. Her breathing was rapid, and they were both sweaty.

"I love you. You are mine forever. He kept kissing her neck, cheeks, whatever skin he could find. When he looked at her, he saw the tears.

"Shit, did I hurt you," he asked, wiping the moisture from her face. But she smiled up at him with that million-dollar smile of hers and shook her head.

"Why the tears then?"

"Because that was perfect, and I love you so much." She tilted her head up and kissed him tenderly, and he hugged her tight and held on to her.

They laid there entwined with one another for a little while longer until Bailey looked at the clock.

"We need to get up and get ready."

He squeezed her tighter and kissed her shoulder. "We still have some time. I want to lay here with you in my arms for a little bit. Then we'll get a shower."

"A shower together?" She asked.

Irish smiled. "I'm a SEAL, baby. I like all types of water sports." He wiggled his eyebrows.

Oh, Lord. She had so much to learn.

CHAPTER THIRTY

Irish and Bailey parked the car and walked down the street to where the local fire department held their haunted house. All of the admission proceeds went to the firehouse.

"Wow! This is awesome," Bailey stated as she clung to Irish's arm. He looked around. The fire department did a great job every year putting the event on. There were Halloween displays everywhere. Some were scarier than others.

As they got closer, they saw the gang standing around, talking to some of the first responders. Irish got a glimpse of Sienna before she saw them. She was hanging out with Alejandra and Cody. The three of them looked festive. Cody was dressed as a grim reaper with face paint and everything, while Alejandra was dressed in a Good-Witch costume.

Sienna finally spotted them and came running towards them. She jumped into his arms and then roared like a tiger, making him and Bailey laugh.

"Oh, Sienna, your costume looks so cute," Bailey said to her as she leaned in and gave her a hug.

"Thank you. Aunt Tenley helped me with my face paint." Irish smiled. He loved how the two leading ladies in life interacted with one another. You would swear that Bailey was Sienna's biological mother.

Tenley and Alex walked over with Potter and Ace. "It's about time you two finally showed up," Potter said, shaking Irish's hand.

"Oh, come on, we are only like five minutes late." Irish tried arguing with Potter, but then a loud squeal by Tenley and Alex, and the site of the two of them jumping up and down ended it as they looked to see what had the women up in a roar.

"They're engaged!" Alex blurted out and then hugged Irish. "I am so happy for you! I told you there was someone out there perfect for you." He smiled and hugged her back. Alex was the one person who did believe he would eventually find the love of his life, and if he was honest, he owed her. After all, she was the one who gave Bailey the push to give him a chance, and she was also the one responsible for helping bring them back together when he acted like an asshole.

He kissed her on the cheek. "Thanks, Alex. You did believe in me, so I owe you at least that and more." He winked.

"Oh, don't worry, I will collect one of these days." Everyone laughed.

"Uncle Ky, can Bailey, Aunt Alex, and Aunt Autumn take us to the haunted house now?"

"You want to go to the haunted house? It is pretty scary," he asked Sienna.

"Uh, huh. I'm a big girl. Plus, Uncle Ace's friend, fireman Russ, said that he would protect us."

"He did, did he?" He asked but looked at Ace just to confirm that was true. They all knew a lot of the first responders in town, but Irish wasn't familiar with "fireman Russ."

Ace chuckled. "It's fine, man. Russ is a buddy of mine. He's a former Marine. He got caught up in some shit during his last deployment about a year and a half ago. You know, wrong place, wrong time."

Irish nodded his head. He knew all too well about the wrong place, wrong time. He had escaped death by mere seconds before.

"Anyway, he busted his hip. They wanted to put him on desk duty, but he wasn't down with it, so he left the Corps and went through the fire academy, passed everything with flying colors, and he ended up with Engine 18."

"That's a bummer. But I'm glad he found his calling with the fire department. If you say it's okay for the women and kids to go, then I'm fine with it."

"He's just going in ahead of them to warn the workers in the house that some kids are coming through and to tone down the scare tactics a little."

"That's cool."

❧

Bailey, Alex, and Autumn walked with Cody, Alejandra, and Sienna towards the haunted house. Even though she knew that Russ was giving the actors a warning about the kids coming through, Bailey was still scared shitless to go through the house. She'd been in haunted houses before, but she always had some male friends she could hang onto and bury her face in their back, so she wouldn't have to "technically" see anything.

As they walked around the side of the two-story rundown house to enter, she caught sight of someone dressed as Michael Myers from the movie Halloween, and she froze. Shit! Seeing him in a movie was one thing, but knowing he was lurking in the house that she was about to enter almost made her turn around. It was just something about that damn white mask and how the scary man moved, showing no emotion. She looked back over her shoulder again, but he was gone. A chill wracked her body, and she pulled her jacket a little tighter around her as she continued through the line.

They had to wait about five minutes to let the group ahead get through before it was the kids' turn.

Alex turned around and hugged her arm. "I'm so happy for you and Irish."

Bailey looked down at the ring on her finger again. She'd done it so many times since Irish put it on there.

"I still can't believe it. I mean, here I was, trying to tell Irish I wanted to have sex with him, and then he goes and surprises me with this," she exclaimed, holding up her left hand.

A sly smile spread across Alex's face. "You and Irish had sex?"

Bailey felt the heat in her cheeks. Alex knew Bailey was a little hesitant to have sex with Irish because she was so inexperienced. She grinned and nodded her head.

"Yes!" Alex exclaimed. But the celebration was short-lived because their group was called to enter the house. Bailey's nerves were off the charts, and she felt as if she was going to be sick. She despised these things but would do it for Sienna.

As they were ushered from room to room, Bailey began to relax. It was obvious the men and women who worked in the haunted house had been warned that kids were coming through.

As they started down a long dark hallway, Bailey accidentally stepped on Sienna's long tiger tail, causing Sienna to fall. Trying to see her way in the dark, Bailey bent down and asked her if she was okay, and Sienna giggled and told her she was fine but that she had lost her shoe. Alex joined them, and Bailey told her what happened. They were all trying to feel around in the dark, but Bailey knew that the next group would be coming soon.

"Alex, you and Autumn keep going with Cody and Alejandra. Sienna and I will keep looking. It has to be here somewhere. I'll try to find one of the workers to help."

Alex agreed and left Bailey and Sienna.

It was only about thirty seconds after Alex left them that Sienna found her shoe under a curtain. As Bailey was putting Sienna's shoe back on, a large hand landed on her shoulder. The move startled her. As she stood and turned around, she came face-to-face with a huge man dressed in a police uniform.

"Ma'am, you need to come with me."

Bailey jerked back and put herself in-between the guy and Sienna. "Excuse me?" She asked.

"A person was injured up ahead, and we are trying to evacuate the house until we can get the individual out." She eyed the guy over. He was wearing a police uniform. "Everyone behind you is being escorted out through the other exits." He gestured toward a door she hadn't even noticed. There was an exit sign illuminated above it. She was still a little skeptical, but if a police officer asked her to do something, she would listen, although her gut instincts told her something wasn't right.

As soon as she stepped out into the dark alley behind the house, she froze. Randy stood next to a black limousine with an evil grin on his face.

"Hello, Bailey...surprised to see me here?" Bailey gripped Sienna's hand and looked at her and saw how wide her eyes were. *Good girl.* Sienna recognized who Randy was from the pictures she and Irish had shown her just in case if he were to show up. She gave Sienna's hand a little squeeze to instill a little encouragement. Bailey had no intention of standing around. She would fight, but her priority was to get Sienna away from the situation. She squared her shoulders and readied herself for a battle.

"Actually, I'm not," she told him. She knew it was only a matter of time before he came after her.

He opened the door to the vehicle and motioned to her. "Get in." When she didn't move, the guy in the police uniform said, "Get in the car, or I put a bullet in the girl." Her blood turned to ice as she feared for Sienna's life. On instinct, Bailey moved Sienna behind her to shield her, but the man was quicker and snatched Sienna from her. Sienna screamed, and the guy covered her mouth to muffle the sound. When Bailey turned back around, Randy stood directly in front of her. She went to strike him, but he caught her arm and stuck her with a needle.

"Ow!" She covered her arm and looked at him.

"You honestly didn't think I wouldn't come prepared this time, did you?"

It made her feel good, knowing that he was scared of her after what she had done to him. He still had a bandage on his forehead where she had hit him with the umbrella.

But her concern at the moment was Sienna and getting her to safety. Not knowing what Randy had injected her with, she probably only had a little time before becoming incapacitated.

She recalled the moves Murphy taught her. She swung her elbow into the stomach of the guy holding Sienna. He dropped Sienna, and while he was bent over, she kneed him in the balls, then punched him in the face. The guy cried out and fell backward onto the ground. Bailey turned to Sienna.

"Run, Sienna!" When she saw Sienna running toward safety, she turned her attention back to Randy. Her vision became worse, and she stumbled when her legs started to go numb. Randy punched her in the head, and everything went black.

"Get her in the fucking car," Randy spat at his friend. Todd lifted Bailey's limp body up and put her in the car. The guy Bailey took down got up from the ground. His face was bleeding, and he was holding his crotch. "Get in and drive, you idiot. That little brat is probably already telling her uncle and his friends. This place is swarming with police, and they will be on our ass in no time. We need to make it to the airstrip."

Irish was enjoying himself. He felt like he was on the top of the world.

"I still can't believe it, man. Congratulations, again," Ace said, and Potter joined in.

"Yeah, if you of all people managed to find a woman to tame your ass, then there is hope for the rest of us," Dino said, joking around.

Irish glanced in the direction of the haunted house and saw Alex and Autumn walking towards the group, but there was no sign of Bailey or Sienna, and that didn't sit right with him.

"Holy crap!" Alex exclaimed as she and Autumn laughed. "Those firemen really know how to put on a haunted house."

"Where is Bailey and Sienna?" Irish asked.

Alex looked over her shoulder back toward the exit of the haunted house. She scrunched her eyebrows together. "Her and Sienna were right behind us, but we got separated because Sienna lost her shoe. We were going to wait while Bailey looked for it, but she told us to keep walking, and she would meet us out here."

Irish looked back toward the building, and his gut twisted, especially when his eyes locked on a buddy of his, who was on the local SWAT team approaching and holding Sienna, who was crying.

"What the hell…" He stated and took off in their direction. The others must have seen what was going on because they were all right behind him. As soon as Sienna saw Irish, she started kicking, and the officer set her down, and she jumped into Irish's arms and hugged him tight.

She was shaking like a leaf. "Honey, what's wrong? Where's Bailey?" She squeezed his neck tighter and started crying harder. He held her close to him and rubbed her back. He looked over to his friend and mouthed, "What happened?"

"I don't exactly know. I was standing along the side of the house with some others on my team when she came running from behind the house. I recognized her immediately. She was crying, saying that she needed to find you."

Sienna pulled back and looked at Irish. "Uncle Ky, the bad man took Bailey. He tried to make me go with them, but Bailey kicked him and told me to run." Irish heard the fear in her tiny voice. "He hurt her Uncle Ky. I saw him hit her, then they picked her up and put her in one of those big cars."

"Irish, I've got my team and the chief heading over," Officer Cade said. He was talking into his radio, relaying the information to someone.

Irish looked at his team. "It was Randy. The fucker must have been watching, and he took her. Goddammit!" He looked at Sienna. "Honey, was it the man in the picture that Bailey and I showed you?"

Sienna shook her head, yes, and Irish felt like he'd been struck by a bus. He was pissed and worried at the same time. If Randy took Bailey, there was no telling where they were headed. Randy had to know that as soon as Sienna told them, he would be a hunted man.

Officer Cade stepped up. "Sienna, sweetie, when you say a big car, can you describe it for me?" She looked at Irish as if she was unsure who to talk to.

He rubbed her cheek. "It's okay, peanut. You can tell him. If you can remember the color of the car, that would be helpful to the police and give them more information to find Bailey."

She took a big breath, and Irish knew that this had to be difficult and very confusing for a six-year-old. But she was a tough cookie and started giving them more details than they asked for, and damn if Irish hadn't felt proud, but on the other hand, he was scared. He knew that if Randy had Bailey, it wasn't going to end well for her.

"Okay, everyone, listen up." The Chief made his way to the front of the large group waiting to hear anything from the state police.

With Sienna's detailed description of the black limousine with the white letters TL on the right rear bumper and a partial plate and the description of the two men, they knew they were looking for Randy Lamont and an unknown accomplice. The information was passed onto the Virginia State Police, and they had their helicopter up in search of the vehicle.

"The suspect's car was spotted on the 264, heading west. We've got a helicopter following them at a distance. They have to know by now that we are looking for them. I've also received word that a private jet landed at the small airstrip off the highway about three hours ago. The plane is registered to a law firm out of Birmingham, Alabama."

Irish clenched his jaw. He knew exactly what law firm that plane belonged to. Anderson Law Firm.

"I've got a team heading to the airstrip to intercept them."

"How can we help?" Ace said.

"Get your vehicles and stay behind my patrol truck. I'll have another unit follow behind you, so other units know you are with us. The local utility company is cooperating and is opening the utility road leading into the airport. It's a shortcut, but it'll be a bumpy ride, so be prepared."

Everyone scrambled to their cars and trucks and headed out.

Bailey blinked her eyes open, and she was greeted by Randy's smugness. She moaned as her eyes closed again. Her head throbbed. She had hoped everything she was remembering had been just a bad dream.

Randy reached over and grabbed the front of her shirt and dragged her off the seat on to the floor, in-between his legs. He licked his lips and looked over at his friend Todd. She had recognized Todd. He was another pompous asshole who hung out at the Country Club. She tried pulling away from Randy, but he held her in a bruising grip.

"Oh no, you don't. You've got a lot of making up to do, my little wife."

252

She jerked her head back and gave him a look that asked, was he stupid. "Your what?"

He ran his finger down her cheek to her neck. Then he cupped her breast and squeezed before running his finger over her nipple. She pulled away, but Todd smacked her in the back of her head. She lost her balance and fell forward. Her face landed in Randy's lap.

Randy laughed. "See, baby. You want my dick so badly, don't you? That military asshole turned you into a cock loving little whore. As soon as we say, I do, I'll give you what you want. I mean hell, I've waited a lot of years to fuck that pussy of yours; I'm sure I can wait a little longer." He kept his hand on the back of her head, forcing her face into his crotch as he gyrated his hips.

She panicked. What did he mean by marriage? She wasn't marrying him. Oh God, she hoped Sienna had found Irish and told him what was happening. That was her only hope of being found.

Randy was still laughing when Bailey opened her mouth wide and bit down through his dress pants into his inner thigh. He screamed and pushed her off him. She tumbled to the floor of the car.

The driver turned and spoke, "The pilot just phoned. The plane is ready."

Randy grabbed her arms and dragged her from the car. Her legs were still a little wobbly, but Randy held her around her waist. She looked around and saw they were outside of an airplane hangar.

"You and I are taking a little trip out of the country," Randy stated as he dragged her across the tarmac toward the hangar. She noticed he was holding a gun in his other hand.

Suddenly, a helicopter appeared right above them, shining its bright spotlight on them. A voice came over the loudspeaker, "This is the Virginia State Police; put your weapon down. You are surrounded."

All hell broke loose as the entire area lit up with spotlights coming from every direction. She was blinded by the lights, as police and emergency vehicles swarmed the area. It was all chaotic as people were yelling from all different directions. She felt Randy loosen his grip. His focus was on something across the way. When her vision focused, she saw Irish, along with a couple of other guys, running across the tarmac. Randy raised his gun. He was going to shoot them. Without even thinking, she reacted and reached for the gun. She and Randy tussled and ended up on the ground. The gun was between them, and they both had their hands on it. The gun fired—the loud sound rang in her ears. She saw the stunned looked on Randy's face before two police officers pulled him off of her.

Suddenly, she got a numb feeling in her abdomen that quickly morphed into a burning pain. She placed her hand on her lower belly, and when she pulled it away, it was covered in blood. *He shot me...* Those were the last thoughts she had before people swarmed her.

"Look! There they are!" Irish pointed, as he, Ace, Potter, and Stitch arrived on the scene. They had been lying back until Randy made his move toward the plane.

"Shit, he has a gun," Potter stated. They were all armed as well. The plan was for them to circle around the plane as the police distracted Randy. As soon as Ace brought the truck to a stop, everyone jumped out and started running. Irish didn't even look until he heard Bailey yell, "No." When he looked over his shoulder, he froze in place as he watched Bailey grab for the gun. They both fell to the ground. He was already moving toward her with other officers when he heard the gun go off. Two officers pulled Randy off Bailey and cuffed him. A couple of other officers had another man on the ground, along with the driver of the limo. His eyes shifted to Bailey lying on the ground. When she lifted her hand from her stomach and he saw the blood coating her palm, his heart nearly stopped.

He slid to his knees by her side, along with the others. Stitch was already lifting her shirt as Ace was calling for the paramedics. But all Irish saw was red. Bailey's red blood was soaking through her clothing and pooling around her. He looked at Stitch as he worked on her. Irish knew from the look in Stitch's eyes when he glanced up that the situation was dire. For the first time in his career, hell, in his life, he didn't know what to do. He grabbed hold of Bailey's hand.

Her face was already so pale. "Come on, sweetness," He whispered next into her ear. The paramedics had arrived and were working to stabilize her. Her eyes opened.

"S--Sienna?" She whispered and tried squeezing his hand, but it was weak.

"She's fine, baby. She did what you told her to do. She found us and told us what happened. We got here as soon as we knew where you were."

"I'm so cold." Someone handed him a blanket, and he covered her legs. "I'm so tired," she said and started to close her eyes.

"No, Bailey. You need to stay with me."

"Randy?"

"The police got him."

He saw a tidal wave of tears in her eyes. "He was going to shoot you guys." She hiccupped and winced from the pain. "I couldn't let him."

He kissed her forehead. "You did good, baby."

He heard Stitch mumble something about needing to get her to the hospital. Within in minutes the EMTs had her on a stretcher and moving her toward the ambulance. Irish walked right behind them and watched as they worked frantically on her. He heard her call out his name, and he ran over to her side and took her hand. She looked up at him. She seemed to be losing focus as if she was going in and out of consciousness, and the tears hit his eyes.

She started to close her eyes. "Keep those eyes open. Focus on me, Bailey."

"Sir, we need to move her now. She's losing a lot of blood, and her blood pressure is dangerously low."

He leaned down and kissed her forehead. "You hang in there, baby. You hear me."

She looked up at him, and her normal bright blue eyes were dull. Irish had seen that look before. Out in the field and most of the time, it turned out to be a tragic situation. "I love you, Ky. I always will. Take care of our girl, okay?"

255

Did she think she was going to die? No, no way was she going to die. He watched as her eyes started to close, and her head fell to the side.

"Bailey, look at me...You fight, baby. I love you."

"So tired...." She said as her eyes rolled up into her head. The paramedics pushed Irish out of the way and loaded her into the ambulance and took off.

Irish was left standing there, watching the ambulance as it drove away with a part of his heart and soul in the back of it. Had he just lost her? He bent over, feeling like he was going to be sick. His body shook violently as he covered his face with his hands.

He felt the multiple hands on his back and knew it was his team. They were there and giving him the strength and support he needed. He needed to be strong, not only for himself but for Bailey as well.

He stood up straight and took a deep breath while he wiped the tears from his eyes. Ace and Potter were standing directly in front of him.

Ace stepped forward and gripped the back of Irish's neck. His team leader had a fierce look on his face. Ace leaned forward and spoke calmly but sternly, "You think nothing but positive thoughts, you hear me?" Irish just nodded his head. He couldn't speak. Not right now when his emotions were on overload. The only thing that mattered right now was making sure Bailey, the woman he loved, lived.

"Come on, man. Let's get you to the hospital," Potter said, opening the passenger door to his truck. Irish looked down at his hands and clothes. He was covered in blood. Bailey's blood. Diego handed him a towel. He tried wiping off what he could. "Don't worry about it, man. Just get in the truck," Potter told him. He slid into the seat while Ace and Diego got into the back seat. The others loaded up in Frost's Tahoe.

CHAPTER THIRTY-ONE

Beep...beep...beep....

It was the sound Irish had been listening to around the clock. He'd been at Bailey's bedside since she was moved into the ICU after making it through surgery. That was four days ago. They usually don't allow visitors to stay overnight in the ICU. Tenley was able to pull some strings with the hospital board, and they relaxed their policies. His teammates and Bailey's friends stopped in every day to get an update. In the days after the shooting, Bailey had been labeled a hero. If it wasn't for her quick actions, Randy could have shot and killed any one of them that day. She never hesitated when she threw herself into the path of that bullet.

Irish held Bailey's hand as he looked her over. Her skin was starting to gain back some of its coloring. When she had come out of surgery, he almost hadn't recognized her. With all of the tubes connected to her and how ashen her skin tone was, he didn't want to believe that the person lying in bed was the woman who held his heart. Sienna had wanted to see her, but he knew Bailey would kick his ass if he allowed Sienna to see her in this state. Thankfully, his mom and dad arrived the day after and had been staying at his house with Sienna.

The doctors had informed him that if it weren't for Stitch stepping in and stopping the bleeding before the paramedics arrived, Bailey would have most likely bled out before they got her to the hospital. Stitch had poured Celox into the wound. Celox is a coagulating agent poured into a wound to stop bleeding quickly. It is used quite often in the military, and by the grace of god, Stitch had some in his medic bag that he always kept in his Jeep.

The door to the room opened, and he smiled, seeing his mom standing there with coffee and a bag of food. His stomach rumbled. He hadn't eaten much in the last few days. Alex had brought him a change of clothes, and the hospital had let him shower there. He hadn't wanted to leave in case there was a change in Bailey's condition. His nerves were taking a toll on him because she hadn't shown any signs of waking anytime soon. Her doctors, on the other hand, weren't as concerned. Their main concern was keeping the wound clear of infection. They also informed him that due to the extensive damage to her reproductive organs, there was a high probability she could never have children.

His mom approached and set the bag and coffees on the table. She leaned down and hugged him.

"How's our girl doing today?" She asked as she straightened out the blankets covering Bailey. Though his parents hadn't officially met Bailey, they already loved her like a daughter and thought of her as part of the family.

He sat back in the chair, never letting go of Bailey's hand. "No change. Her vitals look good, but they aren't sure why she isn't waking up. They say that it could be a good thing that she is asleep because it gives her body more time to heal without her trying to move around."

His mom ran her fingers through his hair, and he could tell she was worried as well. "You need some sleep, honey."

"I'm fine, Mom. I get a few winks here and there. My body is trained for that."

"I understand that honey, but when this little lady decides to wake up, she's going to need you by her side. And you won't be a bit of help if you're falling on your face from lack of sleep."

"I just can't. I feel somewhat responsible for why she's lying here."

"What on heavens earth are you talking about? How were you or anyone for that matter supposed to know that bastard was waiting for her outside the door? The other guy was impersonating a police officer. Anyone would have thought he was with the event. So, don't sit here and blame yourself for something you had no control over."

Irish looked down at Bailey and all of the wires and tubes connected to her. He felt numb and lost. He honestly didn't know what he would do if she didn't wake up. He glanced up at his mom, and for the first time in a long time, she was who he needed.

"I'm scared, Mom. I'm scared she isn't going to wake up. I am scared that Sienna might lose another mom. What has me the most scared is having to live the rest of my life alone because I can never love another woman again. She's my everything. I can't lose her. I can't."

"Don't you worry. This lady is a fighter. She just needs some time to rest and heal. Your friends are all out in the waiting room. They got here right before me. Why don't you take a minute and stretch your legs, go for a walk and talk with them?"

"I don't want to leave her."

"If anything changes, I will come and get you. You'll just be down the hall."

"Okay." He stood and stretched, feeling how good it felt to stand. He leaned down and pressed his lips to Bailey's forehead and whispered to her. "I love you, sweetness. I'll be back in a few minutes."

He gave his mom a hug and kiss on the cheek, and he left the room.

As he made his way toward the waiting area on the floor, he could hear several of the guys talking. Skittles was talking to someone. Was that Jonathan, Bailey's cousin?

He turned the corner and was shocked to see all the guys and even Derek there, huddled together. Jonathan was there, and he was standing next to Ace and Derek. Skittles was sitting in one of the chairs, typing on his laptop. Irish had always been amazed at how fast Skittles could access shit on the computer.

Frost was the first one to see him.

"Hey, man," he said, giving him a back slap. "How's Bailey doing?"

Irish tried to smile. "Still no change."

"She'll come around."

"What's going on?"

Irish saw how Skittles glanced over to Jonathan, and Jonathan nodded his head. Instead of Skittles answering, Derek did.

"Irish, Jonathan's associates uncovered some things that warrant some looking into."

"What kind of things?"

"There is a possibility that Bailey's parents have been lying to her since the death of her grandfather."

Jonathan followed up Derek's sentence, "Long story short, Irish. If your friend Skittles here verifies it, everything belonging to the Anderson's is Bailey's. Her grandfather left everything to her."

"That is a lot of shit to cover up. How would they be able to hide something like that?"

"Simple. For the right price, anyone can get what they want. It's believed that Bailey's parents buried shit deep within corporations. I know for a fact there is a second server that only Bailey's father uses. That is what Skittles is trying to tap into."

"Do you think you'll be able to get in?" Irish asked Skittles as he took the seat next to him.

Skittles just snorted, which to Irish meant he had asked a stupid question. There had never been a time that Skittles wasn't able to get the job done.

After a couple of minutes, Skittles did a fist pump. "Bingo!"

Everyone gathered around as they all watched information appear on the screen.

"Son of a bitch!" Jonathan stated.

"Jesus Christ. Bailey isn't just a millionaire; she's fucking close to a billionaire when you take into account what all of the family businesses are worth," Skittles said as he continued to skim through documents.

"It all makes sense now, why her parents and Randy were in it together. If Bailey married Randy, then he would be entitled to at least half of the fortune legally. He was probably promised a nice piece of the pie.

"Or, they planned on killing her, and then everything would go to them."

Irish bit the inside of his cheek. The more he heard, the more he wanted to go to the county jail and beat the crap out of that piece of shit.

260

Bailey was fighting for her life all because of greed. Hell, if she knew the family fortune was solely hers, she probably would have just given it to them because that wasn't her life. She liked simple and traditional.

"Let's not forget the numerous federal laws that were broken. With this information, her parents are looking at serious jail time."

"What do we do now," Irish asked, not wanting to waste any more time. The quicker her parents were behind bars, the better. "I mean, who do we turn this information over to?"

"I'll make a call to the Sheriff in Birmingham. He has been looking for an excuse to throw Bentley Anderson in jail for years," Jonathan said, then stepped to the side, pulling his cell phone out to make the call.

Irish took a deep breath as he processed everything. This was good news. Once her parents were behind bars, she would be free and without any worry that anyone would come looking for her and do any harm.

"You okay, man?" Ace asked, looking concerned.

"Yeah, just a lot to take in. But this is good news."

"It sure is." Ace went to say something else, but an alarm of some sort coming from down the hall started blaring. When Irish looked, he saw the medical staff and a security guard rushing into Bailey's room.

"Fuck!" He took off running with the team following.

Bailey felt someone stroking her hair. It was calming, and whoever it was hummed a soothing tune.

"Come on, sweet girl. You need to wake up. You've got everyone who loves and cares for you worried sick."

She recognized the voice. It was Irish's mom. She'd never met her in person but had spoken to her over the phone. Her sweet voice and gentle touch was motherly. Something she had yearned for since she knew the type of people her parents were. The soft hands left her head, and she wanted to protest, but something was in her throat. She tried lifting her hand but wasn't sure if she succeeded or not until she heard Irish's mom's voice again and then felt a soft hand take her hand and squeeze.

"Oh, God. That's my girl. Squeeze my hand, honey." She heard the voice say, and then there was pandemonium.

When Irish got to Bailey's room, all he could see were two security guards who had someone face down on the floor while handcuffing their hands behind their back.

Immediately, Irish scanned the room. He found his mom standing between the person on the floor and Bailey. He recognized her stance and knew she was in protective mode.

When the guards lifted the person up off the floor, Irish was shocked when he came face-to-face with Annette Anderson dressed in nurse's scrubs.

Irish looked at the police officers. "What the fuck is going on?"

"This woman came in impersonating a nurse and tried to stick this needle into your fiancé's IV." The officer held up a syringe showing Irish. "But thanks to the quick thinking of your mom, she recognized this lady from photos and hit the alarm on the side of Bailey's bed and intercepted her before she could get near Ms. Anderson."

He looked at his mom and then back at Annette. He walked over and stood in front of her. He gave her a nasty look.

"She ruined everything!" Annette shouted, referring to Bailey.

Irish gave her an icy look. "She didn't ruin anything. You did the moment you gave birth to her. You and your husband were so obsessed with money and glory that you would do anything to get your hands on more money, including money that didn't even belong to you, that you would murder your daughter."

She went to say something, but the officers hauled her out of the room. He ran his hands through his hair and took in a deep breath. All that mattered right now was Bailey and getting her strong, so she would wake up. When he turned towards the bed and met a pair of large, arctic eyes staring at him, his legs almost buckled under him. He worried he would never see those eyes again. He looked to his mom, who was crying as she held Bailey's hand.

He went to the bed and dropped to his knees as his head rested against Bailey's side, and he cried and cried even harder when he felt her hand against his head. At that moment, he knew everything would be just fine.

CHAPTER THIRTY-TWO

Four weeks had gone by since the night they almost lost Bailey. It was early Thanksgiving afternoon. Bailey and Irish both decided they didn't want to wait to get married, so Irish, with, of course, the help of Alex, planned a small ceremony at Ace and Alex's house. Since everyone was going to be there for Thanksgiving dinner, it was perfect.

Irish walked up to Alex as she stacked some of the chairs they used on the patio. He grabbed one and folded it up.

"What are you doing out here? You should be inside with your new bride," she told him as she smiled, but Irish sensed something was off, and he had a feeling he knew what it was. This was the third wedding she had coordinated, and none of the three had been her own. She and Ace had planned their wedding multiple times, but each time something within their schedules caused the postponement.

"I wanted to come out here and thank you again for helping with everything and being there for Bailey."

She quirked an eyebrow at him. "Did you have any doubt I wouldn't?"

"No, you know that isn't what I meant." He bent down and hugged her. "I just mean, I couldn't have done it without you."

She smiled although he could tell it was forced. She turned and started moving the chairs again. "Well, you know I'm becoming a pro at throwing these spontaneous weddings together." She tried to laugh it off, but Irish knew the meaning behind her words.

"Alex, you know Ace would marry you today, right?"

"I know. Don't feel sorry for me. One of these days, I'll get my fairy tale wedding."

As he walked back into the house, he wondered if Ace really knew how Alex was feeling. He didn't want to get in the middle of their business, but they were both his friends, and both deserved to be happy.

He would give it a little more time, but if he didn't see a change in Alex, he would mention something to Ace.

Everyone took their seats around the large dining room table and adjoining tables Alex had set-up to make room for everyone. Their family was getting larger.

Alex finished putting the last of the food on the table. She said a quick blessing, giving thanks for having the best family and friends, and a little prayer for those men and women serving away from home.

"Is there anyone else who would like to say anything?" Alex asked, looking around before she took her seat.

Ace came up behind her and hugged her. "I think you summed everything up, sweetheart." He kissed her on the cheek.

Tenley cleared her throat. "Well, I'm thankful for all of this delicious food in front of us. I don't mean to rude but I have got two very unruly babies in my belly that I think can smell the turkey because one is beating my kidney and the other kicking my ribs." Potter reached over and rubbed her large belly.

Everyone laughed, but then Sienna stood up from her seat.

"Uncle Ace. I have something that I want to share."

Ace smiled at Sienna. Ace was great with all the kids. Irish knew both Ace and Alex wanted to have kids of their own someday but decided it would not happen until after they got married. Another reason for Ace to get his shit together and marry Alex.

"What are you thankful for, sweetie?" Ace asked Sienna.

Sienna stood in between Irish and Bailey at the table and took their hands into her little palms. She looked so cute in her burgundy smock dress and black boots. Bailey had styled her hair up in a pony-tail, then curled the ends.

"I know that you are not my real mommy and daddy. My mommy and daddy didn't want me." She looked up at Irish with the same blue eyes as him, and he just about melted into a big puddle of goo. "But I'm thankful to have you, Uncle Ky," she then turned her head towards Bailey, "and you too, Ms. Bailey."

Irish felt his chest tighten, and he looked over and saw the tears building up in Bailey's eyes as everyone sat in silence while Sienna spoke from her heart.

Irish pulled Sienna on his lap, then clutched her chin, tilting her face up towards his, and he kissed her forehead. "That is definitely something to be thankful for, sweetie. And I speak for both Bailey and I when I say we are thankful to have you in our lives as well. After all, if it weren't for you, I probably never would've found Bailey." She smiled up at him. "There is something Bailey and I would like to give you, and I think now is the perfect time since our family and friends are here to share it with us."

He held out his hand, and Bailey handed him the necklace box containing a silver locket in the shape of a heart that he and Bailey had both picked out yesterday after signing the adoption papers making Sienna their daughter. As he took the box from Bailey, he leaned in and gave her a quick kiss and told how much he loved her. He saw the tear escape from her eye, and he wiped it away before she could.

He looked back at the little blonde-haired, blue-eyed little girl sitting on his lap. He opened the box and watched as Sienna's eyes widened and sparkled as the beautiful locket was revealed.

"Is that for me?" She asked him in a whisper.

"It is," he told her as he clasped it around her neck. It hung low on her chest since it was a little long, but she would grow into it. "It is filled with so much love from Bailey and me."

He looked around the table at all of their friends, and he could see how happy they all were. All of the women were crying, and even some of the guys looked to have tears in their eyes. And people thought SEALs had no emotions.

Sienna took the locket into her hands and flipped it over where both Irish and Bailey had it engraved.

"To Sienna with love from Mommy and Daddy." She read aloud, then looked up at Irish with a confused look. "I don't understand. I don't have a mommy and daddy."

Irish smiled at her and took her little cheeks between the palms of his large hands. "You do now, peanut. Bailey and I signed the paperwork yesterday. You are officially our daughter."

Her eyes lit up, and a big smile spread across her face before she gave Irish a big hug. He hugged her tight as tears formed in his eyes. He felt Bailey's presence before he felt the gentle kiss on his cheek. When he looked over, she was beaming. He winked, knowing she was going to make an awesome mom and wife. "So, I can call you, daddy?" Sienna said as she looked between Irish and Bailey. "And I can call you, mommy?"

He nodded his head, and Bailey said yes. She leaped off his lap and shouted, "Yippee! I have a mommy and daddy!" Everyone clapped, then started digging into the feast Alex had prepared for everyone.

As Irish took the first bite of his meal, he said a silent prayer himself thanking the power above for bringing Bailey into his life and giving him an opportunity for a future he knew he was destined to have.

Later that evening, Bailey took Irish's hand and asked him if he would walk with her. As she walked him down to a dead-end cul-de-sac at the end of Ace and Alex's street, the house she had bought came into view. It was a gorgeous two-story house with a wrap-around front porch.

She walked him up the front steps.

"Baby, are we going to get in trouble for being in here?"

"No, I have permission from the owners." She unlocked the door with the key she had and let them inside.

"I don't understand; what did you want to show me?" He said as they walked further into the house, stopping in the living room. The house was fully furnished and decorated. A twelve-foot Christmas tree stood in the corner, fully decorated with lights and ornaments. But it was when he saw

267

the pictures on the fireplace mantel that she knew he realized what this was.

He turned to face her. "Is this ours?" He asked, and she smiled.

"You've sacrificed a lot by taking in Sienna. Here, you will have not only your office back, but you also have a gym. And we'll have two extra bedrooms for guests. Or, maybe for a nursery, one day." She had been devastated when Irish first explained that the chances of her getting pregnant were slim to none. But until someone told her it was impossible; she would only have positive thoughts.

She watched as Irish toured the house. She couldn't gauge his reaction, and she wondered if he was upset that she did something so drastic without telling him.

She walked over to where he stood by the French doors that opened to the huge back yard with a swimming pool. She wrapped her arms around his waist, and he put his arm around her shoulder. They stood like that for a few minutes.

"Ky?"

"Hmmm"

"Are you angry at me?"

He pulled her around, so she was standing in front of him, then pulled her against his chest. She squeezed his waist, then looked up and locked gazes with his blue eyes.

"Why would you think I would be angry with you?"

She licked her dry lips. "Because I know you don't like it when I spend my money on you."

He grinned, and she felt her insides relax.

"I could never be upset with you for doing something good for your family. This house is beautiful and perfect for our family." He leaned down and covered her mouth with his lips in what she would describe as the most passionate kiss he'd ever given her. As he stroked his tongue into her mouth in such a dominant but tender way, she became so aroused she had to pull back before she made a mess of things. She still had one more surprise for him that was going to knock his socks off, and if that kiss led to anything else, they might just have ended up with an audience. Though it wouldn't have been the first time she was caught with her pants down around the gang. She chuckled to herself.

When they both opened their eyes, he smiled at her as he waggled his eyebrows. "I was hoping we could go tour the master bedroom."

She snorted a laugh and ran her hands up his hard chest. "As enticing as that sounds, I have one more surprise for you." He furrowed his eyebrows, and before he could protest, she continued. "Go through that door," she said, pointing in the direction just off the large gourmet kitchen. It was the door that led to the three-car garage.

Irish walked through the kitchen and opened the door and was greeted by all their friends who stood around a band new dark steel-grey Bugatti Chiron.

He swung his head around where Bailey stood. "What did you do? Do you know how much one of these costs?"

She laughed. "I'd better since I wired the money."

"Why?" He asked, and she walked over and wrapped her arms around his waist.

"Because I love you, and you have given up a lot in your life going out and playing hero and putting your life on the line to protect us here at home. Plus, I know how hard it was for you to give up your Corvette. So, I thought this might be a nice replacement."

He didn't know what to say or do, so he did what he knew what was best for him, and he kissed her.

"Ok, you two. This is a PG area," Diego said, making everyone laugh.

He looked into her eyes and whispered to her. "I love you."

"I love you, too."

He took her face between his palms and leaned down and kissed her. When he pulled back, he smiled. Bailey realized that it was quiet and looked over her shoulder and noticed they were alone.

"They all went back to Ace and Alex's. Sienna is having a sleepover with Alejandra."

Bailey ran her hands up Irish's chest. "She is, is she."

He wrapped his arms around her waist and pulled her snug into his chest, then slid one hand over her ass. He leaned down and suckled her neck, sending her libido into overdrive. Her neck was super sensitive.

"She is. So now that we are alone, how about a tour of the master bedroom?" He wiggled his eyebrows up and down and gave her that flirty grin of his that she loved.

"I think that sounds wonderful. But you have to catch me first."

"Oh, baby, you are so getting your ass spanked for that."

"Bring it on, sailor." She took off running. She made it to the stairs before he caught her. The only lights illuminating the downstairs were the white lights on the Christmas tree. Irish lifted her into his arms. Her legs wrapped around his waist as he devoured her mouth and moans. His one hand cupped her ass, while the other held her head in a possessive grip. She felt on fire. Her hands were in his hair, and she fought for control of the kiss.

When Irish finally came up for air, he said, "Fuck the bedroom," as he walked them over to the Christmas tree and laid her down on the plush rug. He shed their clothes quickly before falling between her thighs.

Before he could get himself inside of her, he heard a low growl. When he lifted his head, he came face to face with none other than Mr. Whiskers. Shocking the shit out of him, the damn cat walked up to him and rubbed his head affectionately against Irish's face.

"Really? Now, as I'm laying here butt naked, you want to be nice?"

Bailey couldn't help but giggle as they watched the "damned" cat saunter his way up the stairs.

Bailey turned her attention to Irish and hugged him. "I love you, Ky."

His eyes twinkled just as he slid home into her. "I love you, too, sweetness."

EPILOGUE

Stitch sat at the dining room table, listening to his close friends and family chat with each other. Thanksgiving was by far his favorite holiday. One, he was thankful for being alive, two, he was grateful for his friends and family, especially those in the room with him and three, he loved the feast of food.

He smiled as he watched and listened to the various conversations being held. It had been an exciting day with Irish marrying Bailey. After everything they had been through in their short time together, they deserved every bit of happiness.

He scanned the room, looking at his teammates, Ace, Potter, and Frost, who have defied the odds of relationships in the SEAL community. Now that Irish was off the market; he was curious who the next teammate would be that caught the "love" bug.

Mia popped into his mind. Now that was a woman he enjoyed spending time around. She was fun, sweet, gorgeous, and wicked smart. He was also very attracted to her, but the problem was, Mia was Ace's baby sister. Stitch wasn't sure how Ace would feel about that. That had been the only reason holding him back, especially now that she was single. Back during Christmas, that wasn't the case. She had been dating a guy back in New York where she lived, but he knew then that the relationship was on the rocks, and it was just a matter of time until it fizzled out, and it had when Mia had caught him with another woman.

He glanced at the empty chair at the table. The chair that Mia should be sitting in and enjoying the festivities like everyone else. Ace and the rest of Mia's family were a little concerned with her abrupt cancellation of attending Thanksgiving dinner.

Stitch didn't know everything about Mia, but one thing he did know was that family time was important for her. So, for her not to come to dinner was somewhat alarming, especially considering she hadn't answered anyone's phone calls or texts.

Stitch felt his phone vibrating in his pocket. He retrieved it and was surprised to see his friend, Sherriff Prescott's name flashing on the screen.

Sherriff Blake Prescott was the head lawman of the little town in the mountains of Virginia where his cabin was located. He was a good friend of his and a former Marine. Stitch always made it a point to reach out to him when he came to town. They would usually have at least a beer together at the local pub.

Not wanting to be rude and talk on the phone at the table, he excused himself and went out onto the back patio.

"Sherriff Prescott."

"Hey, Stitch. Happy Thanksgiving."

"Happy Thanksgiving to you as well. What can I do for you?"

"Well, I have a little situation up here in Sugar Bend."

"And you're calling me, why?" Stitch asked as he leaned against the deck railing.

"Well, I just met an interesting friend of yours."

Stitch chuckled, thinking what friend of his could be in Sugar Bend, considering most of his friends were right in front of him.

"Does this friend have a name?" He replied sarcastically because the only friend Stitch had in Sugar Bend was the Sherriff.

"Does the name Mia ring any bells?

Stitch's blood ran cold.

What the hell was Mia doing in Sugar Bend when she was supposed to here with her family?

Stitch and Mia's story is coming in February 2021!
Pre-order available now!

BOOK LIST

ABOUT THE AUTHOR

Jaime Lewis is new to the indie author world; writing military romance and suspense fiction. Her first book, ACE, from The Trident Series was published in June 2020.

Born and raised in Edgewater, Maryland, Jaime now resides in Ormond Beach, Florida with her husband and two very active boys.

When not working her full-time job, writing, or chasing around her boys, you can usually find Jaime somewhere outdoors. She is an avid sports fan and has a huge passion for supporting the military, veterans, and first responders.

Follow Jaime:

Facebook: https://www.facebook.com/jaime.lewis.58152
Goodreads: https://www.goodreads.com/author/show/17048191.Jaime_Lewis

Made in the USA
Coppell, TX
18 December 2020

45999137R00163